PHOENIX

Apart from the occasional magazine article ('200 mph Driving Tips'), Bob Judd devotes all his writing time to fiction, 'where the truth is'. *Phoenix* is his fourth motor-racing thriller, following *Formula One*, *Indy*, and *Monza*. He lives in London and Palo Alto where he races Lamborghinis and grows sequoias in his back yard.

Bob Judd

PHOENIX

PAN BOOKS

IN ASSOCIATION WITH
MACMILLAN LONDON

First published 1992 by Macmillan London Limited

This edition published 1993 by Pan Books Limited
a division of Pan Macmillan Publishers Limited
Cavaye Place London SW10 9PG
and Basingstoke
in association with Macmillan London Limited

Associated companies throughout the world

ISBN 0 330 32343 1

1 3 5 7 9 8 6 4 2

A CIP catalogue record for this book is available from
the British Library

Typeset by Intype, London
Printed by Cox & Wyman Ltd, Reading, Berkshire

acknowledgements

In researching *Phoenix*, I had the good fortune to meet two distinguished reporters who have both been honoured as Arizona's Reporter of the Year.

Charles Kelly of the *Arizona Republic* helped me find my way around and generously introduced me to sources he had built up in over a decade of reporting. The facts that are straight in here are his. The bent ones are mine.

The Carefree Water scandal is lifted in spirit from an article Terry Green wrote for her paper, the *New Times*, although, as you can imagine, I changed enough of the details to protect the guilty.

'What I want to know is this. Who stole the great song of America, that fine eighteenth-century declaration of freedom and independence; who sold it to the greedy men hiding behind our flag? What I want to know is why the radio sings of the American West in that rinky-dink, honky-tonk, dimestore whine.'

William J. Barnes

'In the lea of the Great Southwestern Volcanic Caldera, a new city is rising.'

Garden's Guide to America, 1947

chapter one

The scene kept coming back, the details so clear I couldn't have just dreamed them. It must have been like that, I thought.

Like this . . .

Across the top of the frame, a black bar for the underside of the car. Across the bottom, another black bar for the surface of the parking lot. In between, the hot blue Arizona sky.

The sole of the shoe is almost new, just a little scuffed on the pale varnished leather, *Florshiem* still legible in gilt as the shoe comes down, out of the sky, to land on the sticky black asphalt. A nice mahogany tassel loafer. High gloss. The mechanic's coveralls are new, dark blue and come down almost to the shoe, showing just a little black silk sock.

Mantovani's thousand strings play 'Charmain' from the hotel's hidden outdoor speakers. Da daa dah, da daa dah, da dahhhh, Charmaaaain . . .

The shoe kicks out of frame and a black hair helmet, blow-dried, shoves under the car, blocking out the sky. The man with the careful hairdo drags in a bundle after him, six red sticks of dynamite tied together with bell wire, and shoves the bundle up on to the bottom of the car. Metal to metal click as four round magnets take hold.

The hair helmet slides back out and the mahogany Florshiems walk away leaving a black lump hanging down from the bottom of the car. The music continues.

Inside the hotel, in the lobby, Barnes is impatient, looking at his watch. He is tall and thin in a light blue seersucker suit, a polka-dot bow tie under a prominent Adam's apple. Barnes is always impatient, his Adam's apple working, his eyes cruising the lobby from behind thick round tortoise-frame glasses. The phone rings and the clerk behind the lobby desk hands the phone to Barnes.

The blow-dry mechanic is calling from a nearby bar where he hangs out but he doesn't tell Barnes that. What he tells Barnes is that he's sorry . . . he couldn't make it. Something came up. But the Cavanaugh and Empire story is hot and he has good stuff. He'd call Barnes when he could get free of the bullshit, OK? The mechanic said he was real sorry it got all screwed up. He said he'd see him later.

Barnes walks out into the parking lot and it is Arizona hot, around ninety-eight fahrenheit, and time for lunch. He has his keys out. The car, the brand-new white Datsun with the lump underneath it, isn't locked. Barnes opens the door, gets in, shuts the door and starts the car.

At the back of the parking lot a plumber in his pick-up truck aims the aerial of a toy radio control at the white Datsun and presses a button on the control box and nothing happens. Barnes turns on the Datsun's radio to get the news. The plumber in his pick-up pushes the button again and again and nothing happens. Then the plumber realises the problem. The problem is that he is in the metal cab of his Ford pick-up and the radio transmission isn't leaving the cab, maybe just bouncing back at him, something. So the plumber steps out of the cab of his pick-up and as Barnes puts his car in reverse and starts to back out, the plumber pushes the button and this time it works and underneath the car, the electric contacts close.

Sending an amp and a half of electric current from a pair of flashlight batteries through two red and yellow plastic-coated copper leg-wires connected by a thin bridge wire inside a number-eight strength aluminium blasting cap. The blasting cap is just over two inches long and about as big around as a pencil. The bridge wire glows, igniting a prime charge, which, in turn, detonates the high explosive base charge. The blasting cap explodes and lights the six sticks of dynamite.

Dynamite burns like a high-speed cigar, a disc of fire moving in a plane through the cylinder of powder at a little under seven thousand miles an hour. Followed by a cone of five thousand, five hundred-degree fahrenheit carbon dioxide, nitrogen, steam, carbon monoxide and nitrogen oxides with an expanding force of a million and a half pounds per square inch, travelling at over ten thousand feet per second.

I knew him. I knew Barnes.

PART ONE

chapter two

We are talking Big Boots here. Really BIGTIME Boots.

These are BIG, STUD, COWBOY BOOTS, standing wide as the Pecos in the desert sand. In the lea of the great volcanic caldera. The big man stands with his eight-hundred-dollar-each Tony Lama Ostrich cowboy boots on the rocks of an old foundation in the Arizona desert sand.

This is MAJORLEAGUE. SERIOUS STUFF.

We are not fuckin' around here. Damn straight. The big man is wearing a red check Royal environmentally conscious Robbins flannel shirt. An authentic dimestore neckerchief, also red, is knotted correctly in front of his soon to be suntanned neck. And he is wearing sun-faded Levi blue jeans, and them Bigtime Boots with them little bumps all over to signify authentic, real expensive Ostrich skin. Full-Quill Ostrich Skin. Money no object. He wears the whole truly cowboy outfit and if you had the outfit you might be a cowboy. But he is not.

I am not. It's not working. I squint into the sun looking out at the Arizona mountains in the morning sun and I have to admit, I am not at home on the range. Even if it is my range.

Riding in on the big silver bird from Denver (from New York, from London seven eye-ball-aching time zones away) just after dawn, I had the feeling that I just might pass. Just an ol' cowhand coming in from the sky. Or what the hell, a guy with a ranch on his hands. Man that busts his own broncs. You know, tough but fair. A man that is at home in the saddle and carries a heavy credit card in his hip pocket. A New Age Western Man.

The feeling didn't last past the first real cowboy in the luggage hall of the Phoenix airport. He was bleary-eye hungover, with a face like an old saddlebag, wearing a sweat-stained Army T-shirt, missing teeth, needing a shave and he was hoisting a dirty canvas bag off the conveyer belt when he caught sight of my brand new bumpy-skin ostrich cowboy boots. 'Shine them fuckers with Clearasil?' he asked without moving his jaw, moving off out the door without looking back.

There ought to be, somewhere, hanging in a closet, a suit of clothes an ex-racing driver can put on without feeling like he is from another planet. Something he could wear so that wherever he goes he doesn't get the feeling that everybody is talking another language and doing whatever they do at half speed.

I liked, no, not liked. Nothing as wishy-washy as liked. I flat-out *loved* being a racing driver, driving racing cars. I am addicted to it and it is all I know how to do. But I don't do it any more. I couldn't if I wanted to. Question is, I thought, looking into the mean, rust-coloured rock of the mountains in the distance, what do I do now?

A racing driver should have one or two fall-back identities lined up for when he climbs out of his car. I thought I did, but when I reached for them they just disappeared. How about: an ex-racing driver adds colour to the commentary direct from the trackside? 'We got fifteen guys, all of them former Indy and Formula One drivers, fifteen guys in front of you, Forrest, standing in line to be colour commentators. We'll call you.'

Well then, how about: an ex-racing driver joins a partnership to sell investment-grade Ferraris and new Hondas? That lasted nearly all winter with phone calls, lunches, lawyers and meetings with bankers. But it was the year nobody was buying old Ferraris and Honda was 'reviewing' their dealer list. So in the end I gracefully withdrew before there was nothing to withdraw from. As anybody who has lost their job can tell you, being an ex anything is depressing work for a man. I mean you tell me; how bad do you want to hear about how I was almost the World Champion? Of course you don't want to hear it. Nobody wants to hear a story that ends in 'almost'. And even if I had been world champion you could probably just about stand to listen to the story for five minutes before your ears turned to cement. Last year's champion was last year.

Not that I want sympathy, sympathy is the last thing I want. Which is just as well, since I don't get any. Well, why should I? I had a good run, made money and hung on to enough squirrelled away in offshore accounts to never have to worry about money as long as I don't spend too much. But oh, God, I miss the heat of slipping into that graceful, elegant, psychopathic, shrink-wrapped super-tech machine with seven hundred horsepower behind my neck.

I miss the cosmic zoom of acceleration and the jolt of getting out there on the knife-edge of control in a hundred-and-eighty-mile-an-hour corner. Zero to a hundred and fifty miles an hour in 4.9 seconds. And yes, I miss coming within an eyelash of killing myself every race or so. I miss the bright and gorgeous people and the reporters who acted as if what I said mattered. Not that I was expected to say much. Like all athletes, I was what I did, not what I said or thought. Being famous, even in a minor way, isn't all bad. Businessmen and politicians bragged to their friends that they knew me. Little boys slid under fences to get my autograph. Breathtaking women came up to me out of the blue and in the sweetest ways you could imagine asked me to bonk their brains out. And now that I don't drive a racing car . . . Only last week the phone rang twice. I have time in the morning and I have time in the afternoon. And let me just check, but I think tomorrow is free. From dawn to sunset. As a man who made a living finding time within the thousandth of a second, that last possible fragment of time when you choose to keep your foot nailed down, hard on the accelerator, picking up speed with the force of an explosion. As a man who was used to the exhilaration of finding an extra fragment of time, I had no idea that one day could contain so much of the stuff. So much empty time. When racing drivers quit driving they can disappear right before your eyes.

I looked up into the soft blue morning sky. No buzzards overhead. Maybe Arizona doesn't have buzzards. But there were birds in the bushes by the creek. And a couple of little brown birds in a saguaro cactus just in front of me were giving me advice; something like get the hell away from our nest before we sing our hearts out. It had never occurred to me that the desert had songbirds. It did occur to me that a bogus cowboy in pimple boots with the new neckerchief had a lot to learn.

My mother was born in 1925 on this land. Dear raging Sally Concannon. The wild and beautiful redhead who was everything a preacher's daughter shouldn't be. She married my father when she was thirty-one, my age, and he was nearly fifty. She must have been bored in a week, in that freezing house in freezing Norfolk. But she stayed with him until I was born, when she went running back to the safety of Connecticut. Sally Concannon Evers and Robert Edgar Ramsey Evers died together a few years ago on the A30 outside of London after years of separation. They'd decided they would remarry, do the whole thing, have a ceremony and reception and rang me up that night to invite me, both of them drunk as coots, celebrating.

My father willed me the Aston Martin, the aluminium body crushed and bloody. And my mother willed me this patch of land that she had been given by my grandfather, land he had purchased for next to nothing when he brought his family here from Missouri after World War One. Ten thousand acres north of Phoenix that I didn't pay much tax on and I had never seen until now.

Maybe, I'd thought one gloomy night in Britain, I could move here. Build a simple house. Why the hell not? Pack a suitcase and shut the door on dark and chilly London. See what's happening in the Valley of the Sun. See if I could get out of the half-speed limbo world outside the Grand Prix Circus Tent that keeps a few sideshows for ex-drivers like me to hang on to until they can't stand the puzzled stares from people they used to know ('Sorry, Forrest, I just didn't recognise you without a racing car.').

When I quit racing I sold my helicopter and dropped the option I'd had on a jet. And slowly I came down to the normal speed and impenetrable maze of everyday life. I found an agent who called himself a personal manager and took twenty-five per cent of whatever he brought in. He didn't bring in much. Evidently the world is not crying out for yet another ex-racing driver. But eventually, after a few celebrity appearances on satellite TV shows that nobody watched, he had got me an assignment from the *Detroit News* for a couple of background columns on the United States Grand Prix, due to be run through the streets of Phoenix that weekend. I was supposed to write it from the driver's point of view. Whatever that is supposed to mean. Driving a Formula One car on the bumpy and rectangular streets of Phoenix is a contradiction in terms. Still, I was willing to give it a try. It didn't pay much but it gave me an excuse to come to Phoenix. And I had an old friend at Falcon who wanted some backup with his board on why and how the Falcon Motor Company should keep on spending the umpteen millions it takes to 'have a presence' in Formula One.

The Formula One Circus was, no doubt, already rolling into Phoenix. And meanwhile I was here, in the middle of nowhere (if you can count ten miles outside of Carefree, Arizona, as nowhere), with nothing but time. Time to look around and see if Forrest Evers might just do something with ten thousand Arizona acres. Farm cactuses, build a resort for the hopelessly bewildered or maybe just camp out under the sky.

Something.

I pulled out a carefully folded old map out of my back pocket, my mother's notes in clear small ballpoint alongside the tiny circles she'd drawn to show me when I was a boy. 'Swimming hole', 'farmhouse', 'eagles' nest', 'barn'; simple places from a simple world before Korea, Vietnam and smart bombs in Iraq.

My mother had warned me that there would be nothing left now but the foundations. Even the eagles, I was sure, would have flown away. Still, I thought it was time to take a vacation from myself and go see it. See where my mother grew up and ran wild. See what there was to see.

So I was happy to find the old foundation of what must have been the farmhouse. To stand there on the rocks that had held up the long-gone house where my mother was born, feel the morning sun on my back and look around, get my bearings. Maybe take a long walk around the property. Maybe not. Checking the map, the creek ran just inside the south border of my kingdom and the land ran a long ways north-east through the hills, towards the mountains.

Something.

A flickering bright spot, reflecting sun. There was a glint through the branches of the trees down by the creek. Well, I said to myself, guess this ol' bogus cowboy'll just mosey on down and see what's kicking up the visual ruckus on my spread.

Like the good ol' cowboy I am, I got back into the Renta-Buick and drove down. Pulled up right in front.

It was an old aluminium Airstream, the last word in 1930s aerodynamic design. From the looks of the cracked tyres, sunk up to the axles in the sand, it had been there for at least five years. There was a smoke- and grease-stained barbecue grill, a washline with some jeans and shirts hanging still as a painting in the dry air, and the lilting water sound of the creek ten yards away. The door was open and I was about to stick my head inside, smelling fresh coffee, when a voice behind me said: 'Who the hell do you think you are?'

'I was just asking myself the same question,' I said, turning around.

She said, 'You look like your mother got you ready. You want a cup of coffee?'

chapter three

'Sally,' she said, holding out her hand, walking towards me, silver bracelets on a tanned wrist, 'Sally Cavanaugh.' She was fine boned, dark and tall, her face oval with large and deep blue eyes and a high forehead in a frame of long dark-brown hair. There was some steel, though. Something behind the smile. But her mouth was wide and generous, and maybe she had a wicked idea and she was trying hard not to laugh.

She looked away at the hills in the far distance, considering, then she looked back to me and her mouth was spreading again into that wide grin. I thought the smile was a good sign. I thought her eyes were as blue as the Arizona sky. And oh, yes, there was a lovely woman on the loose under her faded blue work-shirt. Wobble wobble, she goes. Ding dong, the old Evers salivating sexual dog goes. Wag, wag, goes the tail. Up jumps Forrest. One day I will grow up and become a real adult male, take a more balanced view, bury this dumb and free-floating lurid sexual urge under a mound of responsibility, caring, sharing and, yes indeedy, nurturing. One day I will leave the adolescence of desire and join the sober grown-ups. One day when the sight of a lovely woman ceases to make me feel glad to be alive.

'Where you comin' from?' she said, her dark tanned hand gripping my pale white hand in an honest shake. How, I wondered, did teeth ever get so white. Or was it just her deep tan and a trick of the light.

'You mean I don't look as if I come from here.'

'You don't look as if you come from within a thousand miles of here. And either the sun don't shine where you come from, or you only come out at night.'

She didn't wear make up, she didn't have to, although some

sun-tan oil might have saved her a line or two at the corners of her mouth. Thirty, I guessed. Maybe younger. She wasn't pretty, her face was too strong. But beauty she had plenty of, in her eyes and in her long neck and strong jaw and the grace of her hands. I liked the frank, open way she stared at me, the way you would stare at a man who had just stepped off Uranus. I looked back at her, her grin spreading all the way from her face to mine. 'You've made yourself at home here,' I said, happy to find her on my land.

'You don't *sound* as if you come from here either. You sound kinda English,' she said, stopping and holding her head to one side as if she had heard something odd in the distance. 'Is that accent real or are you just being pretentious?'

'Both,' I said. 'I wouldn't want to fool you.'

'Oh, everybody fools me. If I wasn't fooled so easily I wouldn't be out here in the middle of the damn desert. There's a cup of coffee inside if you like. You got a name?'

'Forrest,' I said. 'Forrest Evers.'

She stopped on the steps of the Airstream for a moment. 'You really buy those boots yourself, Forrest?' she said, disappearing inside before I had an answer.

The Airstream was flooded with light inside. She had cut away the aluminium skin on the north side and tacked transparent plastic sheeting over the frame. The plastic had the tacky and temporary look of all man-made things in the desert. On the other hand the light made it easy to see the oil paintings stacked knee high along the wall next to the bed.

'Are these all painted from around here?'

Sally was pulling two white mugs down from the cupboard over the stove. 'All around here. I paint a lot more than I sell so they kinda pile up.'

I started browsing through them. They had a crude and shaky kid's line, and no perspective as if the figures were drawn by a happy six-year-old. And they were the bright colours children use when they are still innocent enough to believe blue is blue and pink is pink. A bright rainbow-coloured bird flew over a rainbow in a blue sky in one painting. In another, ghosts of Indians floated over the sandy hills. 'I like them,' I said. 'They look like they were painted by a kid.'

'They were, smartass. It took me years to learn to paint that simple. You could buy one for less than the price of a pair of dumb boots. I wouldn't mind a bit.'

'If I had a place to hang one, I'd think about it. I like this rainbow bird.'

'That's a phoenix. You know, the bird that was reborn out of the ashes. Mythical bird, lived for five thousand years, burned to death and rose up from the ashes. It probably wouldn't look good in London. My colours don't travel, they're too bright. Unless you live in the desert or under a neon sign, they look artificial. I've sold a few through a gallery in Scottsdale and a couple in LA. They look OK in La-La Land.'

'That's what you do, paint?'

'I thought you British were supposed to shy away from asking personal questions. Too embarrassing.' She was pouring coffee into the white mugs, the blue coffee-pot steady in her hand. 'Forrest, is that what people really call you, Forrest?'

I nodded, confessing. 'That, believe it or not, is what they call me.' If there were an easier, simpler contraction of the name my mother gave me, thinking it sounded English, I'd love to hear it. For? Rest? Forrie? Forget it.

'To tell you the truth Forrest, I don't know what I do. You can see I'm not much of a painter. I just like the idea of being a painter, you know? It gets me off the hook.'

'What hook? You don't seem all that hung up to me.'

'Oh I didn't mean that. I mean I just get so tired of being the same ol' dumb Sally Cavanaugh every damn day.'

'Everybody gets tired of themselves sometimes,' I said with my usual talent for lo-cal insight, taking a cup. 'I'm glad to see you, Sally. Maybe you just need a little more company.'

'Jesus, company is about the last thing I need. I like it better out here when I know there isn't anybody for ten miles. In fact I don't know whether I come out here to paint or I paint just so I have an excuse to come out here. I just about grew up out here, you know? At least out here I don't get every two-bit con man hittin' on me just because I'm Merrill Cavanaugh's daughter.'

'Oh, I see. Merrill Cavanaugh. *The* Merrill Cavanaugh.'

'That's right.'

'Never heard of him.'

'Well he's not world famous. He just owns half of Phoenix.

Bring your coffee outside and I'll show you something.' She stopped in the doorway, puzzled by something.

'You've been asking a lot of questions about me. What do you do, Forrest?'

'Nothing.'

'You mean you're a bum or another damn playboy?'

'I used to be a racing driver.'

'Racing driver? Isn't that kind of a dumb thing for a grown man to do, risk your neck to go around in circles?' She looked at me, interested. 'That what give you all those lines around your eyes?'

'You're not exactly user-friendly,' I said, following her out down the steps.

'You're goddamn right I'm not. So you were just driving by, thought you'd stop in and maybe pick up a little local colour?'

'My mother grew up around here. She used to tell me about riding horses and swimming in the creek when I was a kid.'

'Where was that?'

'In England. And New York.'

'No, dummy. I mean where was all this horse-riding and creek-swimming going on around here?'

'Right here, I think.'

'Well, she sure picked a good spot. Like I said, I just about grew up here myself. It's a little cool for swimming now, but if you're free and you can find the time, I can recommend it. Any chance I've heard of you? I'm not exactly what you'd call an aficionado of the international racing car set.'

'You know anything about Formula One racing?'

'Sure. It flies in once a year, makes a lot of noise and then it takes off again leaving a lot of mess behind. Just like a damn seagull.'

'That's what I used to drive.'

'Formula One?'

'Formula One. I could have been World Champion.'

'How fascinating,' she said, closing her eyes for a moment. 'What held you back?'

'I wasn't fast enough.' Finally, another smile. A nice, long, slow, generous grin like the first one. Then it faded away and her mouth took on a hard set.

'You see that ridge over there?'

22

She was pointing to what I'd guessed was halfway to the edge of my land, a hill of dirt, rock, sand, dry grass, scrub brush, prickly pear and cholla cactus among the other hills of dirt, rock, sand, dry grass, scrub brush and cactus on the way to the mountains in the distance.

I nodded.

'All the way from the other side of the creek to that ridge belongs to my father. Or one of his damn companies, same thing.'

'Sally, I hate to disappoint you, but that creek or at least this part of the creek is mine. And so is the land to the ridge and on the other side of the ridge and on for another three miles.'

'If you are talking about the land I'm standing on, Forrest or whatever your goddamn name is, you are as full of shit as a pig in the woods. You understand what I'm saying? My Daddy has always owned this land. Always. I don't know what your mommy told you but I guess you are going to have to face the fact that it was a goddamn fairy story. You want to come back inside, I'll show you a map.'

'I don't need a map, Sally. I've been paying taxes on it for ten years. And I am beginning to think maybe I ought to have the junk cleared off. Kind of spoils the view, seeing that old broken-down trailer stuck there. What do you think this property should rent for?' I was thinking I was making a joke. Maybe it was jet-lag, but my intention had been to relax the situation. It was just a misunderstanding. I wanted her to stay.

Sally was not relaxed, she was almost spitting her coffee at me. 'Jesus Christ you got a nerve. Gimme my coffee back. I don't want to see your ugly face here.'

'Sure, take the cup. I've had better coffee from a teabag.' I still thought she was just playing at being mad. And I thought I was too. 'Suppose you show me your map.'

She took the mug, glaring at me, red in her cheeks and her forehead. For a moment I thought she was going to throw the coffee at me and in the silence I could hear the songbirds by the creek as they dropped down off the branches and skimmed along the surface picking off the rising insects. The sun had real heat in it although the air was cool. Sally turned and went back inside the Airstream. I waited outside. After a while she stuck her head out.

'Well goddamn, Forehead, get your dumb ass in here and look at this map.'

The map was a white sheet of paper on the dinette table, a photocopy of the original from the Maricopa County Recorder's Office. A large section of it had been lined with light blue magic marker. Handwritten across the property were the words, *Airport Development Corporation*.

'Sally, look, I'm sorry,' I said. 'I don't know what this map proves. But I'm sure we can straighten this out.'

'Damn straight we can straighten this out. You get your pretentious British ass off my property and that'll end it right there.'

I was going to point out that I wasn't really British, as if that would have mattered, when I heard a brake squeak, the sound of a large vehicle sliding across dirt and stones and then coming to a stop and an engine running.

He was around six foot six, broad across the shoulders and getting out of a grey Ford van that had stopped an inch from the back of my rentacar as I came out of the Airstream. He slammed the door shut and there was a large white star on the side. EMPIRE it said in bold letters under the star.

'This man botherin' you Sally?' he said, not taking his eyes off me. His wrists were the size of my forearms.

'Goddamn it, Orrin, you get the hell out of here.' Evidently Orrin was not one of her favourites.

He didn't seem to mind. What he minded was me. 'You know you are trespassing here,' he said, not taking his eyes off me.

'Looks to me like you are lost, Orrin. This is my land, and you are on it.'

'Bullshit,' he said like it had a fine flavour . . . his favourite word. 'You get back to wherever the hell your home is and don't you come trespassing here. Could be dangerous, you know, this part of the country, trespassing. Folks don't like trespassers around here.'

'Orrin,' she said, 'you get your dumb ass back in that van and you get the hell out of here, you hear me?'

Buzzards forty miles away would have heard her. Orrin gave me a little nod. 'Love your boots,' he said. Then he got back in the van, backed up and drove away.

'And you get the fuck out of here too, before I get really mad,' Sally said in the same sweet voice.

I suppose I was overtired and under sensitive, but some basic nerve gets twisted when you get pushed around on your own land. 'Let's be fair about this Sally,' I said walking up to her. 'What would you say was a fair rental for ten thousand acres with a sizeable creek running through it? One thousand five hundred dollars a month, would that be too much?' Her face was turning red under her tan. A kind of mahogany. 'Figure one thousand five hundred dollars a month that's what, eighteen thousand dollars a year over the past ten years you've been squatting here, you said. That's one hundred and eighty thousand dollars you owe me in back rent.'

She was bending over picking up a good-size stone. She did a little wind up, throwing her leg up in the air like a pitcher and threw a three-pound rock through my RentaBuick's windshield. The next rock was a lot smaller, she threw it sidearm from five feet away and it hit me in the stomach. Maybe I should have tried to calm her down, said something like I'm sorry, I'm sure it's just a misunderstanding. Let's have dinner, or another cup of your excellent coffee.

But it was hard to think clearly because she was screaming. When you are being stung by a swarm of bees, you don't stop to think and wonder how you got into this mess, you just run. I got back into the car in a shower of rocks she was slinging by the handful. I jammed the car into Lo, lurched forward, making her jump aside and land on her butt. I kept my foot buried on the gas, spinning and turning in the dry dirt, sending up a shower of rocks and accelerated out the dirt road. The windshield had a hole the size of a grapefruit, the window on the passenger side was cracked, and both of the headlights smashed.

Fuck you, Sally Cavanaugh, I thought. Fuck you. In the rear-view mirror she was still sitting in the dirt, giving me the finger.

The windshield was so smashed and cracked I had to lean over and peer out the hole. The wind in my face made my eyes tear and I had to slow down. Take my time. Enjoy my scenery. A mile down the road towards Carefree, I stopped to look at a fence. Something else I hadn't expected to find on my land.

The poles were weatherbeaten to silver grey, the barbed-wire rusted, but they were in good shape. Keep out or keep in, it didn't say. Somebody was maintaining them.

chapter four

Naturally I could have stayed in a simpler and far cheaper hotel. It's hard to justify the $325 a day the Arizona Biltmore charges for a room and I didn't even try.

You approach it by way of a winding suburban drive past the sprawling homes with the wide lawns and evergreen borders on the shores of the golf club. These are the homes that corporate America used to aspire to in the days when Life was a magazine, tail-fins were taken seriously and Cadillac was the mark of excellence. Homes where the dreams of gin and tonics out on the terrace listening to the hum of the swimming-pool filter and the distant click of golf balls come true with stunning boredom. Half of the sprawling stucco ranch-style houses are empty and for sale now, their owners' hearts bursting from all that golf or their bank accounts drained dry by the Savings and Loans scandals that were invented right here in Phoenix, America's tenth-largest and fastest-growing city. Just around the corner from Frank Lloyd Wright's old stomping grounds.

Frank Lloyd Wright designed the Arizona Biltmore (or he helped design it) (or a student of his designed it) (depends on which plaque you believe) and it has that dark, art deco, pagan temple look of the 1920s. There should be Packards, Pierce Arrows, Stutz, and Deusenbergs parked out front of its vast lawns and grey-stone-slab façade. My RentaBuick, with the hole in the windshield, smashed headlamps and pockmarked with rock dents, staggered past the entrance like a refugee. I hid it in the parking lot behind a hedge.

The Arizona Biltmore is not a hotel. It is a Resort. Capital R. The grass grows electric green under the spray of hidden sprinklers making small rainbows in the sunlight. Flowerbeds bloom preposterous purple, a backdrop for the corporate execs in their daffodil-and-carnation play-clothes in a big rush to get to their golf, tennis, swimming and horse-riding. They had to hurry. Their holiday had limits, as in two weekends and a week in between because they had to get back and get lined up for the sales conference on the twenty-third. My holiday stretched out over the horizon. All the way to a hole in the ground. So I took my time going up to the reception desk. I asked to see the manager.

He was an earnest man in a plain, small office, anxious to know whether there was anything he could do. Was my room all right? My room was fine and my bed had room for five. Peachy marble loo. Loved the terrace.

Who handled his border disputes, I wanted to know.

'I'm sorry?' he said, raising his eyebrows and retreating that small distance into professional hotel rectitude. He was about thirty-five and I would guess that it had been years since he had lost control. But then you never know.

'Solicitors, lawyers,' I said. 'Your hotel has over two hundred acres surrounded by the city. There must be a firm of lawyers who look after your property agreements.'

'A firm of lawyers,' he said slowly as if I might be thinking of digging post holes in one of his perfect greens. His hair was high back and sides, showing a lot of scalp above the ears. A very clean man.

'I have some property outside Phoenix,' I said. 'And I thought you might know the name of a law firm that handles property disputes.'

'I see. Yes. Well we use a company called Behrman, Siskin and Victor. I can give you their number if you wish. Just a moment while I write it down.' He looked up the number, started to write it down, then stopped midway, looking up over his glasses. 'I wonder if I might ask you a personal question, Mr Evers? Where, if you don't mind my asking,' he smiled, 'did you get those boots?'

'Yeah, hi. Hello?'

A woman's voice. It sounded like she was chewing gum. Or maybe chewing on a pencil. I was sprawled out on my bed with room for four more bedmates. I pictured what she looked like; short, dark, pudgy. Curly hair, chubby cheeks? Maybe nineteen. A little husky in the voice. Tough but sexy with a boyfriend who worked for the telephone company. A touch of loneliness in her voice. Nipples like . . . I had to do something about my sex life. It had been weeks. My mind was slipping.

'Uh, hello. Is this Behrman, Siskin and Victor?'

'Yeah, right.'

'Can I talk to somebody about a property dispute.'

'What's the problem?'

'Maybe I could talk to Mr Behrman.'

'I'm the Behrman in this firm. Judith Behrman, OK? What's the problem?'

I erased my mental picture of the woman. She was mid forties, iron hair. Proper suit, pearls at the neck, drank martinis and smoked cigarettes nonstop.

'I'm sorry, I'm not used to the principal of a law firm answering the company phone.'

'A lot of people find it disconcerting. I'm not big on pomp and circumstance.'

'You do work for the Arizona Biltmore, Judith?'

'Yeah, some, but they're there since 1928. So it's not like we're breaking new ground in the neighbourhood. You want a list of references first or you want to take the risk, tell me what's your problem.'

'My problem is that I own ten thousand acres around ten miles north-east of Carefree.'

'And?'

'And somebody else is claiming they own it.'

'You pay taxes on this land, Mr uh . . . '

'Evers. Forrest Evers. I've been paying taxes on it for around ten years.'

'And you have a deed.'

'Sure I have a deed. But it's in London.'

'Yeah, I thought I heard that in your accent. But I wasn't sure. Could have been a Connecticut accent. Who's the other party, Mr Evers, claiming they own your land?'

'Call me Forrest. I'm not sure.'

'You want to take a guess, Forrest?'

'There's a woman named Sally Cavanaugh who has a trailer parked by my creek and who threw a stone through my windshield.'

'You want to sue for assault, trespass?'

'I don't want to sue anybody. She said her father had owned the property for years. I think she said his name is Merrill Cavanaugh. And there was some cowboy in a van who tried to throw me off my land. The truck had a star on the door and it said "Empire" under the star. Sally Cavanaugh has a map she showed me that has "Airport Development Corporation" written across half of my ten thousand acres. She said, and I don't know, maybe she's right, she said the map was copied from a map in the county records office.'

'Well obviously I need to know a lot more, Forrest. Why don't you do this: bring any documents you may have down to my office and we'll have a talk. But in the mean time, if you like, I can give you a guess right now.'

'Sure, guess.'

'My guess is that if it is Merrill Cavanaugh, and if a cowboy in an Empire truck tried to throw you off your land, my guess is that they have been encroaching. It would not be the first time. And I'll take it a little further than that. My guess is that they have wrapped up your property as legal as the eagle on a dollar bill.'

'Are you telling me you think there's nothing you can do about it?'

'Listen, Forrest, if they have been encroaching on your land, there's a lot I can do about it. Just don't get your hopes up.'

'When can I come in and see you?'

'I'm in court the next couple of days. What about Monday?'

'I'm going back to London then.'

'Well, when you get back to London, fax me your deed and we'll start from there.'

chapter five

The Phoenix Sun building has the grace and charm of a cement brick the size of a city block. Unfortunately it is the size of a city block. But then news factories are not famous for their architectural distinction. This is where Arizona's largest newspaper is written, edited, composed and printed. Every morning at 2 a.m. the trucks roll out on to the streets of downtown Phoenix with half a million copies of the *Phoenix Sun* on their backs. FRESH NEWS OF MORE DISASTER.

The lobby, just off Central Avenue, was as smudged and ink-stained as an old typewriter, and stuffed with security guards wearing black security-guard suits. How many security guards, you may ask yourself, does it take to check an ex-racing driver into the *Phoenix Sun*? The answer is three. One to sign you in, one to ring upstairs somewhere and see if anybody really is expecting you. And one to glare at you as if you were a sexual pervert. You never know, masturbation could break out in downtown Phoenix at any time.

There was a dark-brown marble wall behind the sign-in desk with PHOENIX SUN in large and dirty chrome letters underlined with the thought 'Great is Truth and Shall Prevail' in small, dirty, chrome letters.

I wondered if Great Truth was what had caused this outbreak of security. Or was a gang of terrorists blotting their notepads? If the *Phoenix Sun* really needed all this protection, it wasn't for telling Great Truth. Newspapers aren't built on Great Truth; newspapers are built on wars, rumours, rapes, murders, sex and wacky stunts. Reporters probably told the truth when they could but it was rarely great. Reporters stood on the sidelines with their notebooks out, more pushed around by events than pushing them. But then, what did I know about being a reporter? Still, when did ignorance ever slow down an opinion? I was here to learn, and I had everything to learn, no heavy braking into the hairpin required.

The security guard with the phone in his ear gave me a *Phoenix Sun* VISITOR badge to pin like an accusation on my dark green shirt. Dark green golf shirt, tan cotton pants, mahogany loafers and a big badge that said VISITOR. I looked like the perfect Phoenix citizen. Number Two Guard pushed the elevator button and when the bell went *ding* he automatically said 'let's go' to the opening elevator doors. Number Three gave me a grudging, go-ahead nod. 'Just don't play with yourself,' his look said.

I followed Number Two up to the third floor, across one half-acre newsroom and into another; rows of desks, men and women with the edgy pallor of fluorescent light, some staring at the walls, off into space or into their video screens, some joking over plastic cups of coffee. They were at home in their club and VISITOR following behind Number Two Guard didn't rate a second glance.

Number Two led me to the far end of the room where a tall, thin man with a big Adam's apple and horn-rimmed glasses was leaning against his desk, staring into his video display. He wore a seersucker suit and he looked like a high-school science teacher. 'How you doin' Evers. I'll just be a minute,' he said without looking up. Deep voice, echo chambers in the Adam's apple. Punched a few buttons, looked at the screen, saying, 'Roy Vespers called me from the *Detroit News*. He said you knew fuck all about being a reporter. I told him I'd babywalk you for your first five minutes.' He kept pushing buttons and staring into the screen.

'Think I'll be able to learn anything in five minutes?' I said.

He pushed a button, the screen flickered and went blank, and then he stood up. 'I think I can show you enough to get you into deep shit,' he said, smiling. 'I'm Bill Barnes,' he said. 'Vespers said you were a racing driver and now you were going to be a reporter. Where'd you go wrong?'

I laughed. 'Well, I was a racing driver. I wanted an excuse to come to Phoenix, so I said I'd write something on the Grand Prix for the *Detroit News*. Nothing to do with "great truth prevailing".'

32

' "Therefore we shall weep and wail".'

I looked puzzled.

' "Great is Truth and shall Prevail", you must have seen it in the lobby downstairs. It comes from the Old Testament, Ezra, chapter four. The Jews are telling themselves that unlike the Babylonians' their new city will be fair and just. "Great is truth and shall prevail." ' He paused for a moment for effect. ' "Therefore we shall weep and wail." Laura Elisabeth Richards. The clods who put that up in the lobby didn't know the half of it. They still don't.'

'Laura Elisabeth Richards?'

'Dead writer. Died in Gardiner, Maine, 1943. No, nobody's heard of her. But she won the Pulitzer Prize for a biography about her mother, Julia Ward Howe, who wrote "The Battle Hymn of the Republic". Little Laura Elisabeth also wrote *Snow White* and something called the *Joyous Adventures of Toto*, which I think is the original *Wizard of Oz*. So she probably had as much to do with defining the American dream as anybody before Disney fucked it up. She wrote a poem that added that little undercut, "Great is truth and shall prevail, Therefore we shall weep and wail." And I liked that. So I wrote a piece about "Laura Elisabeth and Great is Truth" but they spiked it. There's a lot this paper won't print.'

He looked down at the blank screen for a moment. 'You be careful, Evers. You never know, you might like playing reporter. The pay's lousy, the hours stink, but there is the lasting satisfaction of seeing people wrap fish with your prose. You know anybody here?'

'Not really. Unless you want to count a woman who was throwing rocks at me this morning. I can't say I know her but I won't forget her for a while either. Sally Cavanaugh ring a bell?'

He took off his glasses, and rubbed the bridge of his nose. 'Oh, God, yes,' he said more to himself than to me. Then, looking up again, 'Yes indeed. Sally does throw rocks.' He paused for a moment, thinking of something. 'OK,' he said, bending over the keyboard and looking at the blank screen. 'First thing you gotta do is sign in. Tap this key. Now type in my name and the password.' He typed but nothing showed on

33

the screen. 'You don't see anything on the screen in case somebody is looking over your shoulder.'

'You handle a lot of sensitive stuff?'

'Some of it is touchy, yes. OK, I've typed in "Barnes" and I've typed in my password,' he paused for a moment, 'Sally.'

'Not just a casual acquaintance,' I said.

'Not just a casual acquaintance. You could say I liked her and that would cover about ten per cent of it. Look,' he said, 'I'm late and I've got a lot to cover. But if you're free tonight maybe we could break bread together, huh?' His Adam's apple bobbed up and down when he talked and he had a way of looking you directly in the eye as if he was challenging you, challenging what you told him. I liked him.

'I'm free tonight, tomorrow,' I said, letting it hang.

'Great. You can tell me how you got to meet Sally. You must be amazing fast, or unusually offensive. Maybe both. I knew Sally for a year before she started throwing stuff at me.' He looked at his watch. 'Let me show you how to work this little monster before I run,' he said.

'OK, now you see I got these baskets up at the top of the screen, these little icons. This one is my personal file, move the cursor over to it and press enter. Now I go to command D for my day notes and you can look at my notes, although I'd just as soon you didn't.'

He took a couple of minutes to show me how to type and edit a story, how to store it, and how to send it. 'Don't worry if you don't understand everything I'm showing you. Carla over there' – Carla, black curls, red lipstick, double chin and dangling gold earrings, waved back from two desks away – 'can show you what's what if you get stuck. Now if you want to erase something, hold down the command key and hit "K" for kill.'

He did and the screen went blank again. We both stood up. 'Goes into the spike file for twenty-four hours.'

'Spike?'

'Yeah. There used to be a spike on the city editor's desk. They stuck the stories they killed on it and once a day they pulled them off and dumped them. Pleased to meet you Evers,' he said. 'I've got to go, but you're welcome to stick around and see if you get the hang of this thing. And listen, if anybody wants to know I'll be with Bobby Roberts at the Jardin Hotel bar then at the Red Rooster Bar around three. Where you staying?'

'Arizona Biltmore.'

'Sleeping rough?' His eyebrows arched up over the tops of his glasses in mock surprise. 'I'm impressed. If you want to be a reporter you're going to have to lower your standards. Pick you up at seven thirty? We'll have a drink at the bar, you tell me about Sally and then I'll show you what makes this Cowtown tick.'

He picked up his notebook and tucked it in his back pocket. 'Amazing tits,' he said, moving away, smiling, waving, gone.

And so I sat down to play. The screen was blank, reflecting my state of mind. Ignorance may not slow you down on the way to an opinion but it can stop you dead in the face of technology. I tapped the sign-in key and the screen came to life. I tapped in 'Barnes' and then his password, 'Sally', and the icons came up in a row across the top of the screen. Signs from some obscure civilisation that hasn't died yet. I moved the little cursor across the row of figures and, what the hell, punched the command button and 'N'.

The screen flickered to life. There were random phrases, dates. 'Roberts-Empirio', 'Admiral Boyce', 'San Diego delivery route?', more names. 'San Diego', 'Las Vegas', 'Chicago', places, names of banks. I don't remember much except the name Empire jumped off the screen at me in two or three places. Obviously these were files of Barnes' notes. Notes he'd asked me not to look at. I pressed the esc. button to escape and the icons came up again, glowing on top of a blank screen. I made a mental note to ask him about Empire over dinner, and maybe bring up San Diego to see if there was a story there he was working on. After I'd asked him about Sally.

Carla was only too glad to come over and give me a short tutorial on typing and editing and she showed me creased pictures of her three nieces; round smiling faces, three young girls in small medium and large on somebody's green lawn under a blue sky.

There is nothing to driving a computer. As long as you don't scream out loud and put your fist through the screen when you accidentally hit the wrong key and erase half an hour's work. A whole sentence gone. Speed, evidently, was not going to be my major strength as a writer. I had always imagined that since phrases always came easily to my mind, that the words would lie down on the page or the screen with equal ease. Those easy phrases not only wouldn't lie down or stand up, there weren't any. Nada.

What I was trying to start to write was a quick survey of the Formula One season that was just about to kick off. Phoenix was the first race of the season and I thought I'd pass on a few of my general thoughts on Ferrari's progress over the winter, and Nigel Mansell's new determination, etc. But as soon as I started to write it down it sounded as if I'd read it before. As if I was just copying what the real journalists had written and I had nothing new to say. Had nothing to say at all.

My mind drifted back to my last race at Phoenix, the year before, in the first practice session Friday morning. The sky was overcast and the track (if you want to call the rough city streets with portable concrete barriers a track), the track was hard to read at first. The cars hadn't been out long enough to lay down a coat of rubber from their racing tyres and the concrete and tarmac surfaces had different levels of grip. Tricky as a snake with hips. I was out early, working up to a reasonable speed, finding the limits.

Phoenix was a nasty, street-fighter track. Most of the turns are the simple, flat, ninety-degree left or right; the everyday turn left on to Adams and then right on Seventh variety. Stand on the throttle, stand on the brake, turn, stand on the throttle. No finesse, no great long swooping 165-mph corners to separate the men from the boys. Just point and squirt.

You don't sit in a Formula One car, you lie down, strapped in tight to the chassis, with your shoulders and head elevated just enough to see over the cowl. With the suspension rock-hard and a grand total of one inch of suspension travel, you bounce and vibrate with the car. So your head bounces like a jack hammer two feet off the ground, jarring your vision. With three-foot high concrete barriers all around the track, it all looks the same concrete grey. Not only can you lose track of where you are, even if you know where you are, you can't see much.

Name

Sitzplatz/Seat, Dest.

Row **8**

Seat **F**

LH3085

FRANKFURT

42

MÜNCHEN

I was coming into the hair-pin turn before the main/pits straight. It's a long, slow double apex, the trick being to get on to the throttle as soon as you can. You clip the first apex just coming off the brake coming into the corner, ease on the power around the corner and hard on the power just before the inside apex coming out of the corner. So the textbook says.

I was coming into the corner, just clipping the inside, coming off the brake and there was a damn Dallara, spinning in front of me. Normally a Dallara is a pretty car, sleek as racing cars go. At that moment it looked as big as a barge, stretching like a steel barrier across the track. There was nothing I could do. It was twelve feet away and I was headed for it at eighty-five miles an hour. Its four wheels were locked, the car was sliding sideways turning away from me, headed out towards the wall. I started to get back on the brake, seeing the car loom larger, moving left, oil streaks down its side, grey smoke and chunks of rubber spewing off the bottom of the rear tyre.

I didn't miss it, it missed me, Vesco letting off his brakes and the car rolling out to the outside of the track in the microsecond when he must have seen me. I got hard back on the throttle and headed up the straight, a half-gallon of adrenalin free-basing through my veins.

The main straight is wide and over a half-mile long. It ends in a right-angle turn, normally a good place to pass. Floating up the straight in that accelerated compression of time called speed. Tunnel vision, blurred at the sides and at the end of the tunnel, there was another car up ahead, yellow, a Lotus, moving slowly, probably just came out on the track. I went through the gears catching him quickly, and as the corner loomed up he moved over giving me plenty of room as I got on to the brakes and changed from having seven hundred horsepower screaming at the back of my neck, squashing me against the car with the G-force of acceleration, my cheeks flattening against my teeth, changing from that violence of wind and noise into the reverse effect, standing on the brake my whole body suddenly taking on multiples of its weight, the straps of my harness digging in, cutting me into sections.

The track is full of little corrugated ripples and as I get really hard on the brakes, slowing down from one hundred and ninety-five miles an hour down to eighty in just slightly under two seconds, when the right front wheel hit a slightly larger ripple, bounced off the ground, locked in mid-air, and the left front, having plenty of traction, pulled me into the wall.

Just like that.

The left front tyre hit the wall, tore off, and I spun once, knocking the concrete again and backed down the escape road. I remember sitting there in the helpless fury that you have when something breaks, diluted with the gratitude that it wasn't a bad crash and that I wasn't hurt. I remembered that breathless racing of the heart and the weak feeling in my arms when the shouting . . .

. . . no not shouting.

Silence.

The newsroom was dead silent and urgent whispers boomed off the walls. Carla, green silk blouse, dangling gold earrings, was bending over me telling me that they had just heard from the police. Barnes. Blown up. Killed. Barnes had been killed. Barnes who was here a few minutes ago.

Down in the street below, a siren was screaming. And in the distance, in the bright blue sky, a puff of smoke was hanging in the air like a balloon, drifting away.

chapter six

Glue Los Angeles, with its big, wide streets, no centre and no pedestrians, on a rubber sheet. Now stretch the rubber sheet several miles in all directions. Now you have some idea of Phoenix.

Phoenix stretched on and on and on and on from the hospital window. The wide, flat streets marked off the big squares that were once farmers' fields. The eye could travel for miles and see the endless litter of one-storey shopping malls, launderettes and Pizza Huts, factory shoe-outlets and Nissan Dealers. With empty lots and suburban houses scattered among them. Then for no reason, mirrored towers of office buildings would stick twenty or twenty-five storeys in the sky. Then more empty lots and laundromats and Burger Kings. Then an unexpected eruption, another cluster of office towers. Off to the right, in the distance, Camelback raised a red hump of rock alongside Paradise Valley, the Beverley Hills of Phoenix where the Gold-waters lived.

Phoenix, according to my visitors' map, had sixty-three shopping centres, twenty-three riding stables, one hundred and three golf courses, and, as far as I could see, no pedestrians. At 9 a.m. on a Friday morning, the streets of Phoenix looked like the city had been abandoned to the scattered crawl of automobiles. Down below, on the track, I could see the pre-qualifiers making their last desperate rush to qualify for qualifying, the scream of their engines remote complaints from another time zone. Another life.

The nurse behind the reception desk at Phoenix General Hospital had cheerfully asked with a flat East Texas twang what I was doing 'in these parts'.

I told her I was in Phoenix for the Grand Prix.

'That old thing?' she said. 'They had the Grand Prix last year and nobody come. Shoot, there was a ostrich race the week after?' She said it like a question, just making sure I was catching her drift? 'And more people come to watch the damn ostriches run than paid all that good money to see those little bitty foreign race cars.'

There were two kinds of people in Phoenix that week. People who cared about the Grand Prix. And people who didn't. The didn't-give-a-damns outnumbered the fans two thousand seven hundred and fifty eight to one. And half of the fans had flown in on charter flights from Tokyo. Most of Phoenix was aware of a Formula One Grand Prix World Championship Race in its midst the way you might be aware of a fly in a pool room . . . vaguely irritating, but not where the action was.

The Grand Prix course was laid out on the downtown Phoenix streets, blocking some and cutting off others. One building isolated in the middle of the track houses a mortuary where, the story went, a cadaver sat bolt upright, eyes wide open when a Formula One car went shrieking by. 'What the hell was that?'

'That was a Formula One car,' the mortician said.

'Oh,' said the cadaver, 'is that all.' And lay back down.

Formula One were setting up their billion-dollar global tent in Phoenix and the owners, drivers, mechanics, physicists, sponsors and the rest of the performing troupe were as provincial as any other circus come to town. Some of them had read the local paper and they knew a reporter had been dynamited. But it didn't bother them and they didn't think about it. This is America, they thought. They blow reporters up all the time, don't they? Did you see Mansell's lap time?

I didn't blame them. Phoenix wasn't their town. Their town was a jumble of airport lounges, restaurants with the menus in a foreign language and high-tech workshops and wind-tunnels in rural England, Italy and France.

It's human nature, I thought, staring out at the bright blue sky and the empty shining streets. Blood leaking out from under your neighbour's door will make you weak in the knees. But if a man is murdered with an axe in another country, a sparrow on your lawn with a bent wing will get more of your sympathy.

Barnes had not died. He lay three rooms away from the empty room I was in, in intensive care, within ear-shot of the

Formula One cars. The blast had shredded his legs below the knees, torn off an arm at the elbow and taken off the back of his head. A week after the blast no one could bear to tell him he was dying. They had taken off both thighs and his other hand, beginning with the fingers and working their way up, day by day. So much carpet, felt, fibreglass, plastic, chrome, paint fragments and bits of Japanese steel had shrapnelled into his flesh that they had to keep amputating to stop the gangrene. The gangrene spread anyway. I had wanted to tell him how sorry I was. That dinner could wait. That I would wait. I wanted to tell him that I had liked him in the ten minutes that I had known him. Next to the awfulness of what had happened to him, none of that seemed important now.

Barnes was now a national figure. Network news carried nightly reports on his condition and the halls of the hospital were choked with reporters waiting for the inevitable.

The *Phoenix Sun* said over a hundred national reporters were working on the story. And the Phoenix police had assigned over a hundred and fifty officers, they said, to solving the crime. Justice would be done. As if there was any justice for taking a man's hands and legs, his mind and his life.

I had seen Barnes on his bed and I wish I hadn't. I had not been allowed into the intensive-care room, I could only peer with the newsmen and women through the smoked observation window and see the mass of dressings and tubes that had been a man. And if you want to know what a septic and draining stump of a leg looks like, I don't want to tell you.

A surgeon told me Barnes was able at first to raise a finger to recognise the doctor's presence, but that was all. It was a miracle, he said, that Barnes had lived at all, let alone this long. Barnes had always fought. He would go down fighting.

The difference between the cool and muffled rooms of Phoenix General, the tight-lipped, exhausted doctors and nurses moving past, lost in thought, the difference between the hospital and the paddock of the Phoenix Grand Prix, was total.

You could be forgiven for thinking the reason nobody was on the streets of Phoenix at ten o'clock on Friday morning was because they were all jammed into the Formula One paddock. Except these were not normal pedestrians. And this was not a normal paddock. This was the first practice day in the United States' only Formula One Grand Prix.

First the paddock. The paddock in Phoenix won the Evers Pits award for the worst paddock in Formula One racing. Monaco is bad, but you forgive Monaco the lack of space because you forgive Monaco everything (if you didn't there wouldn't be a race there). Besides the country is so small they'd have to annex part of France to make more room. Mexico is worse. Except Mexico is so poor and starving you expect the pits to be the dirty, run-down places they are. Phoenix didn't have those excuses. Central Phoenix measures twenty-five miles by twenty-five miles. Phoenix is not small and it's not poor, but you'd never know it from the cramped concrete alley they call the paddock.

Never mind. Your typical Formula One Paddock Creeper is an adaptable creature . . . bright, rich and sometimes famous.

The Phoenix paddock was a narrow strip of concrete, bordered by the campers of the racing teams on one side and chain-link fence and parking lots on the other.

Campers?

Campers were a definite step down in the world for most of the teams who are used to their forty-five-foot-long leather-lined and well-stocked rolling 'hospitality facilities' where they like to rest their drivers and entertain their corporate sponsors and favoured members of the press. But there was no room for the usual Formula One Showboat in the Phoenix paddock and they make do with these little Winnebegos.

As a result, the movers and shakers in Formula One didn't hide in their motor homes the way they do in most races, they strolled up and down the narrow concrete strip. It was March and the air was cool but the sun was as intense as Khartoum.

Jackie Stewart, hand-tailored Savile Row pale lime-sherbet linen sports jacket, ash-grey Dunhill flannels, hand-made Löbb casual loafers, three times World Champion, moves quicksilver through the crowd, hawk-eyed, quipping and smiling, on his way to set Bernie straight on something, pausing to hear how this journalist has lost weight and that one is looking forward to Jackie's annual shooting match at Gleneagles.

Barnes sitting in his car backing out. The force of several dozen shotguns coming up through the floor of the car, a million and a half pounds per square inch shattering the tar, paint and steel of the underfloor into shrapnel, rising up at the speed of over a thousand feet in the first thousandth of a second on the crest of the shock wave inside the car.

Phil Hill, World Champion in 1961, wears a blood-red Ferrari shirt in honour of his old team. He stops to tell two journalists about the time Olivier Gebendien stumbled into the wrong bedroom in Monte Carlo as, in the background, Jean Marie Balestre, FIA President For Life, has his arm around today's Ferrari driver, Jean Alesi, telling Alesi something as the photographers keep a wary distance.

A gorgeous woman with long tanned legs and red satin hot pants edges through the crowd with a long-lens Nikon pointing between her legs and nobody looks twice because former World Champion Alain Prost is sticking his head out of the little Ferrari hospitality area. He is on tiptoe, too short to see who he is looking for.

Barnes is dying. His body inside the balloon of five thousand five hundred-degree blast of nitrogen, steam, oxides and debris, his lower legs, gone.

There were ten minutes to go before the first morning practice, the warm up before the timed qualifying in the afternoon. I was headed for the concrete bunker they call the media centre, the sound of Formula One racing engines starting up obliterating any chance of conversation. Still one loud voice soared above the noise.

'Daddy look,' she said, just behind me. 'Daddy, this is the oak-head who tried to run me over.' Her voice was loud enough to make heads turn.

chapter seven

'Hi, Pine brain, 'member me?' Sally was smiling, cheerful, holding her hand out.

'Sure,' I said. 'You're the little peach who threw a rock through my windshield.' I took her long slender fingers in my hand and gave them a little friendly squeeze.

Sally's voice was the same and her eyes were still blue and her mouth had the same wide grin as when I'd first seen her by the creek, but this was a different Sally. No more country girl. This was a sophisticated urban woman in a flimsy swishy little dark blue nothing. Her hair had that slick and casual tossed-around look only available at heavy salon expense. Classy little sandals and dangling turquoise and silver earrings to set off her eyes and show just a touch of the artist.

'You come out on my land again,' Sally said in a nice friendly voice, Pepsodent teeth gleaming, 'and I'll shoot you. Won't I, Daddy?'

She had freckles on the bridge of her nose. Very rare, freckles on a dark tan. Reluctantly my eyes shifted to the weathered brick standing behind her. Daddy. Daddy had little beady blue eyes. Wide, flat, lipless mouth; wide, flat, zero-expression face. A little sunburn on top of a seventy-year-old tan. Brillo hair you could cut your hand on.

'Merrill Cavanaugh,' he was saying by way of introduction.

'Forrest Evers,' I said.

'Yeah, I know who you are.' Just a tic of a smile to let me know he was accustomed to holding the high cards. 'My daughter tells me, Mr Evers, that she was a little short on the hospitality the other day.' There was a web of deep lines around his mouth and his eyes. He was dressed in a kind of blue-grey mechanic's coveralls, with a lot of straps and belts. But it didn't look like he was planning on crawling underneath any cars, the coveralls were silk. It made him look like a butch transvestite at a garden party.

'She's a little old to be throwing rocks,' I said.

'Oh, you get used to that,' he said. 'You ought to see her throw credit cards around.'

'Shut up, Daddy. Don't be rude. You'll give this candy-ass Englishman the wrong impression.' Her smile stayed lit. She was enjoying this. I gave her a nice big grin back.

'You a fan of Formula One racing, Mr Cavanaugh?' I said, counting freckles on the bridge of his daughter's nose.

'Merrill, please, call me Merrill. Mind if I call you Forrest?'

'He's no Forrest Daddy, he's a Walnut,' she said, batting her eyes at me. 'A real off the Wahlll Nut.'

'Shut up for a moment if you would please, Sally,' Cavanaugh said, not looking at her, studying me. 'No, Forrest, I'm not a fan, although I admit I do enjoy the excitement. Tell you the truth, it's the money that interests me. There's one hell of a pile of money here and I like the smell of it.'

Behind him, Ken Tyrell was waving his arms at Bernie Ecclestone, the man who runs Formula One racing. Ken kept pointing to the track, Bernie, in a crisp white shirt, was solid stone. Whatever it was that Ken wanted, Bernie was not giving him any this afternoon. Behind them, a tanned and heavily muscled Phoenix cop in short pants with a white helmet with a .38 strapped to his belt rode by on a bicycle. The bicycle said 'Police' on the frame and there was a little American flag fluttering on the handlebars.

'I'll let you in on a little secret,' Merrill said, leaning towards me, lowering his voice. 'One of my outfits has a piece of that Italian Strada Rossa Team for the season. If you look real close you can see our logo on either side of the nose. Six inches by five and a half goddamn inches. Now that is what I call a high-rent district. We paid about a half a million dollars to stick those little decals on the nose of that car. You heard of Darvol?'

'Darvol,' I said. 'Doesn't ring bells. I can't say that I have.'

'Nobody else has either. So let me tell you, Forrest. Darvol is one of our leading developers in the Southwest; leisure complexes, resorts, retail environments.' Sally was looking off to the middle distance. Reminding me that her eyes were the same blue as the Arizona sky. Cavanaugh's eyes were the same blue only faded by the sun. 'There's a lotta real-estate buyers in Germany and Japan and we'd like to put their money to work for us here in Phoenix. I mean we're not parochial. We got a couple of tie-in deals with a Japanese bank, brings us a few foreign investors, and we give them a little insight into how to get things done around here. A kind of a mutual back-scratching. But we thought it was time we spread our wings a bit, developed our own contacts overseas.'

He leaned closer, another confidence. 'Sally says you used to drive these damn things. You know how to play this game maybe you ought to run a team. The way that Strada Rossa outfit' – he jerked his head back, indicating the pits – 'is spending my money I got to think there's a lot of profit in it. For somebody. I guess I'm a little spoiled, Forrest. I'm used to a generous return on my money and I can't help thinking that there may be a smarter way to go about this.'

'You're worried about your sponsorship,' I said.

'What I'd appreciate, Forrest, is a little advice from you. You're the only American I know of in this damn sport. And I can't help but entertain the suspicion there ought to be an American team. Maybe you could give me a little advice on the subject.'

'Sure, I'll give you advice,' I said, 'for what it's worth. But I'm not sure I know what you want advice about. Are you thinking about investing in your own Formula One Team?'

'Oh hell, not my money. OPM.'

'He means Other People's Money. He doesn't like spending his own money, do you Daddy?'

'Oh, I'll spend money to get money. Money's not a problem. You see, I had my own team I could call it "Darvol", like "Benetton", or "Marlboro", instead of just a couple of stickers on the nose.'

'You are talking about a lot of money. I'd guess Marlboro Mclaren's budget is over a hundred million dollars a year. And they get their engines free from Honda.'

'I know that,' he said with the straight lip, no-expression, brick face. There was a scream of racing machinery from the pit lane as the morning practice session opened. We waited for the sound to die down as the cars drove down the track one by one.

'Partly it's a question of technology,' I said. 'There are several Americans in Formula One racing, but they work in Europe because that's where the autoclaves, the wind-tunnels and the rest of the whole technology is. So even if you had an American team, you'd have to have your base in Europe, and preferably England.'

'Shit, Penske runs his Indy team with cars they build in England, I don't have a problem with that. I'm here to tell you that money is not a problem. And if money is not a problem then finding the right people shouldn't be your insurmountable obstacle, should it, Mr Evers? England or Timbuktu. I don't think we'd have a problem with geography.'

'Putting together a team that is going to be capable of winning the World Championship in two to five years would take at least twenty million dollars.'

'Who said anything about winning? I just want to be there, Forrest, I don't have to cross the line first. Anyway what's this problem you've been having with my daughter?' Sally smiled happily.

'Well, I don't know as I'd call it a "problem",' I said, keeping it friendly. 'It's more like a puzzle. Did your daughter mention that she's camping out on my land?' I said, keeping the conversational cannonball rolling.

Sally mouthed 'fuck you' to me, with a little smile. No hard feelings.

'Don't misunderstand me. I don't mind, Merrill. I don't mind at all. Sally's welcome to stay on my land as long as she likes. Throw rocks all day long if that's what she wants to do,' I said.

She said, 'See, Daddy? A real Timberhead. Solid mahogany wahlnut Forrest fruitcake.'

'Oh, shut up for a minute if you would please, Sally,' he said, his lips barely moving. He had a habit of running his hand over the Brillo bristles on his head when he talked. 'The two of you are worse than a couple of damn kids.'

He put his arm around his daughter. 'Mr Evers, Sally tells me you believe you have a claim on a sizable chunk of real estate the other side of Carefree. Well, let me tell you, if you

47

want to make a complaint, I'm sure, depending on the validity of your claim, you'll have redress under Arizona law. I can recommend a good lawyer, specialises in that kind of thing, if you like.'

'Sally says one of your companies claims to own my land.'

'Did she now?' It was a trick of the light, no doubt, but his old eyes seemed to brighten. 'Well I'll tell you what, Mr Evers, I have a lot of companies. And together they do own a considerable amount of land.' A Formula One engine came to life in the pits behind us, screamed, coughed, and died. 'Why don't you come out to the house real soon, bring your papers, have a drink and we'll talk about your land and mine. I'm sure we can sort something out. I can't say for sure, but it might just turn out that we're neighbours. I'm neighbour to a lot of folks in Phoenix.'

'Daddy likes to keep in reach of everybody's pockets, don't you, Daddy?' Her smile stayed fixed.

'I'm afraid I never did get around to teaching you manners, did I, Sugarpuss?' He gave her another one of those imitation smiles that he had, although it could have been a gas pain. It was gone when he turned back to me. 'She was always too pretty to spank, even when she was a little baby. Damn shame, probably would have done her a lot of good. You take me up on that drink, Forrest, hear? I'd like to hear what you think about running one of these teams.' His head tilted back, a man of authority.

'My God, Merrill Cavanaugh offering to buy a drink.' A confident, friendly voice boomed behind me. The little quickie grin on Merrill Cavanaugh came and went. 'I hope somebody got that on tape,' the voice went on.

He was about thirty-five, sticking his hand out for a shake. 'How do you do. I'm Bobby Roberts? Friend of the family you might say. I saw you race here last year, Forrest. I'm not mistaken am I, you are Forrest Evers? This here's Jenny Webb. Say hello, Jenny.'

'Hello,' said Jenny, cheerful as a bird. Bobby had the casual look of money and time to spend. Southwestern American Country Club with a nice tan and a face handsome enough to sell cigarettes or designer silk shirts. Sunglasses pushed back on his long blonde hair. Friendly green eyes. Pink linen shirt and floppy pistachio trousers. Two-hundred-dollar Super-trick white and multi-dayglo electra-colour Reeboks with wrap-around, high-tech, action-air, see-through, auto-pump support system and white and pink leather-and-foam tongues that stuck out like a pair of thirsty dogs. Right there on the cutting edge of fashion, Bobby was.

Jenny was right alongside, curled around his arm, and Jenny must have been Miss Kansas. A break your heart face. Or maybe she was Miss Midwest or Miss Universe and Miss Milky Way. Jenny was the prettiest woman I had ever seen and Jenny looked straight through me as if I weren't there, smiling her all-purpose pageant-winning smile. Bobby's ultimate masculine accessory.

'See what a little corn'll do for you,' Bobby said to us all, the proud owner. 'Eat more corn, Sally, and you could be as pretty as Jenny.'

'Fuck off,' Sally said, smiling, still smiling. Was I the only human being in Phoenix who wasn't smiling? I thought for an instant. Followed by an image of Bill Barnes. Bill Barnes was a long way from smiling. It made me think of something, some connection I couldn't quite reach. Then I remembered.

'Don't get to see much of you, these days, Bobby,' Cavanaugh said, looking hard at the man.

Bobby didn't seem to notice.

Bobby said, 'Anything you need to know about Phoenix, Forrest,' Bobby said, 'don't ask Merrill here. Merrill probably owns it, and if you're not real careful, he'll sell it to you. And keep the deed. If you want to know something in this town, Forrest, ask me. I'll tell you where the money is.'

'Maybe there is one thing you could tell me,' I said. 'What was Barnes going to talk to you about?'

'Well I guess you got me there, Forrest. If it's important to you I hope and pray he's gonna get better so you can ask him.'

'He told me he was meeting you at the Jardin hotel.'

'Your name is Forrest?' said Jenny, wrinkling her perfect tiny little nose, her voice as flat as Kansas. 'Like the trees?'

'Any man big enough to wear those boots, Jennysweet, can call himself anything he likes,' Bobby said, with a knowing nod to me. The instant buddy. Man of the World. 'I'm sorry Forrest, I just can't help you there. If Barnes told you he was meeting me, I'm not surprised. He's an investigative reporter and you know they'll rarely tell you who it is they're really meeting. Bill's a friend of mine and for all I know maybe he was using my name as a cover. Maybe not. Whatever. Poor man, he didn't get to tell me about it. You'll excuse us, I want to talk to my friend over in Ferrari. Nice to meet you,' he said to me. Jenny's little bottom, in little white shorts, waved wobble-wobble goodbye.

'If Bobby has a friend in Ferrari,' I said, 'he doesn't need enemies.'

'He may not need 'em,' Sally said, looking after him, no smile at all, 'but he has plenty of 'em. Makes new ones all the time.'

'You two'll have to carry on squabbling without me,' Merrill Cavanaugh said with an old man's feigned regret. He watched Bobby and Jenny turn into the Ferrari courtyard where the tablecloths were red and the waiters wore yellow shirts with a black prancing horse on their breast pockets. He turned back to us, 'I want to go over to the Strada Rossa pit, act like I know what's going on.' He went off into the crowd, a little stiff in the joints, legs like commas, white shoes wide apart.

Sally and I stood there for a few beats, looking at each other, the sound of the cars out on the track rising and falling, the crowd finding their way around us.

'Well do tell me, Mr Racing Driver, who do you pick to win this Grand Prix?' Sally batted her eyes at me.

'You always throw rocks at people or is that a special gesture?'

'Just at the rude shits,' she said. 'Believe it or not, for a while there I was glad to see you. I thought you might be somebody new. I get so tired of the same old assholes around here. I mean it really pisses me off when you come on all friendly and then you pull that dumb shit about owning my land. It just isn't funny, you know?'

'If you'd paid taxes on it for ten years I don't think you be laughing either.'

'Look at me, Forrest, I am not laughing. I am so weary of the old hard shell act. You're just like every other man around here. You know what a walnut is, Forrest? It's a nut with a hard shell, but it ain't that hard to crack.' She stopped, looking up at me. Then she put a hand out, just lightly resting on my crossed arms, those deep blue eyes looking up. 'Look, Forrest, I'm sorry. It's really nothing to do with you. I know I'm a little freaky today. Bill Barnes was an old friend of mine and I just feel so bad.'

'So he said.'

'You know Bill? You really talked to him? I thought you were just teasing Bobby. What'd he say?'

'He said you'd been close.'

' "Close".' Sally closed her eyes for a moment and when she looked at me again, her face was a shade harder. 'Yeah, you could say that, I guess.' She was interested in the ground for a moment, then looked back up. 'I don't know if you're married or not, Forrest, but take it from an expert, don't get involved with a married guy. Or a married woman, you know what I mean? That's really what he called it, "close"?'

'Have you been to see him?'

'I couldn't bear it. They say he's conscious.'

'Sometimes,' I said. 'But I think you're right not seeing him. I don't think he recognises anybody now. And I wouldn't have recognised him.'

'I never heard him mention you. Where'd you get to know Bill?'

'I don't. I only met him for around ten minutes at the newspaper the other day. But I liked him. We were going to have dinner together and he was going to tell me about this gorgeous woman who throws rocks at strangers.'

'You got to admit, Forrest, you're stranger than most. And you have to get rid of those boots.' Then the smile left and the pain came back into her face. 'Oh God,' she said, looking off in the direction of the hospital, 'I hope they find the bastard that did that to him.'

'They have enough cops working on it,' I said, the way you do when you don't have anything to say, wanting to keep talking to her.

'Yeah, but they don't want to know anything.'

'But you do.'

'Of course I do. You staying here long?'

'I hadn't really thought about it.' I had thought about it. I had a ticket for a flight out to LA Monday morning after the race and then on to London.

'Well, think about it,' she said. 'Do you good to stick around. Get out of this damn city. This damn town is going to keep on growing until it reaches LA. They got whole grids of streets out on the desert. Streets with names just waiting for some developer to come along and plug in the houses. Put a wall around them and call it a secure community.'

'That's real pretty land that you or I own.'

'Daddy owns. But that's what I mean. Arizona just doesn't know what to do with cities. Cities need limits and Phoenix doesn't have any. What I'm getting at is you look like you need a little fresh air, Forrest, see the colours of the desert. Get a little sun on that pale face of yours. That'd bring you back to life.'

'I didn't know I'd been away.'

'There's a whole lot you don't know,' she said.

Looking over her shoulder, in the distance, I thought I could tell which window in the hospital I had been looking out of. Which window was next to Barnes.

'Tell me,' I said. 'I'd like to know.'

'Well, for a start, you crack open a walnut,' Sally said, 'and you get these little bitty broken bits on the inside.'

'I wasn't talking about myself. I meant Barnes.'

'Bill Barnes is not any of your damn business,' she said, turning and walking away into the crowd.

chapter eight

Sunday. Race day. Welcome to the bunker. Inside the low, flat, concrete block it was thick with cigar and cigarette smoke, men and women jammed in like refugees and thick with the noise of typewriters, teletypes, printers and three hundred people talking at once.

Up on the walls, on fifteen monitors, Alesi's Ferrari, a fuzz of angry red on the phosphorescent screen, jinked left, and almost took the lead from Senna in a fuzz of red and white. The silent fuzz balls were still side by side going down the main straight. The TV screens cut to a view from a camera at the outside of the first corner, fuzz balls headed straight into the lens, Alesi out-braking Senna for a moment at the end of the straight, locking his wheels, ducking in on the inside. Cut to the camera looking down the short chute to the second corner. Alesi had overdone it, went wide, Senna cut inside him to take the lead back again and the French journalist sitting next to me said zat zee leetle bastaird, Al Lazeee, wooed be a great drivair when he grow up.

I hadn't planned to be in the bunker. I had thought I would be different. I thought I wouldn't watch qualifying and the race on TV, in the concrete bunker, the way the racing journalists do. No, I'd watch from the stands. See the race the way the paying public sees the race. See what the people come to see.

There is something eerie, for me, watching a Formula One car on television. It seems so easy. Television gives you the illusion of being behind the wheel and you think, that's fast, but it's not that fast.

And it is true, it is not that fast. The car is much, much faster. Because television doesn't give you the vibration of seven hundred horses screaming at thirteen thousand revolutions per minute vibrating the pedals, the wheel and your spine. Television doesn't give you the heat, or the noise, or the gravity multiplied two, three, four and five times, slamming you back and forth and side to side. It doesn't give you the irritation of an engine that feels as harsh as trap rock and wouldn't pull the skin off a banana below 11,200 rpm then comes on full whompf at 11,300, a seven-hundred-horsepower on-and-off switch. It doesn't give you the grit in your face, the smell of the exhaust and the sense that the car is right up on the edge and the front wheels are starting to lose it, that the car doesn't want to turn in now, at this speed on this surface, right now. It wants to scrub off a little more speed before it turns in and if it doesn't turn in right now, in another ten feet it is going to scrub off a lot of speed against the concrete barrier that is a thirtieth of a second away.

TV doesn't give you the hyperspeed zing of a second broken down into a thousand fragments or the impact of the rubber on the concrete.

Television doesn't give you any of that.

I thought sitting in the stands might give me some sense of the speed and the force. Better than TV. It might even be fun, I thought. Some of the excitement, none of the pressure.

I was lucky. As a journalist I had a free pass to any seat in any stand, as long as a paying customer wasn't sitting in it. So I didn't have to pay $200 to find out that from the grandstands opposite the Phoenix pits you couldn't see the track. That unless you are sitting in the front row, leaning over, the only thing you can see on the track is the tops of drivers' helmets as they zing past. Or that on the corners, the stands are built to show you the absolute minimum of track. And that there are no scoreboards and that the PA system isn't strong enough to hear a single strangled word.

So the spectators at the track in Phoenix never knew what was going on, what the times, the speeds, or the places are except for one or two leaders. An hour out cruising the stands was enough to explain why so few people were in the stands. Unless you brought your own portable TV set, you couldn't see the race from there.

Maybe they should have found the guy who built the stands for the ostrich races.

I went back to the bunker to 'see' the race. The smoky, noisy, bunker crowded with journalists from all over the world 'reporting from trackside' and lit with long, bright fluorescent tubes. It was like an underground school for the study of some distant battle in history, like Thermopylae or Okinawa. A big, bare room filled with rows of old brown fibre-top school-room tables with brown metal folding legs, the table tops cluttered with ashtrays, laptops, styrofoam coffee cups, reporters' portable computers and press releases. The silent TV monitors showed the action on the walls and minutes later, bulletins of lap times and interesting little facts were printed out stacked neatly by category and by time of release in plastic dispensers along the wall.

A question for my column. If this race wasn't for the benefit of spectators who couldn't see it, and it wasn't for the journalists who didn't see it either, except what they were shown on television, who was it for?

And what was I doing there except hanging on? That was the real reason I didn't want to go back into the bunker. It wasn't just the distance that TV put between me and the race and the car. It was the distance between myself and the journalists. The distance between who I had been and whoever the hell I was now. I had been a player. Now I was just another bogus minor scribe on the sidelines feeding off the faxes, press reports and TV screens. Now I was playing at being one of them and we were all embarrassed about it.

'Great to see you, Forrest.' 'What's happening, Forrest?' they said, their eyes on the screen, not waiting for an answer. There wasn't any answer.

In the meantime Senna, who was thirty, a year younger than I, who speaks six languages, who will not watch television for fear of diminishing his eyesight, who has trained his heartbeat to slow down by five beats a minute below normal, who is paid over a million dollars a race, who carries a Bible to read on the long flights, and who has won the world championship three times, Senna won.

Later that evening, as the teams were pushing their cars up ramps and on to the big transporters to take them back to the airport and back to Europe, and as the journalists and the fans crowded sixty deep at the Phoenix Sky Harbor International airport, anxious to check in before the flight home took off, I sat at Barnes' desk in the *Phoenix Sun* newsroom, trying to put words to screen, trying to find some excitement in a race that already seemed like a rerun.

Barnes was dying.

I wrote, 'Thirty thousand horsepower tore around the streets of Phoenix today in a storm and fury that ended as predictably as an apple dropping towards Newton's bald dome.'

Tripe. Start again.

'The crisis in Formula One racing today . . .'

What crisis? They have more money than they can count and four billion TV spectators a season.

Start again. I needed a jump start.

I started fooling with the buttons and thought, What the hell, let's see Barnes' notes. Maybe there is a little nugget of local colour there to get me started. I punched Command, 'D', for day notes, Barnes' notes.

Nothing. The screen was blank. I tried it again. Nothing. Now I was curious about 'Empire', the company name that had been on the side of the van on my land, and I wanted to know what Barnes had found out about them. I wanted to find out who Barnes had been talking to. What he was researching. What story he was working on.

Nothing.

I tried it several ways. Nothing.

At 6 p.m. on a Sunday evening in the vast grimy newsroom of the *Sun*, most of the grey metal desks were empty. Here and there, in silence, half a dozen newspaper journalists bent green and flickering faces over keyboards, peering into video displays.

The man nearest me looked up when I said, 'Excuse me,' his boyish face wrinkled in mild irritation at being interrupted and from trying to remember who I was.

'What's happening?' he said, scratching his chest through a T-shirt that said, 'No Shit, No Flowers.' He was about twenty-six or twenty-seven, his story in broken paragraphs on his screen.

'I wonder if you could give me a hand with the computer?' I said nodding towards Barnes' desk.

He looked over at the blank screen and pushed-back chair where I had been sitting. 'What, Barnesie's?'

'My name is Forrest Evers, and Barnes was going to let me use his desk for a while to write up a little piece on the Formula One race before I go back to London. I'm probably just pushing the wrong buttons,' I said, 'but I can't call up his notes.'

'Oh yeah? What do you want to look at his notes for?' He wasn't angry yet. But the look on his face said he could be soon. 'Notes are like underwear,' he said. 'They are personal, secret and sometimes nasty. You don't show them to anybody you don't want to. What's your reason?'

'No special reason. Except that Barnes' notes were there when he showed them to me. And now they're gone.'

'Maybe he erased them. Most writers aren't exactly wild about having somebody else look at their notes.'

'He didn't come back.'

There was a pause while he looked at me. 'He was blown up half an hour later,' I said.

'Kevin Turnbull,' he said, holding out his hand. People in Phoenix are great handshakers. 'Let's have a look.'

Turnbull bent over the keyboard. 'Barnes give you his password?'

'Sally,' I said. Turnbull pushed the buttons on Barnes' terminal. He tried different combinations, different ways, and there was nothing. Plenty of Barnes' old stories, plenty of the phone numbers and addresses he kept for research. But no notes.

'Could anybody erase his notes from another terminal?' I asked.

'Not unless they knew Barnesie's secret password, and I don't know anybody except you and Barnes and maybe the city editor who does. And not unless they know something I don't. I mean anything is always possible with computers. Some weirdo, maybe, with access to the mainframe, could probably erase anything he liked. But if Barnesie's notes were dumped, I'm about ninety per cent sure somebody must have come in to Barnes' desk and erased them.' He looked up at me with a reporter's curiosity. 'You're going back to London tomorrow, Evers?'

'I have a ticket for a flight out tomorrow, Kevin. But I think I'll stay for a while. What do you know about the Red Rooster Bar?'

chapter nine

Even in March the Phoenix sun shines down with a spotlight intensity, drawing Americans from as far away as Maine and Alabama to the Valley of the Sun. They come to doze in the hot winter light and feel the warmth in their bones as their skins turn carcinogen-brown and their blood sizzles.

Come spring the rich take off for Aspen, Jackson Hole and London. While the rest go back inside and turn on the air-conditioning.

But in the winter, rich and poor, they all come to Phoenix. Millionaires fly in from San Francisco to hook up their satellite dishes and uplink codes to the billions streaming from transponder to transponder in the stratosphere, twenty thousand miles above the equator.

Widows and divorcees from Minneapolis come clutching their Savings and Loan bank books and photographs of children who have children of their own. Freelance pilots drive up from Miami to fly real-estate developers who like shopping from the sky, and small-time dealers slip in quietly from NY and LA to take their cut from the tidal wash of hash, crack and grass that flows in from Mexico and Central and South America.

Old Mafia dons fly in on their own jets from Chicago to retire and keep their hand in a few legitimate enterprises and streamline the local call-girl operations. They bring their wives, their girlfriends, their families and a few extra guys they keep busy watering their lawns and keeping the girls in line. Autoworkers from Detroit drive through in their Winnebagos and Dodge Wanderers on their way to Disneyland, slow down, and stay for the cheapest fully equipped (PLUS FREE PARKING!) North American condominiums under the sun.

Bankers, businessmen, plumbers and funeral directors came

from all directions when business was booming. And even when it wasn't the golf was always good.

In the distance, a loudspeaker quacked the names of two-somes and foursomes ready to tee off, and I rolled over, opening my eyes. Ninety million miles away from the fastest-growing city in America, a single light source framed the heavy drawn drapes in my room with stripes of glowing white light.

Time to get up.

Shower, shave and pull on my yellow socks, turn on the radio for company, the quiet ceremonies of a single man. My body has a few scars, a long purple one down one shin that I shattered in a Formula Three crash when a front upright let go. And there is a jagged half-dollar sized disc on my back where a universal joint separated from a half shaft and flung a piece of shrapnel into my back to nestle next to a kidney. But apart from the memories of old lovers and other injuries, my carcass carries very little excess baggage, although I had to admit I had picked up seven pounds since I'd stopped driving. I couldn't see it, but the scales did.

When I had been driving in Formula One I'd pictured myself retiring to a luxurious life alongside an uninhibited and generous woman; a life of swimming-pools, tennis at the country club and dinner with friends at the conversational end of an expensive restaurant table. I pictured myself travelling to the paradises they build for the tasteful rich in the third world, and diving naked into the sea at night in Tahiti.

None of that happened. When I quit driving, I slid for a while. I ate too much and I drank too much, thinking I was celebrating my escape from the confines of a Formula One cockpit where you are allowed almost nothing to eat and absolutely no alcohol to drink because every extra ounce of weight will cost you time around a race track, and every alcoholic drink has the potential of slowing your reaction time by a crucial half of a thousandth of a second. So after I stopped driving, I gladly drank and ate what I felt like until I saw a bloated face staring back at me from my mirror one hungover morning. The crags on my face were filling in, my eyes carried luggage and my mouth was beginning to gape.

Not celebrating, drowning.

So I did the sit-ups, the push-ups and all the rest of the

exercises that are almost as boring to hear about as to do. I did them every morning out of some need to feel that I could go back to being a racing driver again if I wanted to. Even though I knew I never could.

But at least I could feel, in the air-conditioned air of my room, and, now that I had pulled the drapes back, the sun heating the blue carpet, at least I could feel the ache and the strain. Barnes had no legs. And now, according to the morning paper, no hands. They had to keep cutting off parts of him to stop the gangrene. What does it take, I wondered, counting push-ups, what state of mind, for one man to blow the legs off another? What was the prize?

I took the paper with me to breakfast. I had slept late and the wives and the children were already splashing in the big pool in the distance, while the husbands in their shorts and T-shirts, looking like oversized schoolboys with hairy legs, the husbands were herded into a sales meeting in a conference room behind me. They had left the windows open and I could hear their hearts sinking as a hard American voice sounding like George Bush fought the feedback on the mike. 'OK fellas, let's take another look at those sales objectives for the South-west Region again. OK?

'OK, we know those quotas are tough, twenty-two per cent up over last quarter. OK, we know it's tough out there. We all know there's a recession out there. Nobody ever told you it was going to be easy. Reach your quotas and I guarantee you a six per cent bonus.'

His voice lowered a few confidential notches and I could picture him bending to the mike. 'But I know and you know you are not the kind of guys who are going to be satisfied with just making your six per cent bonus for making your quotas. If all you want to do is just make your quota all I got to say to you is pack your bags, goodbye and good luck. Making your quota this quarter is not going to be enough. Not nearly enough. That's the downside. The upside is, the guy who is willing to go out there body and soul, the guy who is willing, and I know he's right here in this room, the guy who is willing to go out there and break his heart for his company is going to break the records and win that one hundred and twenty five per cent bonus and the Silver Anniversary Edition Lincoln

Continental Town Car because WE HAVE SIX GREAT NEW LINES TO SELL IN!'

Followed by the sound of hearts sinking as the husbands considered the possibilities of escape to Mexico.

Pretty women in candy-stripe dresses moved among the tables on the shady terrace, and the sun flung dancing coins on the fresh white linen tablecloths. Muesli with hazelnuts was thoughtfully chewed and perfect black coffee thoughtfully sipped while the guest considered his paper and his day.

The front page blared the arrest of Dick Esmond, a small-time street operator. A doughy face stared out from the grainy front-page news photo, hair carefully combed, wearing his best white shirt, hands cuffed behind his back, surrounded by serious detectives. A small-time street operator, the newspaper said, as in makes bets, runs little rip-offs like selling polished lead bars as discount silver. Knows guys who could rough somebody up if you wanted. Knows a few guys, know what I mean? A small-time dipshit who had told Barnes he had a hot tip for him at the Jardin hotel.

The largest manhunt in Phoenix history ended today when Dick Esmond walked into the Phoenix Police and Public Safety building 620 West Washington with his lawyer and confessed to the dynamiting of THE SUN star investigative reporter of the year, Bill Barnes.

Barnes won national prominence with a series of articles first printed in THE SUN exposing corruption in the state legislature and naming Phoenix developer Merrill Cavanaugh in a bribe scheme. Barnes was named Arizona reporter of the year earlier this year.

The reporter has been in intensive care in Phoenix General Hospital since the bombing last Wednesday where his condition continues to be listed as 'critical.' The reporter lost both legs and part of an arm in the bombing and early this morning surgeons amputated his left hand in an effort to stop the spread of infection.

Phoenix police had been searching for Esmond since the bombing as Barnes was reported to have named Esmond, the Mafia and the Empire corporation in a statement to witnesses before he lost consciousness. Barnes has been unable to speak since entering the hospital.

Sources close to the State Attorney General's office say that Esmond's lawyers are offering a deal. In exchange for leniency, the unofficial sources say, Esmond could be persuaded to tell the story of who was behind the bombing of the reporter. While detectives on the case say Esmond had no grudge against Barnes and was likely to have been a hired hand, no details of any deal have been released.

No doubt police investigation is an art and a science. This was their town and no doubt they knew what they were doing. But I thought it was strange they would plea-bargain with a dynamiter in exchange for a story. What 'story'? The story I wanted to know was the story Barnes had been working on.

Another article in the paper made two assumptions. One that somebody hired Esmond. And that whoever hired Esmond was reacting to something that had already been printed. That theory may have included half of the crooks in Arizona. Barnes had been a prolific investigative reporter. But it didn't make sense. Killing a reporter for something he already wrote might seem like revenge, but it wouldn't change anything. If anything it would stir up the story again. There had to be a better reason. I could just let it go. But what else had I to do?

If I put off seeing the lawyer about my land until the afternoon, I could stop by the Red Rooster around lunchtime, around the time Barnes had planned to go there. I had the time. I had plenty of time. Time to finish my coffee and wonder what the story was that Barnes had been working on. What had he found that attracted six sticks of dynamite?

On the way out a clerk behind the desk in the lobby stopped me and handed me a message. It was wrapped around a rock.

Forest, (Or is it Forrest?), How about trading the pleasures of the Biltmore pool for sand, dirt, cactus, coral snakes, mesquite and gila monsters? Your place or mine? 2nd and final notice. SALLY. 271 8298.

'Your place or mine.' I knew my deed in London was solid and the land was mine. On the other hand she was on the land and there was always the possibility that they had done something nasty and legal. I wondered if she had seen her father's name in the paper. Sally was spiky and tough and I was glad to hear from her.

I took the RentaBuick back and apologised for the hole in the windshield. 'Don't worry about it,' the check-in clerk said, pushing back her hair and not looking up. 'Happens all the time.' I drove out in a device called a Buick Reatta. It looked like a Reebok with wheels. Full-race boat-tail rear deck. Tasteful chrome-style accents. It went forward, if you want to talk about performance. Fuzz balls on the carpet, banana balls under the hood. Solid mush. Jesus, I missed driving a single-seat, spine-vibrating, balls-out racing car.

The Red Rooster Bar, like most of Phoenix, is in a mall. You'll find it just off Indian School, between a sporting goods store and a porno bookstore with a liberal lending policy on bazooka-bazoomer monster-tit videos.

Inside, the Red Rooster had the air-conditioning up hi and the lo-cool decor of the charcoal-grey eighties. Grey carpets, smoked-glass mirrors, black leather swivel bar-stools with a little red rooster embossed on the back for that classy, extra fifty cents a drink touch. At twelve thirty in the afternoon, while their corporate brothers were snapping shut their corporate big-money-is-just-around-the-corner notebooks and trooping into the Arizona Biltmore Wright Room for a sandwich and lemonade lunch, a couple in a back booth were taste-testing each other, squirming slowly while maintaining a seated position and two men in dark blue Kool-King Air-Konditioning overalls were shooting pool.

Three men in slacks and sport shirts were sipping on short beers, looked up to see who was coming through the door, saw me and went back to staring at the bar, uninterested. Two more could be truck drivers at the end, and one flash-looking tall gent stood alone at the near end. Heavy indifference from all of them.

The Nevill Brothers were coming through the sound system, voices as deep as the Mississippi, *Brother Blood, Brother Blood. We're of the same spirit, of the same mud.*

I ordered a Calistoga water from the bartender, depressing

him further. *We're from the same water, we're from the same love.* I said hello to the thin dark man at the near end.

'Who the fuck are you?' he said.

'I'm a friend of Bill Barnes.'

He was tall, with weak little brown eyes set close to a long thin nose. Bright red shirt opened to the third button. Thin gold watch with a gold mesh strap on a hairy wrist. He looked down at his watch, a prize possession. 'From what I heard, Barnes was short of friends. He had friends, he wouldn't have all those extra shoes now. Frankie . . . '

One of the men at the far end of the bar pushed off and came over. He had on a dark blue designer shirt with almost no sleeves, all the better to show off the biceps. Clear eyes, an eager smile for the white teeth to shine in. 'Frankie, this guy says he's a friend of Bill Barnes.' He turned to me. 'Whattaryou, a detective, a cop, another newspaper reporter?'

'Usually,' Frankie said, bulking large behind me, 'the newspaper reporters buy us a drink.'

'You've had a lot of reporters in here?' I said, signalling the bartender.

'We always get a lot of reporters in here,' Frankie said from behind me, 'they come here to brush up on their vernacular. Gimme a Bloody Shame, if you would, please, Max,' he said to the bartender. 'They like to believe we have connections.'

The bartender poured tomato juice into a glass and added horseradish, lemon juice, Tabasco and Worcestershire sauce. He placed the glass on the bar with care.

'Another spritzer, Max,' the tall thin one said. 'Charles Lawrence,' he added looking at the bottles behind the bar. 'If we had one guy in here asking us about Barnes we musta had fifty.' The bartender placed a tall fizzing glass on the bar in front of Charles.

'Barnes came in here a lot?'

'Yeah, a lot. He was always pushing some angle for some story he was going to write. Cheers,' he said, lifting his fizzy glass.

'Cheers,' I said, lifting my water. 'You have any idea what he was working on last week?'

'Look,' said Frankie with just a trace of Boston in his voice. 'Let's set something straight here, shall we? First you should be aware that when it came on the TV that somebody blew up Barnes, a cheer went up at this bar. My personal opinion, if that is what you are after, is that the guy is a copper-plated asshole. I know he sold a lot of newspapers but he hurt a lot of people too. Good people.' He took a drink of his Bloody Shame, the tomato juice staining his white teeth. 'You are not in the middle of a Bill Barnes fan club. The guy was a loner and there is a reason.'

'Is, Frankie. *Is* a loner. The guy's not dead yet. You see,' Charles said, not looking at me but at the door as if he was expecting somebody, 'a lot of people jump to the conclusion, a guy gets blown up, presto, the Mafia did it. Every time something happens, "Boom, the Mafia did it." '

'Barnes is supposed to have said the Mafia did it. You're going to tell me the Mafia didn't do it.'

'I don't have to tell you anything. Look at what happened; you tell me. Dynamite,' he said, arching an eyebrow. 'Dynamite? What are we talking about here, a Wells Fargo stagecoach? Assuming that there is a Mafia, and personally I don't think there is, apart from maybe a few sick old bastards sitting around their swimming-pools in Palm Beach and waiting to croak. I mean there are a lot of organisations out there now. But assuming just for the moment that there is that old Mafia, they would never use dynamite. No professional is going to fuck around with dynamite. Too clumsy, too unpredictable. No finesse. They'd go plastic. A little Semtex, as they say, goes a long way.'

'The other thing is,' Charles said, 'if the Mafia did it they would have done it. They would have vaporised the sucker. The guy that did that job would not,' he said, regarding his glossy black pointed shoe, 'be allowed to shine a man's shoe. Know what I mean?'

'You've told this story before.'

'About fifty times. Which is the other thing. You're never going to see the Mafia whack a reporter. You whack a reporter and you get fifty of them coming out of the woodwork. Is that what you are, another fucking reporter?'

'You could say that,' I said. 'What are you guys, PR for the Mafia?'

They both smiled at that. Frankie said, 'You're not from around here, right? Can I give you a piece of advice?'

'Shoot,' I said.

'The sun out here is magic on skin problems. You take those boots outside in the sun, they'll clear up in two, three days.'

It takes just a minute for the eyes to adjust from the gloom of the Red Rooster to the high noon billion-watt Phoenix sun. The world is overexposed, comes out of the white light slowly, the details faint at first. Especially if the sun bounces off a wide van windshield on to the side door when you come out. Not just a van. A grey van. Outside, in the mini-mall parking lot, with the sun blazing on its windshield, there was a grey van just like the one that had the big cowboy inside telling me to get off my own land. There was a star on the door and EMPIRE written beneath it.

chapter ten

'Wahlllnut,' she said. She sounded pleased. 'Where are you?'

'Outside a bar called the Red Rooster looking at a grey van that says Empire on the side.'

'Seems a strange thing for a grown man to do in the middle of the day.'

'I got your rock.'

'Well, goody. I don't know what it is about you, Evers. I don't know if I even like you, but I feel like I know you.'

'I thought you might know something about the van.'

'Van? Evers, you have the charm of a broken foot. What van are you talking about?'

'I thought you might know who normally drives it.'

'Sweet Jesus, you're playing detective, aren't you. Well, congratulations. You've tracked down an Empire van and you are off to a flying start, Wahlnut. I think Empire has around fifty of 'em.'

'What do they use fifty vans for?'

'Hell, I don't know. It's a big company, Forrest. They have a lot of stuff. If you're all excited about Empire ask Bobby Roberts. He does some kinda work for them. I mean he's on their board, but I'm not sure what the relationship is. Are you calling about my message or is this just a business call?'

'You sound pretty feisty this morning.'

'Of course I'm feisty. It's one of my better features. I was just going out the door.'

'From the Airstream?'

'From my house. The Airstream doesn't have a phone.'

'Do you have Bobby Roberts' phone number?'

'Three-three-six. Oh-four-oh-six.'

'You know Bobby pretty well.'

'Fax, three-three-six, oh-four-oh-eight. Mobile phone, oh-eight-nine-seven, nine-eight-seven-two. I know him all too well. We were engaged.'

'I'm sorry, I didn't know.'

'Don't be sorry, it was once upon a time, a long time ago. Bobby has his moments but I don't miss any of them. Maybe you should talk to him. If I was up to talking to Bobby I'd ask him about Bill.'

'Bill?'

'Barnes, Bill Barnes. Bobby'll lie, count on it. But you'll get a lot more out of him than a Empire van. I'm running late now, I'll see you later.'

'When?'

'Finally. You say when.'

'I'm seeing a lawyer about getting the squatters off my land this afternoon. How about tomorrow?'

'Tomorrow afternoon. Whereabouts?'

'Your place or mine. I thought maybe you could show me the prickly pears.'

'Can you swim?'

'Sure.'

'Too bad. See you at two at the Airstream.'

'Mr Roberts' office. How may we help you?' She had a Southern voice, somewhere south of Memphis where there was no hurry at all.

'I'd like to see Bobby this afternoon.'

'May we know who is calling?' She pronounced it 'cowling'.

'Forrest Evers. Mr Roberts and I met at the Formula One race this weekend.'

'I'm sorry Mr Evers, Mr Roberts is out of the office at this point in time.' Tie 'em, she said. 'How may we be in touch with you?'

'I'm staying at the Arizona Biltmore. You expect him back this afternoon?'

'Well, that's kind of what I'd have to call an open question. Depends on whether ol' Bobby Boy gets a snootful at lunch. He gets a snootful at lunch it could be Tuesday.'

'You're saying Mr Roberts is not a fun employer?'

'Mr Roberts is a triple-A turd.' Tehhhhrrruud, she said.

'You'll tell him I called?'

'Just a minute, Mr Evers, I do believe I detect Mr Roberts' shadow looming across my desk.'

I waited.

'Mr Roberts says that he has four fifteen open for you.'

'Lucky me,' I said.

'Don't count on it,' she said.

I stood watching the van, dug in my blue jeans for another quarter and dialled again. 'Hi,' she said.

'Judith?'

'Yeah?'

'I'm Forrest Evers, I called you last week about ten thousand acres north of Carefree?'

'Yeah, I remember, you thought Cavanaugh was encroaching on your land. We've been doing some heavy digging on your behalf. You calling from London?'

'I'm still in Phoenix and I'd like to see you. When's a good time?'

'Where are you now?'

'A little mall off Indian School near Central.'

'Now's the best time. You're five minutes away.'

A five-minute drive will take you three miles in Phoenix in the middle of the day. Maybe folks in Phoenix nap during the daylight hours. There were a few cars here and there. Some of them moving. And twice I saw a bus. But the town seemed to doze under the sun as if it were formerly inhabited, the only surefire sign of life the traffic lights turning red and green and, after a while, back to red again.

Behrman, Siskin and Victor are on the top floor of a tall glass and chrome tower with NEW CENTURY in six-foot-high chrome letters over the entrance. Across the shining monkey-dick pink marble lobby to the bank of elevators, an elevator car waited patiently, its doors open. It might have been waiting since last Saturday. I pushed the button for the nineteenth and top floor where there was a wonderful view in all directions.

Judith Behrman had a wide, old-fashioned oak desk, heaped with folders, papers and three computer screens. There were four other desks scattered across what looked like a half-acre of grey carpeting, but nobody was sitting at them.

'They're all at lunch. I try to do without. Pull up a chair.' I sat on the secretarial swivel chair next to her desk. For a man used to the cramped complications of London offices, the empty space was astonishing. 'Looks like you have room to grow,' I said.

'Most of our research is done freelance so a lot of the people who work for us don't work here. But yeah, we have room to grow. You could die from all the room we have to grow in. We arranged the financing for this building and did all the legal work,' Judith said. 'So we got stuck with it. There are eleven other tenants in New Century and room for a hundred fifty-three more. Anybody tells you Phoenix is a boom town, Mr Evers, take what they say with a half-ton of salt. After the Savings and Loan scandal broke I have to tell you the boom in Phoenix just went piddle into the sand leaving a lot of guys with limp dicks in their hands.'

She threw her head back and stretched a tanned arm to take in the three thousand square feet of office space around her and the desert air beyond. 'The wide, open spaces of Phoenix, Mr Evers, are in the office buildings. If you're looking for an office to rent, I can give you a choice of around twelve thousand, move in tomorrow.' Judith Behrman was short with short curly hair and a streetwise smile that made her little cherub face go round. Not the iron-grey haired lady in a grey flannel suit that I'd pictured from talking to her on the phone. Large green eyes, but I wasn't looking at her eyes.

'I see you've noticed my boobs,' she said. She was wearing a tight black T-shirt.

'I suppose they get noticed quite a bit.'

'It's my choice, you know? I mean I could wear baggy blouses and walk around hunched over, and hope nobody'd notice. Or I could have 'em fixed. But they're an asset in front of a jury. Women sympathise 'cause they know what a pain in the ass they are and men tend to pay attention to every word I say. You want to talk about your property, Mr Evers?' She had a husky voice with a little rasp.

'The deed's in London, but . . . '

'Like you said. I know. Don't worry about it. I pulled a copy out of town records. You ever talk to the trustees of your mother's estate, Mr Evers?'

'I'm not even sure who they are. There's a firm of solicitors in London that deals with them, Cox something and Cox.'

'Cox, Carleton and Cox, Mr Evers, and you ought to talk to them, because what you have in this particular parcel is around half of what you had before.'

'I don't understand, I've paid the taxes.'

Judith stared off towards the west coast. 'People think land is permanent. Like it is always going to be there. But out here, Mr Evers, it is not uncommon to find your land has disappeared overnight into somebody else's pocket.'

'What are you telling me?'

'Did you notice a drop in taxes one year?'

I had to think for a moment. 'About five years ago. They went down a bit, maybe twenty, twenty-five per cent,' I said.

'You didn't think that was the least bit strange.'

'Taxes fluctuate. Go up and down.'

'Well maybe they go down in London or Cornetto Land but I have to tell you, Mr Evers, that the last recorded fall in taxes in the United States was 1776.'

'What are you telling me?'

'I'm telling you that the trustees of your mother's estate around five years ago sold five thousand acres to a company called Skyway Development Corp which purchased the land on behalf of the State of Arizona under eminent domain for an airport that was never built.'

'Nobody ever told me anything about it. I mean if the state was going to purchase the land for an airport, why didn't the state just buy it from me?'

'Because the state didn't want it.'

'But they bought it anyway.'

'The state didn't buy it.'

'I must be asking the wrong questions. Can you just tell me what happened?'

'Sure, although I have to guess at some of it.'

'Just tell me.'

'You sitting comfortably?'

'Tell me.'

'Right. A group of Arizona State legislators were on the board of directors of a company they set up called the Skyways Development Corp. They then passed a law proposing a feasibility study of construction of a new airport outside of Phoenix, on your land.'

'A feasibility study?'

'Who's going to object to a feasibility study? "Air traffic in the Phoenix basin is going to increase two hundred and seventy-five per cent in the next ten years and the time to start planning for it is now." That kind of crap. Nobody is going to object to doing a study about planning for the future. Doing something, that's different. Under a subclause in the bill they allocated ten thousand dollars for an airport feasibility study.'

'So they hire consultants,' I said.

'They don't hire anybody. Skyways Development, acting on behalf of the State of Arizona, pays your mother's estate ten thousand dollars for five thousand acres of your land.'

I thought for a moment. 'That's two dollars an acre.'

'Two dollars an acre. A fine deal for the state. And after four years, their obligation to the state subsides, and they offer to buy the land from the state for one hundred per cent profit to the state, for twenty thousand dollars. And indeed, Skyways Developments purchased five thousand of what used to be your acres from the state of Arizona. So, they made ten thousand dollars profit for the state of Arizona and they are now the legal owners of that land. At a total out of pocket cost of twenty thousand dollars.'

'I didn't sign anything.'

'You didn't have to sign anything. The executors of your mother's estate did.'

'So I'll sue them, take them to court.'

'From what little I know of the British legal system, Mr Evers, you will break your heart and your bank trying to sue your solicitors. And I hate to tell you, your prospects here are worse. Simon, Roberts and Phillips filed for bankruptcy the week after the transaction. They no longer exist as a company. You are also an absentee landlord, so it's not as if you can count on drumming up popular support around here.'

'Let me make a guess here, Judith. Simon, Roberts and Phillips are the Arizona legislators who set up the Airport Development Corporation.'

'Simon and Phillips were state legislators, yes. Roberts is a local attorney.'

'What about the Airport Development Corporation?'

'An inactive and wholly owned subsidiary of the Darvol Corporation.'

'Who the hell are they?'

'I doubt if I'll be able to tell you much about them because they are an offshore company, registered in the Bahamas. As you may know, offshore Bahamas companies are not famous for answering their phone calls.'

'Offshore meaning untouchable under US law?'

'Well, occasionally they are touchable. But a lot of times by the time you've managed to pry one open they've moved the assets to another shell. You want a cup of coffee, Mr Evers?'

'No thanks, I feel plenty alert.' I also felt sick, the way you feel when you come home and find your front door is open and a burglar has taken everything he could carry and slashed the furniture.

'Mr Evers, the lawyers your mother appointed as trustees of her estate stole her land or rather the land she left to you and they did it as legal as an eagle. I don't know the property but I'd guess, going on what property is going for out there now, that it's worth around twenty-five thousand dollars an acre. If you wanted to buy it back it would cost you around a million, a million five, maybe even two million depending on the water situation.'

'But how the hell can they own it if they got it through fraud?'

'This is the West, Mr Evers. According to some native Americans all of the land from sea to shining sea was obtained through fraud.'

'You mean there is nothing you can do about it.'

'As I told you before there is a lot I can do about it. But it will be expensive and it will take time and considering that you would be going up against the resources of the Empire Corporation, I don't think your chances of success are worth a damn.'

'You're telling me to take a million, two million dollar theft of my property and do nothing about it.'

'I'm telling you that it would cost you a good deal more than that to try to get it back.'

'Through legal channels.'

'Through legal channels. I had one kinda goofy idea. For fifteen maybe twenty thousand we might get some tame legislator to reintroduce the airport feasibility study.'

'That would get my land back?'

'That wouldn't get your land back. But it might slow them down from building a few hundred condos as your next-door neighbours.'

'Let me ask you one more question. This Roberts who is a local attorney. Would that be Bobby Roberts by any chance?'

'Mr Evers, can I give you a piece of advice, no extra charge? Forget Roberts. He's a sleaze ball, a small-time sleaze ball. He owns a couple of race tracks which is a licence to print money. And he is a lawyer. I don't think you are going to get anything out of him without serious risk of doing serious financial damage to yourself. I expect the only reason the other two brought Roberts in on the deal was to have him put up the cash. If you really want to get your property back, there's another possibility, but I wouldn't recommend it. You ever hear of Merrill Cavanaugh?'

'I've met him,' I said.

'Well then you know you could lose the rest of your land if you are not careful. On the other hand he's one of the people who make property move around here. Merrill Cavanaugh was the man Bill Barnes was writing those articles about before that terrible accident.'

'Accident?'

'I'm sorry, it's just a lawyer's caution, creeps in now and then. I mean before some bastard blew him up.'

chapter eleven

You can take it as given that crawling along the streets of Phoenix from tower to tower in a Reebok RentaBuick, waiting for the lights to change or waiting for the woman with the tight silver curls, driving a Chevrolet Citation, the one with the heavy dust coat and a loose rear bumper, waiting for her to make up her mind whether she is turning left from the right lane into Chicken Cortez or right into the oncoming traffic as her flashing rear light suggests, believe me your mind will automatically slide into neutral. From Judith Behrman on the top of her tower, down to the street and across half of Phoenix, crawl crawl across the nowhere landscape of sunshine drive-ins and traffic in lo, and up again to Bobby Roberts on the top of another glass tower. Why does a city with several hundred square miles of empty lots need skyscrapers? Glass office towers rose up out of the dirt, scattered across the landscape, shining like mirrors. Were they high-rise ego trips for the real-estate developers and bankers who made it big? Was there some fundamental corporate psychological need to be sky high, way up there where the eagles fly? Are the skyscrapers in the desert the real totem poles of the twentieth century? Or just the cheapest way to stack white-collar workers? Whatever else they were, they were empty.

The El Coronado lobby directory listed insurance companies, land developers, a couple of dentists, a few lawyers and ninety per cent empty space. Like Judith Behrman, Bobby Roberts had the whole top floor to himself. His receptionist sat behind a blond wood desk facing the elevator doors. Behind her, across an acre of new beige carpet, in the windows that went from floor to ceiling, the empty sky was bright blue and the grid of Phoenix trailed off into the dull smog of the distance. Her desk held a video screen, a fax, a word processor, a telephone, a chrome nameplate that said 'Yvonne' and Yvonne's elbows. Bobby's office, with tasteful chrome letters on the door that said 'R. Roberts', was off behind temporary walls to the left. All that empty space gave me the impression that Bobby was not paying rent on the majority of it.

Yvonne's chin rested in her hands, studying me as if I was the first two-legged man she had seen. 'Goodness,' she added after a pause. She had wide green eyes and blue eye-shadow, and a fuzzy cloud of blonde hair. 'Y'all don't look like I expected,' she said with a magnolia drawl.

'What'd you expect?'

'A little bitty man, like a jockey. I thought all you English racing drivers were the size of a duck.'

'I'm not English.'

'Coulda fooled me. Wherever you come from sure scared the hell out of them boots.' You could drive around the block in the time it took her to say 'boots'.

'Them boots are ostrich skin, ma'am,' I said, 'and proud of it.' A little John Wayne into the timbre of my voice, there.

'They look like goose bumps to me. You're not scared of heights are you? Or are you worried about our Mr Roberts?'

'You said he was a turd.'

'Triple A,' she said with a smile that came and went. 'Although I suppose any woman from Alabama with a ten-year-old daughter gets involved with a turd like that probably deserves what she gets. What she gets is pain.'

'I'm sorry.'

'Don't be. Pain sharpens the mind. Keeps a heart from going soft. Don't let me put you off him, Mr Evers. Let Bobby do that little thing himself. You can take a seat if you like.'

I sat down on a sofa the colour and lumpy texture of oatmeal. 'Does it bother you being in a half-empty building?' I said.

'Hard to tell, isn't it, whether Phoenix is growing or shrinking. I don't mind, being on my own here, it's preferable to the alternative. On a slow cloudy day I sometimes go over to the window and I look out at all those other glass boxes in the distance and I picture each one of them with just one person in them, you know, nose pressed to the glass on the top floor, looking out to see if maybe there is somebody else out there, trying to figure out what happened, where all the people went. Most days, though, it's real busy. Bobby has what you'd call a high energy level.'

'Well I'm glad to hear it,' I said. 'What's Bobby do most days besides cause pain?'

She drew herself up, rearranging things on her desk, not looking up. There was a little quaver in her voice. 'You'll have to forgive me, Mr Evers. I've had a little shock today and I guess I have been a little unbusinesslike if you know what I mean.' She looked up, under control now. 'Mr Roberts should be with you just as soon as he is available.' She started punching buttons on her keyboard, peering into the computer screen.

'I didn't mean to offend you,' I said. 'Is it OK if I call you Yvonne?'

'Yvonne's OK,' she said. 'Yvonne is just fine,' she said between her teeth.

She busied herself with the keyboard as if I had been hung up like a coat to await Mr Roberts' arrival.

I waited a while. 'Are my boots that bad?' I said.

'They're not bad, Mr Evers, they're hilarious. Goddamn hilarious,' she said, her voice flat. 'You'll have to excuse me Mr Evers but that is it for small talk. That is all the small talk I can take today.' Her mouth started to wobble and tears rose up and ran over, down her cheeks. 'Goddamn it,' she said rubbing the heel of her hand across her cheek. She started to fumble in her bag for a Kleenex, a woman on display and no place to hide. She said, 'I am thirty-two years old, I have a degree in economics that has never done a damn thing for me, and I can tell you that being trifled with, if that is not too old-fashioned a phrase, makes you feel, makes me feel like shit on a stick.'

She looked up, tears gone and green eyeshadow smudged. 'And I have had enough promises about how we're gonna do this and pretty words about how nice it's gonna be when we do that. And then that's all it was, a lotta damn words. And I swear to God that the next asshole who makes a pass at me is going to get his balls dropkicked over to New Mexico and if you . . . ' she stopped. Then she looked at her computer screen and began to type.

Type, type, type.

I waited a little. 'Yvonne, I don't want to interrupt but I wonder if Mr Roberts knows I'm waiting for him.'

'I have no idea,' she said, still typing.

'Would you mind telling him?' I asked.

'Mr Roberts is not in at present,' she said.

I got up and put my hands on her desk, leaning over her. She had a musky, sexy scent of perfume with a sour sweaty note. She seemed to be deleting files from the computer. 'Would it be too much to ask where Mr Roberts is at present, Yvonne?'

'Most likely he's half a mile up seventh getting shit-faced at Brownies.'

I stood up. 'Thanks for your help, Yvonne,' I said. 'I hope you feel better soon.' I pushed the elevator button, heading back to the Buick Reebok.

'Fuck you,' she said as the doors were closing.

The parking lot behind the wide, one-storey building that called itself Brownies was half-full at five on a Monday afternoon. The back entrance leads through the kitchen, into a time warp. 1950s red leather banquette seats along the walls, Frank Sinatra crooning underneath the clash of dishes and the mumble and shrieks of a crowd three deep around the bar. There were plain tables with red-check tablecloths for serious steaks, and a few tables still held late lunchers into their fourth or fifth martini. Except for the short skirts some of the women were wearing it might have been 1957 with the waiters in white shirts, black bow ties and aprons and the cigar smoke heavy enough to lean on.

'Forrest!' Bobby stood up and bellowed across the dining-room. He was at a round table with four other men and two women and he was waving me over with a drink in his hand, his arms open wide like I was an ol' war buddy.

'Forrest am I glad to see you. How the hell are you? What kind of trouble you getting yourself into and how can I help? And what the hell are you drinking?' Bobby looked a little bleary in the eyes but he still looked good, light tan gaberdine suit freshly pressed, light-blue button-down Oxford shirt, pale green tie. He was tanned and relaxed. His blonde hair had that tousled look that came from a hairdresser who read *Gentle-*

men's Quarterly. A hairdresser who knew how Redford's hair-dresser did it.

'Water,' I said.

'Jesus, don't drink that shit, we need all the water we can get for the golf courses. Let me introduce you to these good folks, Forrest,' Bobby said, his arm sweeping around the table to include the circle of faces looking at me with mild curiosity.

'Pay attention here,' he said to the table. 'This here is Forrest Evers, one of the great all-time racing drivers, isn't that right, Forrest?'

'Nobody has ever accused me of greatness,' I said.

'OK, a not so great Formula One driver. Be what you wanna be. Now listen, Forrest, I want you to meet State Senator Leon Hodges' – a middle-aged businessman in a blue shirt and a solid blue tie, suit jacket hung on the back of his chair behind him, nodded in my direction – 'and his personal assistant of the week, Sharon Kelly.'

'You cut that shit out, Bobby,' Sharon said, 'you gonna get your face smacked. Sharon Kelly,' she said to me, 'Clerk of the Civil Appeals court and don't you ever believe a damn thing Bobby says.' Her mild round face with freckles and no makeup smiled welcome.

'Sam Cantucci, proud owner of Twin Star Developments . . .' A small, bald thin man in a dove-grey suit and conservative tie waved his cigar hello to me.

Bobby pointed to a man across the table who looked young enough to be a student at North Utah State Teachers' College, short back and sides haircut showing mostly scalp, white shirt collars splayed over a check sport jacket. 'State Representative Philip Causton.' State Representative Causton paused mid-drink, Adam's apple swallowing, to acknowledge the introduction. Bags under his eyes showing that he had grown-up habits.

'And his very special friend for today, Lila Wells.'

Lila Wells, a fifty-year-old woman with bright red hair and a frilly pink low-cut blouse showing a lot of freckles, gave Bobby the finger. 'Same old joke,' she said to me, 'Bobbie's a little crude sometimes but his heart's in the right place. You just need to give him a little room to keep from getting spilled on.'

'Little luncheon club we got here,' Bobby said taking another large gin and tonic from the tray of drinks the waiter had set down in the middle of the table. 'And Phil and Tom who represent law and order in this town in the form of deputy police chief and assistant State Attorney General.' Blank stares from two men who would never give anything away for free. I gave a friendly, casual, all-purpose Evers nod of the head as Bobby went on, enjoying himself. 'Course our little luncheon circle if we don't get off our ass and get out of here is in serious danger of becoming our little dinner circle.'

'The only person at this table who's been sitting on his ass since lunch is you, Bobby,' Sharon said, looking at me.

'What brings you here, Forrest,' Bobby said, flagging a waiter and making a circle with his hand to indicate another round of drinks.

'I went up to your office. Your receptionist thought you might be here getting shit-faced.'

'You saw Yvonne?'

'I saw Yvonne. Not a happy woman,' I said.

'No, Forrest, I am alert to that little thing, Yvonne is not a happy woman. But she is correct in that I am happily on my way to becoming entirely shit-faced if that is all right with you. In fact I hope you take up my invitation to join me,' he said looking around the table for approval. No nods of approval. 'Tell me, Forrest,' he said, leaning into me like a poker player who's bluffing a four card flush. 'Maybe you can answer one of life's little mysteries. Why is it,' he said, slowly leaning back and raising his voice, talking to the table, 'why is it just because you fuck 'em once or twice they think you owe them the rest of your life?' He took a cigar from his breast pocket and sniffed it.

The Assistant Attorney General and the Deputy Police Chief pushed their chairs back, standing up. 'Nice to meet you,' the Deputy Police Chief said, scanning the room for any other familiar faces, nodding from time to time. 'Good talking with you,' the other man said. 'You need any help around here, you let me know.'

'I'll do that,' I said.

Bobby put his hand on my shoulder, a friendly gesture. 'How you getting on with Sally? I don't want to tell another man how to go about his business but you could do a lot better in this town. I mean there's a lot of good pussy in Phoenix, you don't have to go around with somebody's humped half of the men in town.'

'I thought you used to be engaged to Sally.'

'Oh, Christ, years ago. We were just a couple of kids. Good to see you again, Forrest. What can I do for you?'

'Good to see you too, Bobby,' I said, hearing my own voice drop down a notch to the level of true sincerity. 'I don't know if you can help me or not, but you may know that I am not just here for the race.'

He spread his hands, palms out to show me nothing would surprise him and he had nothing to hide.

'I've got a little money. And I've got a little stake out north-east of Carefree.'

'Nice country out there. Lotta very attractive opportunities.'

'Lotta opportunities,' I said, chiming in. There are times I wonder if I shouldn't have been an actor. Deep furrows in the brow to indicate deep concern. 'But you know I'm not at all familiar with the property market around here and I thought I might take you up on your offer to act as a kind of guide.'

'What kind of property are you looking for?'

'Oh, I've got one or two million,' I said in the casual off-hand way that people who have millions to throw around like to dismiss the size of their fortune. 'And I like it out here. I like the feeling of space, I like the clear sky over my head. So I'd like to get involved, if you know what I mean. I don't mean totally involved, no more than five million at the most. I'd like to find and invest in some property that is prime for development. Something I could hold on to for a year or two and then turn it around to somebody who might want to build a mall, or singles and retirement condos.'

Bobby's face took on the serious look of the big-league businessman. 'Well of course I'm sure you appreciate, Forrest, I am an attorney, not a real-estate agent, I don't have a licence, don't need one. But you have come to the right place. Phoenix is a tricky market now and I wouldn't like to see you get burned. On the other hand,' he said, waving his cigar, 'this is a hell of a good time to buy, hell of a good time. If you make the right connections here, there's nothing you can't do or change. Boundaries, taxes, laws . . . This is God's own country, Forrest. And I have his fax number.'

'What kind of attractive opportunities are you talking about, Bobby?'

'Tell you what. You got any place you got to be? You able and willing to take a couple of hours, go look at a couple of places, see what you think?'

'I guess I could spare a couple of hours,' I said, looking at my watch as if I could just squeeze it in.

The parking lot was still hot from the day, but the day was beginning to cool. Bobby sagged a little against the door of the big silver four-wheel drive machine with over-size tyres, a big triangulated roll-over cage and the six long-range Hella driving lights mounted on top of the roll bar. 'Something I can brag about at the club, being driven by a Formula One driver. You ever drive a Range Rover, Forrest?'

chapter twelve

'You gotta admire,' Bobby was saying, head back, soaking up the sun and the sixty-mile-an-hour breeze, 'you gotta admire the balls of some of these operators.' He cocked an eye at the Range Rover's speedometer, leaning forward against his seat-belt.

'Keep to the limit if you would, please, Forrest. The police out here'll bazooka you for going fifty-six. I know it seems like crawlin' to you, but we'd better keep to the double nickel or some gung-ho asshole twenty-year-old cop is gonna come after us with his siren screaming like we ran over a pregnant nun.'

I slowed down all the way from sixty-two to fifty-five. The endless scroll of saguaro and cholla cactuses, sagebrush, sand, rocks and dirt rolling past and a mountain range a hundred miles away made any speed on the ground seem as slow as the hour hand on a waiting-room clock. Saguaros grow an inch or two a year. Joshua Trees grow whatever fraction of a millimetre it takes to raise their hairy branches twelve feet above ground in a thousand years. Survival out here has nothing to do with speed. Pterodactyls were plenty quick.

The air was bright and clear, and in that vast landscape Bobby's Range Rover crept across the surface, a bug on the ocean. After twenty minutes, the mountain range was still just as far away. Bobby had closed his eyes, resting.

'You were talking about balls,' I said to wake him up. 'And operators.'

Bobby's eyes opened and he sat up, stretching, looking for something. 'I'll show you,' he said. We passed an outcrop of dark red rock and he smiled, recognising something. 'Show you what I mean. See that golf course over there?'

Unless you were clinically blind it would have been tough to miss. I had been seeing the golf course long before his arm pointed to the swath of neon green that cut across the desert. Cactuses paled next to its brilliance and sprinklers added sparkle to emerald fairways that had been laid over the landscape like Astroturf.

'What you are looking at is the Punta Verde Golf Club. That sucker is green from pure, clean, drinking water,' Bobby said from behind his dark sunglasses. 'A million and a half gallons a day so a few retired fuckers can ride around on their golf carts on green grass.'

'You're telling me there's so much water around here,' I said, 'that they sprinkle the golf courses with drinking water?'

The desert stretched out in front of us, low, flat houses stuck into the rock and hills here and there, but nowhere was there a sign of water. The sun blazed overhead for an ambient ninety-five, two per cent humidity. With the top down on Bobby's Range Rover, the leather seats were hot to the touch but the breeze of dry air kept us comfortable.

'No. Shit no, Forrest, that's my whole point. There's no water at all. What I'm saying is what I was saying to you before. You have to know your way around out here. You can change the law, taxes, boundaries, change any damn thing you like, if you know the right people.'

'If you know these friends of yours,' I said, thinking suddenly of Barnes.

'Yeah, that's right, friends of mine. But you still have to know your way around. The equation is not that simple. Never was. What you know still counts just as much as who you know. Like right now, you could buy development land in the town of Carefree no trouble at all. A lot of guys would love to sell it to you. But you'd have a hell of a time developing anything on it.'

'Even if you had the balls and knew the right people?'

'Even if you had the balls of a buffalo and the Pope was your brother-in-law. What I'm saying is, right now you can buy all the development land you want in Carefree. Only problem is you can't build anything commercial on it as long as Punta Verde is suckin' up their water.'

I looked over at Bobby, the breeze adding to his tousled look. He said, 'You see that's Carefree's aquifer that's watering those golf courses. If Carefree doesn't put a stop to Punta Verde sucking up their drinking water, they could be clean out of water in fifteen, twenty years.'

He stretched, waking up a little. 'What Arizona state law says is you have to guarantee a hundred years' water supply before you can develop. Which means that if you are a developer in Carefree right now sitting on a big parcel for development you are shit out of luck.'

'No water, no new shopping mall.'

'Absofuckinglutely. Now the developer of that little twenty-five-thousand-acre Punta Verde estate and three others, all of which have golf courses, is a property development division of Texxon.'

He paused for a moment to emphasise the importance of the corporation. 'You better believe those fuckers are slick. What Texxon did was get state permits to tap into the aquifer for drinking water for their developments, right? Mean time they told Carefree they were going to build a pipeline to run in agricultural water from the state aqueduct so, please, couldn't they just use this irreplaceable several-thousand-year-old ground water for their golf courses just for a little while, while they get their pipeline built. Couple of payouts and promises here and there and yes indeed, Carefree grants Texxon temporary permission to siphon off a bit of their groundwater until Texxon gets that pipeline built.

'Well a few years pass, and the pipeline isn't built and Carefree begins to notice their aquifer is sinking out of sight. Carefree bitches and the boys from Texxon say, "Hey fellas don't worry about it. We're working on it." So Texxon does a deal with the City of Phoenix to *sell* the drinking water they are sucking up from under Carefree to Phoenix. In exchange, and this is the beautiful part, in exchange for the privilege of being allowed to *buy* the water, the city of Phoenix is building a pipeline free of charge to bring in agricultural water from the state aqueduct for the green, green grass of the golf links.'

'So instead of watering their neighbour's golf courses, the Carefree ground water now waters the city of Phoenix,' I said, watching a man in a canary-yellow shirt, bald as a baby bird, riding along the fairway on his golf cart. The cart made dark tracks in the wet grass.

'Yeah, well they will when the city of Phoenix builds an aqueduct out to Punta Verde and Texxon's other developments. Meanwhile they're treating the fairways to a little million and a half gallon a day drink of the best drinking water in the state of Arizona. But you got it. Texxon gets their water for nothin' from Carefree's aquifer and sells it to the city of Phoenix for a free aqueduct and a little profit on the side.'

'Leaving Carefree high and dry.'

'You get a winner, you're gonna have some losers, Forrest. Balance of nature. You see, there isn't anything out there you can't do if you know two things, what you're doing and who the good people are. Take the next left,' he said, his eyes closing behind his sunglasses.

'The good people,' I said. 'People you know,' I said.

Bobby nodded, smiling vaguely. 'I know 'em all,' he said.

'Left' was a dirt road, heading out into the open desert.

'Place I want to show you,' he said, 'is a four-thousand-acre undeveloped parcel that belongs to some friends of mine.' Bobby stifled a yawn, the gin and tonics picking up speed in his system under the hot sun, percolating in his brain. 'It's listed as agricultural land, which means the taxes are close to nothing, and you'd have to negotiate water rights. And you'd have to get a couple of variances passed before you could pass it on for development. But it is,' he yawned, 'a beautiful spot and if you're willing to put in the time and the money it could be worth something.

'There's a ridge running through it where the Indians had a Kachina, an ancestor, a kind of a mythical god so there is supposed to be some kind of religious significance attached to the place. That's one of your tougher variances, it's not easy. You're going to need to find a couple of tame Indians in the BIA, and it'll cost you about as much as the land, but it can be done and I can help you there.

'For example, maybe you could make the Kachina into a tourist attraction, get the state to declare a couple of hundred acres around it a state park, sell the 'authentic' dolls at a little souvenir store and raise the value of your land while lowering your tax liability. Once you get into it the possibilities multiply.

'Anyway, from this ridge where we're going you can see for hundreds of miles and not see a soul. Makes you feel like maybe the best thing would be to just let it be, you know. Everybody feels that sometimes. Like it'd be a shame to fuck it up with another prestige, high-security, armed-response, semi-retirement, environmentally responsible, new-age, adult leisure community with swimming-pools, choice of golf courses, community centre and two- to three-car garages 'cause you can't get to any place else without driving for half an hour. Free personal psychiatric counselling with low no-load deposit and all that shit,' he said, grinning, enjoying his rap.

'I mean it is a beautiful spot but some smart operator's gonna get rich developing it and it might as well be me or a friend of mine. Anyway we'll just have a look. Maybe give you an idea of what your money can buy.' Bobby closed his eyes and smiled peaceably, his head rocking with the bumps in the road.

As cars go, the Range Rover is a tractor. It's a pleasantly disguised tractor, and it is probably the best road-going four-wheeled cross-country device you'll find parked in front of a country club. But it is still a tractor. Underneath its glossy British aluminium skin there are two massive solid axles, carrying a tractor-size differential each and four fat, wide, off-road knobby tyres, giving the Range Rover the unsprung mass of an International Harvester. Add the aerodynamics of a brick and a body that sits high over the wheels like a shoe-box on roller skates and what you have is not exactly a sports car.

All that heavy cast iron and rubber bounds up in the air over every lump, and on a rough dirt road, the suspension has a hard time keeping the tyres in contact with the earth over fifty miles an hour. At sixty-five, the suspension gives up; the wheels stay semi-retracted as they kiss the tops of the ridges. I eased the car up to eighty, the big knobby tyres skimming across the washboard, a plume of dust rising behind us. Bobby's shoulder leaned against me and he began to snore.

I flicked the steering wheel sharp left, pulled up hard on the hand brake, and dropped the clutch, then let go of the steering-wheel, then the hand-brake. The car pirouetted nicely, skittering on the loose dirt as Bobby's sunglasses flew off. It took Bobby a couple of beats to focus on where he was and what was happening. It takes just a little while of staring at a dirt road disappearing behind you into the dust at eighty miles an hour before you adjust to the fact that you are going backwards and you have no idea of what is going to happen next, whether you are about to hit a cliff, a ledge, ditch, dog, car, truck or whether you are going to have another instant of life to think about the question.

Bobby said what the pilots say on the flight recorders before they hit the mountain. He said, 'Oh fuck.' Then he said: 'HOLY FUCKING SHIT, WHAT THE FUCK ARE YOU DOING? TURN THIS FUCKING THING AROUND.'

I flicked the wheel again, let out the clutch and floored it and we were heading forwards again, although if I were the passenger I would have had serious doubts about whether we were going to get around the corner coming up that rose up slightly and then disappeared. Probably to the left.

Bobby stared at the corner, his mouth wide, his cheeks bulged by the wind. He said: 'AAAAAAAAAAAAAAAAARRGGGGHH-HHH.'

I kept my foot down and cocked the wheel a little to the left then back right, steering into the skid, just clipping the inside of a small rock on the edge of the ditch on the left side of the road as we touched the inside of the curve, went over the crest of the hill, and then the car was airborne. Peace and quiet for a moment.

The road did go left, but it bent right first and there was plenty of room. Plenty of time.

Bobby went 'AAAAAAAAAAAAAARRGGHHHHH' some more.

We landed like a brick in the middle of the road, the Range Rover slamming down on the bumpstops, losing its poise and letting go sideways on the rebound. 'What I want to know, Bobby,' I shouted, tromping down on the accelerator as the car bounded like a loose pig towards the side of the road, 'is why Barnes was going to meet you.' Bobby stared at me, eyes wide, as I kept my foot down and got the car straightened out.

'Stop the fucking car,' he said. He had to shout to make himself heard but there was just a touch of a quaver in his voice.

I flicked the wheel, pulled the hand-brake and we were heading backwards again, this time down a sharp dip in the road. I was looking over my shoulder, working out how hard we would bottom out. With the clutch in and the car coasting backwards downhill at, say seventy-five, the sound of the wheels, pounding over the rocks, sending up a plume of stones and dust, sounded like surf. I had to shout over it. 'What was Barnes going to write about you?' I said.

Bobby was looking over his shoulder, straining against his seat belt to twist around. His face had gone white and he was gripping the back of the seat. 'Fuck you,' he shouted, out of breath. 'How the fuck would I know? I didn't see Barnes.'

The Range Rover hit bottom, bounced, the dirt road rose up again and the car hit again, harder, crashing down on the bumpstops.

There was a moment while the forces of two tons of Range Rover slamming down on to a rising dirt road at seventy-five miles an hour, there was just a moment there while the several tons of impact, having jammed the springs down flat, wound up inside the frame and chassis before they decided which way those tons of force would unload. A few thousandths of a second pause while, just behind the crest of the hill in front of us, the dusty yellow roof of a pick-up truck began to rise.

Normally, when you are driving, you have several ways to control the car; you can step on the brakes, turn the steering-wheel and/or feed more or less power into the situation through the accelerator and/or the gears. In a racing car, at racing speeds, those three elements of power, brakes and steering are all intricately interrelated. You can, depending on the situation, steer the car with the throttle, send the front end of the car into a slide with the brakes. You can, in some situations, get on the power sooner by turning into a corner a few milliseconds later. None of the above apply to a Range Rover going backwards uphill up a narrow dirt road, crashed down on the bumpstops at seventy-five miles an hour. So it probably made very little difference that I turned the steering-wheel, cocking what used to be the front wheels, left, hoping to get out of the way of the pick-up truck, especially since the back wheels let go like the legs of a grasshopper, SPROOOOOIIIIINNNNGGGG, followed by the front wheels, SPROOOOOIIIIINGGGG, and we were airborne again, the back end of the car lifting like a jet fighter taking off an aircraft carrier, up into the Arizona sky, and the roaring stopped for a moment as we had a glimpse of the old yellow Chevvy pick-up truck, dust as thick as pottery on the faded yellow paint, and a mildly quizzical face of a man with a red beard peering out behind the windshield just coming up over the crest of the road. The back end of the Range Rover continued to rise and all we saw was the deep blue of the early evening Arizona sky.

Followed by the deep brown of Arizona dirt. The back wheels crashed into the road first, my left foot was bounced off the clutch and my weight shifted on to my right foot mashing the accelerator to the floor so the rear wheels started churning forwards, as if the Range Rover had decided that the last place it wanted to go was the ditch. That they were churning in the opposite direction to where we were going may have had some braking effect.

But not much. By the time the car's front wheels hit the road behind us we were already heading into the ditch and catapulting up and over, rolling into the cactus and rocks of the desert.

A car rolling over and over across the desert makes an awful noise, a non-stop roar punctuated by the whang of metal on rock and you think that the car is not slowing down, is never going to slow down before it splats like a tomato against a rock face.

Eventually the car rolled one last time on to its wheels, rose up for one last quarter-turn, then gave up and fell back again.

The cloud of dust that we had been in the middle of drifted away.

In the distance I heard a voice. It was calling, but I thought it could wait, and I closed my eyes for a moment.

I woke up when hands were carefully unbuckling my seat-belt and the bearded face of the man in the pick-up truck was peering into my face with concern. 'You hurt any place?' he said. 'You think you broke anything?'

I shook my head no.

'Don't you fucking touch me,' Bobby said.

I got out of the Range Rover to have a look. 'Warren Palmer,' the man with the beard said. His face was pale, as if he worked in a mine, and his eyes had maps of the Grand Canyon around them. 'You folks sorta flew over me,' he said with the beginning of a smile. 'Most people,' he added, 'prefer driving forwards.'

Bobby was swinging his legs out of the car. The Range Rover

looked a mess. Both headlights were smashed, the body looked as if it had been stoned by a mob and the row of lights along the top of the roll bar were smashed and crumpled foil, except for the one light at the end that had been ripped out of its socket and hung dangling from a yellow wire.

'You,' Bobby said to me, 'you, are going to be one sorry son of a bitch.'

The man with the beard held out his hand to Bobby. 'Warren Palmer,' he said. 'What happened?'

'This son of a bitch tried to kill me,' Bobby said. 'Stupid asshole is supposed to be a racing driver and he can't even keep a car pointed in the right direction.'

'I'm sorry, Bobby,' I said. 'I didn't mean to crash your car.' I started to walk towards the battered machine. 'I thought you might want to tell me about what Barnes was going to write about you and your "friends".'

'You're goddamn right you're sorry,' Bobby said, feeling his elbow. 'You're gonna be the sorriest son of a bitch for fifty miles. If you want to know something, why don't you just ask?'

'I did,' I said. 'You wouldn't tell me.'

Warren Palmer was walking around the car. 'Four-wheel drive, izzit?' he said to nobody in particular. 'Doesn't look too bad. Suppose she still runs?'

I looked at the car, considering the possibilities of its still being able to function after rolling over several times.

Bobby said, 'Don't even think about it, Evers. I wouldn't let you drive a shopping cart.' He walked over to the Range Rover, and with the slow delicacy of a cowboy getting on to a horse that has just thrown him he climbed into the driver's seat, felt his elbow for a few moments and turned the key. It started first turn. He bent forward over the stubby gear levers, putting the car into four-wheel drive. Then he looked around both ways to see if there was any oncoming traffic out on the desert, raced the engine and looked at me. 'If you want to know why Barnes was coming to see me,' he said, 'you can kiss my ass.'

Then he let out the clutch and the silver and dented Range Rover lurched off slowly, climbing over the ruts, ridges and gullies of the desert, making a two-wheel path through the cactuses, down into the ditch, up on to the road, up over the hill, and out of sight, leaving a long tail of fine dust glittering in the late afternoon sun in its wake.

'Looks like you could use a ride,' Warren Palmer said.

Later, as the dust plumed behind us in a red Arizona sky, he said, squinting into the sunset through a windshield glowing with several years' accumulation of dirt, 'For a while there, I thought you were going to die.'

'The thought crossed my mind,' I said.

'Is that a special wish of yours? Most folks prefer to wait.'

'Oh, I'm happy to wait. I was trying to avoid running into you.'

'I guess I'm grateful for that, although I'd guess if you didn't make a habit of driving around backwards at a hundred and twenty miles an hour, taking evasive action wouldn't be such a problem.'

'We were only going around seventy-five.'

'Oh, well then,' he said, grinning, 'barely creeping along. Of course speed is entirely relative to your local environment. I came out here about twenty-five years ago, just kinda drifting in a nice mauve fog of psychedelics and paranoia. I was so stoned so much of the time, folks called me Wheat Thin. You know, like those crackers, Stoned Wheat Thins? And one morning to my immense surprise, I woke up naked in the desert. I guess everybody else had just moved on and left me behind. Or maybe I was just too stunned to know what was happening. I don't know whether it was me or them. But I woke up alone and stark naked in the desert with the sun just coming up. And the first thing you notice about the desert is that it makes one thing perfectly clear. If you don't get your ass in gear, you die. You can do either one, get your shit together or die. The desert doesn't give a damn one way or another. But it is tough to stay alive out there and that makes people kinda thorny. Any place special I can let you off?'

'Where are you headed?'

'Just into Cave Creek to get drunk and fall down.'

'Is that anywhere near a taxi?'

'You come on in with me to the Mine Shaft bar and I reckon we can fix you up with a ride.' He took his eyes off the road for a moment to look at me. 'As long as you don't mind somebody else doing the driving.'

chapter thirteen

Behind the smoked glass, in the sea-green light of the intensive care unit, Bill Barnes was wrapped in bandages. His eyes were visible but they were shut. No forearms now and stumps for legs bundled in seeping white gauze. Hovering over his head, in a horrific parody of TV, a monitor showed his pulse, temperature and breathing patterns in moving graphs.

There is a nightmare I remember, my own little in-head video that comes screaming back to me in the dark times when I cannot sleep. A dense wall-to-wall screen of the faces, the endless Italian crowd, dark faces silent, peering, pressing forward, hoping for a look. The police are trying to clear the way for the ambulance, its blue light rotating. And there is no sound except my breathing, around me the silence is total because we all know that the man is splintered and charred and dead inside his blackened car from the impact, the explosion and the fire that burned with the intensity of a blowtorch before they finally put it out. And the crowd turn from the ambulance to look at me with their dark eyes and they know that I have killed him.

'Mr Evers.' A tug at my elbow. A nurse is standing beside me, her face framed with bright red hair, a little turned up nose, bright blue eyes and freckles. A kind and brave face that faces death on every shift and spits in his eye. 'Maureen', her name tag says. 'Mr Evers, please. It's almost ten p.m. Visiting hours are over.'

PART TWO

chapter fourteen

The morning was bright and clear with the sparkle that high barometric pressure gives to the light on the best sunny days. Eighty-three degrees at 8 a.m. with four per cent humidity. It was going to be a hot, dry Arizona spring day. A good day, as the warrior said, to die.

Barnes died early that morning, before sunrise. The news spread from the radio and television to the newspapers and coffee tables at the Biltmore. Commentators meant it when they said Barnes lived the reason men and women became journalists in the first place. He lived, as one anchorwoman put it, to tell the truth. And to expose the greedy and the crooked who wrap themselves in the prestige of public and private office. To bang down their doors and to prove in print that the Emperor has no clothes and his hand in the till. Barnes was, the reporters said on that morning, the best investigative reporter in America, the man who was unafraid to stand up. Who should have and would have won the Pulitzer Prize. The kind of man who gave the News Business a power and a purpose beyond entertainment. Who upheld the truths we are said to hold self-evident.

More teams of investigative reporters were on their way to Phoenix to take reporter's revenge. To find out who had hired Esmond, the street thug, to kill Barnes. And to find out why. Esmond was telling the police he'd be glad to tell them who was behind the conspiracy. If they'd let him plea bargain. The trouble was he kept changing his story.

I watched *Good Morning America* in my room, read the papers in the dappled shade on the terrace at breakfast. And, in the Buick marshmallow they call Reatta, switched on the local news. I was going to see the daughter of the man they rarely mentioned, except to say that Merrill Cavanaugh had been the subject of Barnes' most recent series of exposés. And had been one of the names erased from Barnes' file.

The desert air was clear and bright, vapour trails crisscrossing high overhead as the reporters flew in and out of Phoenix, to and from Chicago, Dallas, Boston, Atlanta, LA and New York.

Whatever it took to uncover the bastards behind the bastard who put the dynamite under Barnes' car, they would do it. They would conduct the Barnes version of the Warren Commission in public, in the press and on the air, they said. 'Meanwhile, in Scottsdale,' the radio said. Along with 'more news after this important announcement'.

I wished the police and the reporters luck. More luck than I had in my clumsy attempts. The police had the man who had set the dynamite and they said they were looking for the real criminals who had put him up to it. Some of the best reporters in the country were on the case. The FBI was involved. What the hell was I doing? Just because I had met Barnes, just because I had liked him. Just because I had nothing better to do.

I had everything better to do. As an investigator into the death of another man I made a hell of a racing driver. It was a good day to die, I thought, and here's to the former Forrest Evers the former investigative reporter, righter of wrongs and general avenger of the public conscience. Let the fraud slip below ground quietly where he can do no more harm. No ceremonies please, and no flowers. Be glad he's under the ground. He's going to need a place to hide when Bobby starts flinging his lawsuits around. So far I had managed to trash one thirty-five thousand dollar Range Rover, and enrage a hundred-dollar-a-minute lawyer. Let's see a little damage limitation around here. Pull the grass over the dummy's head before he hurts somebody. Bury him with his pimple boots on. Or Rock-Hoppers as the case may be.

I was coming back on to my land, sun reflecting off the windshield, feeling some old pull of affection for the slow roll of the hills, and a fresh irritation at seeing somebody else's fences running across the grain, when out of the high left-hand corner a rock flew in a slow arc overhead.

I saw it in that staccato motion, dotting across the blue sky the way you see when you are not really paying attention, standing on the Reatta's brakes to keep out of the stone's way, thinking, 'She's got an arm.'

The Buick skidded to a stop, a cloud of dust carrying on, leaving the red car cocked at an angle on the dirt road.

'Hey, Wahlnut,' she called down, bounding down the slope, her shadow running like a black stripe across the hot hillside. 'You're early.'

'Usually you let things slide for a moment or two before you start throwing rocks,' I said out the window. She was thirty yards away in a white shirt with rolled up sleeves and cut-off jeans and I was leaning out of the car window.

'Just trying to get your attention. I'm glad to see you.' She half ran, half skidded down the slope to the car, opened the door and got in. A hot young woman in a small car smelling of hot young woman. She tossed her fine glossy hair. 'What happened to your pimple boots?' she said.

'Do you miss them?'

'Yeah, a little. They made you seem kinda helpless. Like the Hollywood Cowboy, you know, has stuntmen do all the real cowboy stuff. Now you don't look like you need help so much. More like a dude with a lot of money to spend on lightweight hiking boots.'

'Sure is tough to get your footwear to hit the right note around here,' I said.

'We just going to sit here?'

'Where to?'

'Up the road a piece. I'll show you.'

There wasn't much of a trail, and sometimes it seemed to just disappear. Sally walked easily, she'd been here before, she knew where she was going. She also seemed heat-proof. The temperature had risen with the sun. And although the air was so dry it didn't feel like a hundred degrees, the temperature readout in the Reatta said it was a hundred and four. After a few minutes' walk I was sweating heavily and the light made me squint. Sally, dry as a bone, was a moving shadow in front of me.

Sally said, 'Keep your eyes open, maybe you'll see something. Maybe a little horny toad. Most of the animals in the desert sleep during the day to keep out of the sun but you might just see a family of Gamble quail marching single-file through the mesquite. They're real cute, with a feather sticking out of the top of their head like an Indian.'

'They probably have spikes,' I said. 'Everything else in this desert seems to prick, sting or scratch.'

'For a full-grown man, Evers, you are a real baby. There's plenty of room between plants, cause their roots have to spread out so far for water. Besides, if you had to fight so hard for survival, you'd be prickly too. But not nearly so pretty. Look at all the flowers. Don't they just make your eyes ache with all that colour?'

The colours weren't the shy, watery colours of the English garden. They were hot pink, vermilion and blazing yellow. Every tree, bush and cactus that morning seemed to be wearing an umbrella of flowers, a Las Vegas strip for bees, screaming; 'ME, ME. PICK ME, SUCK ME, MAKE ME WRITE BAD CHEQUES.' I wondered if the flowers for Barnes' funeral would be so bright, so blazing with life.

'You know Barnes died this morning,' I said.

'I know. I woke up around four and I thought I felt something and I wasn't sure but I thought of him, and I felt relieved. Like thank God that's over. And I went back to sleep. Then I heard it on the news when I got up.'

'I thought you'd be more upset.'

'Oh yeah, upset. I was upset. I was real upset six months ago when he said he couldn't meet me for dinner, and I said, 'How about later?' and he said, 'Maybe in a year.' I was upset then.

'I thought: You stinking son of a bitch to lead me on with all those plans of the house we were going to build in the mountains and the books he was going to write and the paintings I was going to paint. It was a pretty picture and I loved it, and I didn't give a damn if he had to leave his wife and kids. I loved him. And I could have sworn he loved me. And he just tore up my pretty little picture like it never meant a damn thing to him.'

'I thought you were upset about him when I saw you at the race track.'

'Of course I was upset. Everybody was upset. Well, you know I really had been wishing ol' Barnsey'd get hit by a bus or something. And when he got hurt like that, oh shit Forrest, do we have to talk about this? I'm glad he died this morning because he was suffering so bad and there was no way he was going to live and thank God now it's over. I'm sorry he died. I'm sorry I ever knew him. But I've done my mourning for him and I feel like he died a week ago. Everybody knew he was going to die. Let's not talk about it for a while, if you don't mind. Let's change the subject. Tell me what happened to you.' She stopped and turned, facing me.

'Nothing happened to me.'

'Yeah, nothin'. A little kid has something to hide and you ask him, what you got there, Donnie? And he goes, "Nothin'." You know he's hiding something. But don't worry about it, Forrest. You want to carry something nasty around with you, don't let me hold you back. But it looks to me like it is about time you dumped it. Got rid of it. I mean I have known one or two men in my life and I have never seen one who is wound up as tight as you are.'

'Maybe it comes from living in London. I don't like talking about myself.'

'I know the feeling, I mean, I've heard about it. But it is strange, you know? I don't know who you are, Wahlnut,' she said sitting down on a large rock, studying my face. 'I don't have a clue. Except two things. Maybe you know what I mean. Maybe not. But I feel a kind of pull towards you, Wahlnut, and don't you go feeling put upon. It doesn't have a thing to do with romance, although God knows you look good enough. But I feel like there is something between us, do you know what I mean? Like we are carved from the same bone.' She said it like a question. 'And I've thought about it and at first I thought that maybe it's that we are both artists.'

'I don't think I'd make much of a painter,' I said. 'I can't even draw a straight line.'

'Of course you are an artist. Think of yourself in a racing car, streaking across the countryside describing arcs and curves like you are a dancer across the landscape. And the colour of your car is like a moving brush just skimming the surface before it disappears. If I were painting you driving a racing car, I'd paint the car blue, a deep blue like outer space, a temporary brush stroke. But that's not really it at all is it? What I feel in my bones is that something nasty happened to you. Blunted you. Made you shrink.'

'It hasn't been an easy year.'

'Why, because you're not racing any more?'

'That's part of it. But it's just part of it.'

'Tell me the other part. See what happens.'

I looked at her intense face, her soft eyes, and thought, what the hell, I'll risk it. 'I killed a man,' I said.

'You mean you had an accident?'

'No, it wasn't an accident.'

'You did it on purpose, killed him?'

'I planned it and I did it. And when it was over I felt like I should have been caught and punished. I felt like I had done something monstrous and disgusting like raped a baby and everybody knew about it and I felt like I had stuck my arms up to the elbows in the man's blood. The other thing was, what made me feel bad, what made me feel the worst, was that I was glad I did it.'

'But you weren't caught. You're still walking around in your cowboy boots and your high-price hiking boots.'

'Well, nobody knows for sure that I did it,' I said. 'Except me.'

'If you like,' Sally said, 'I'll punish you.'

We were climbing and the heat was making us sweat. Sally was in front of me, her long legs, strong and tanned, making the pace. She said between breaths, 'I wish you could have known my Daddy when I was a girl. He was something. I mean you see him now and he just sort of bumbles around. But when I was a little girl, nobody could stand up to him. Once I heard him shouting on the phone and I asked him who he was yelling at, and he said, "The damn fool who thinks he's the Governor."

'And when the Governor of the State of Arizona came to our house that afternoon, with his tail between his legs, I answered the door and he said, "Excuse me, I have an appointment to see Mr Cavanaugh." Nobody could stand up to Daddy except me. So I thought, I can get away with anything. And you know what? I was right.'

'Getting away with something isn't the hard part,' I said.

'Anybody can get away with something. It's living with yourself that's hard.'

'Phooey. Living with yourself isn't hard at all. Easiest thing in the world. It's living with somebody else that's hard. I'll bet you're just a big old pussy cat around the house.'

'Yeah, a real pussy cat,' I said. 'Just feed me twice a day and put water in my dish. And you are the tiger.'

She looked back at me, not sure what I meant.

'Difficult to live with.'

'I'm not difficult, I'm impossible.' She looked around for another rock big enough to sit on and found one. There was a pause while she looked off into the hills. 'Tell you the truth, Forrest,' she said, looking up at me, 'you act like a cowboy without his horse. Kind of clumsy and on the ground. Maybe it's time you looked for a place to settle down.'

'Is that what you meant by punishing me?'

'I wasn't hinting that I want to live with you, Forrest, if that's what you think. Like I said, I'm kinda drawn to you in some weird way, but I'm not even sure I like you. How'd you kill this man?'

'With my car. I made him crash in a race.'

'Shit, Forrest, people crash all the time in racing cars. Isn't that why people go to watch the damn things? Sounds to me like you are being a little heavy on yourself.'

'Like I said. Nobody knows.'

'I know.'

'But you don't believe me.'

'Oh, I believe you all right. Look at me, Forrest, tell me what you see.'

I took Sally's face in my hands. 'Looking deep into your eyes,' I said, 'I see a goofball.'

She laughed. 'See what I mean? We are a lot alike.'

I kept her face in my hands, kept looking at her. 'I see a little girl still trying to get her father's attention. A little girl nobody can say no to. And if they do, she's a big girl now and she'll just blow them out of the way.'

'Forrest, I have to tell you nobody in America now calls a woman over fifteen a girl and gets away with it.'

'Too bad. The more I see of a boy or a girl in what passes for a grown-up, the better I like them.'

'Yeah, well, just don't call 'em that. You call a cowboy "boy" you'll get your balls in a sling. A woman'd probably just take your head off. What were you calling me? A pushy little spoiled brat? That I push people out of my way? You mean like Barnes?'

'I don't know anything about Barnes,' I said. 'But if Barnes was killed by a rock, I'd be suspicious of a little long-legged girl I know,' I said. 'Where's this swimming hole you were talking about?'

'You don't know anything about women either, do you?'

'I'm happy to learn,' I said, taking her hand and pulling her back up.

chapter fifteen

The stream was deep, fast and clear, running along the bottom of a ravine covered with coyote bush, cactuses, ironwood and mesquite. It was about four feet across and it fell off a shelf of rock into a deep wide pool that was as blue as the Arizona sky overhead. Our shadows circled our feet.

Sally walked out on a rock that overhung the pool, pulled off her white shirt, slipped out of her cut-off jeans and kicked off her dirty white Nikes. She turned to face me, her breasts jiggling, a trickle of sweat running down to her navel, a little puff of silky hair between her thighs lighter than I'd expected. 'Well, Off-the-Wahlnut,' she said, 'are you going to just stand there gawping, or are you going swimming?'

She turned and dived, her body an arc in the air, her hands straight out, breaking the surface, gliding into the water, toes pointed, the water going 'ploop'. I could see the pale glimmer of her shape, making frog kicks along the dark blue of the bottom. It took her a while to reach the other side, then she came up, erupting out of the water, shaking her head and blowing air, the water spraying out into the dry air, sparkling in the light. 'Come on, Wahlnut,' she said, taking a deep breath. 'It's perfect.'

In one motion I unbuckled my belt, unzipped and hooked my thumbs behind my trousers and pulled off my pants, underpants, socks and a little extra effort for the lightweight hiking shoes, tossed my shirt into the air and before it landed jumped in head first, folding at the last minute into a cannon ball, making a boom of an impact and sending spray ten feet into the air. Hot, sweaty and dusty as I was the water was liquid ice, numbing my bones before I touched bottom. I swam underwater to where her feet were bicycling, grabbed an ankle and pulled her under. She had a kick like a colt.

We swam back and forth twice and floated on our backs, feeling the blazing sun and the freezing water before we climbed out, hoisting ourselves out of the blue water on to the warm flat rock. We stood up, facing each other, out of breath, water streaming down. 'Don't worry about towels,' Sally said, 'in this desert air you'll drip dry in about two minutes flat.'

'I wasn't worried about towels,' I said.

'Oh, I thought that was a towel rail.'

Sally's mouth was wet and fresh and her skin pebbled with goosebumps that softened under my hands.

'You feel like my cowboy boots,' I said.

She said, 'We can't do this.'

'You're worried about getting pregnant or AIDS.'

'Or herpes or God knows, hoof and mouth disease? No, there's ways around that. It's not that, Forrest. It's just too soon. I don't even know you.'

'Have you ever really known anybody in your life? Really?'

She looked me in the eyes, and her eyes softened and she said, 'No. Not really.'

'Neither have I,' I said. 'But we could try.'

Her breasts were small and perfect white against her tan and they were mostly wide and pink, intensely sensitive nipples, puckered from the cold and widening in my mouth. 'Amazing tits,' Barnes had said.

'There's no place,' she said, 'it's all rocks and grit and there's ants in the grass.'

'I'll lie down,' I said, holding her hand, lying down on my back on the flat sandstone rock, pulling her down to me. Sally bent over me, kissing me with her wide fresh-water kisses, the first touch of her body cold from the water, and then warm.

The rubbery squeak of cold, watertight resistance giving way with her loosening thighs to the delicious warm and slippery slow sliding up and down and around. The sun was on my face and I closed my eyes and we clung to each other like survivors on a raft.

'Forrest, that's awful. Look what you did, you're bleeding. You've rubbed your back raw on the rock.' We were lying side by side, Sally up on her elbow, peering over me.

'I had help,' I said happily.

'I'm sorry. I really didn't plan this.'

'Well, I'll give you Forrest's Law of Probability. Nothing,' I said, 'ever happens according to plan. If you had planned it, it probably wouldn't have happened.'

'Well, I don't think we should plan to do it on a rock again.'

'Not this afternoon, Sally.'

'Why did you do it?'

'Because you are beautiful and sexy and it has been a long time, and I am powerfully attracted to you, and I like you . . .'

'I mean why did you kill that man?'

It took me a little while to shift gears, to stop thinking of all the reasons I had made love with Sally and why I was already thinking of doing it again, taking more time. 'I don't think I had any choice,' I said.

'Isn't that what the murderer always says?'

When we stood up, the flat sandstone where we had been lying had wet patches drying in the sun. I felt as if the bony places on my back had been sandpapered. And I looked at Sally's lovely face and her sad and troubled eyes and I didn't mind a bit. Small price to pay. We kissed lightly and awkwardly touched each other. The new person. The sweet taste. The wonderful places, here and there. Delicious kisses.

'Not standing up,' she whispered in my ear, cupping me lightly in her hand.

'And not lying down,' I said. 'It's your turn on the bottom, I don't think I'd like you with scabs on your back.'

She pushed me in.

And jumped on top of me driving me down to the bottom of that dark and freezing pool. Her mouth found mine before I came up for air.

We came up gasping, arms around each other, kicking to stay afloat. 'I can't possibly tell you how much you excite me,' she said to the rocks behind me.

'Try.'

'Let's make love here, in the pool. Like this.'

'Sally we can't. It's freezing. We'll drown.'

'Try,' she said.

I tried and it was difficult, staying afloat, keeping my head above water, hands and feet treading water, but I thought I was about to manage it, Sally's legs tight around my waist, when I saw the first one floating through the sky, cherry red against the blue, falling towards us, making a sputtering, fizzing sound.

chapter sixteen

The fizzing little red ball made a little 'plink' in the water about six feet away and I thought it was a joke. It was just a cherry bomb.

I was thinking some dumb camper, maybe. Or some jumpy thirteen-year-old kid out on his trail bike, a pocket full of firecrackers, looking to blow up a few rattlesnakes, maybe pop a couple of saguaros, maybe scare the grown-ups, get revenge.

I was wondering where he was hiding when the cherry bomb went off with a damp 'plooop' six feet underwater and a giant rubber hammer pounded my legs and stomach black and blue and a steel vice clamped shut on my balls.

Sally screamed, her fingernails digging into the back of my neck, and high overhead another red ball was falling out of the bright blue sky.

It splashed two feet behind me. For a microsecond or two as I watched the red ball slowly sinking in the clear water, its fuse glowing and smoking, I considered picking it up and throwing it out of the water. How much damage can a cherry bomb do to your hand underwater, I wondered in that instant before I realised that these were not normal fireworks and that it might just take your hand right off at the wrist and I was churning arms and legs, charging in the water like a runner, trying to get away from the impact with Sally's arms and legs around me, taking her with me, her head on my shoulder.

The second cherry bomb went off with another innocent watery ploop, a little louder than the first, but nothing to prepare me for the blow that hit me in the back, knocking the wind out of me.

The third went off behind Sally just before it hit the water. The blast deafened me, the flash stinging my eyes with hot grit.

I don't remember a fourth, but there must have been a fourth, maybe more because the next thing I remember was Sally tugging at me, pulling my head up above water. 'Forrest,' she was saying, 'Forrest, move, damn you. Move something,' when another cherry bomb turned into a bright orange fireball tearing a hole in the air next to her face.

Then it was quiet.

Sally was floating face down, a red rag of blood around her in the blue water. I rolled her over and hauled us towards the edge of the pool an armful of water at a time. There was no sound.

Sally was breathing, but she didn't look good. The side of her face was flaming red, her hair above her left ear was burned away, and when I held her head up out of the water, little pin dots of blood rose out of her cheek. Her jaw chattered as if she were freezing. I pulled myself up out of the water, holding her hand to keep her above the surface, then I bent down and reached under her arms and pulled her up. She sat on the flat rock, naked, and looked at me trying to focus, blood from her face dripping down her body, her mouth open and bleeding, her chest heaving.

Silence. I looked around for a sign of someone, a noise, something moving. Nothing.

I rinsed out my T-shirt and held the cool cloth to Sally's wounded face. Her eyes squeezed shut and she made a little whimpering sound. The bleeding wasn't as bad as I thought at first, the burns had cauterised her cheek, but the skin around her temple was black.

'Hold still,' I said as she flinched and pulled back from me.

'You hold still, Wahlnut. I don't want you touching me,' she said turning away. Her voice sounded as if she were in another room, some place behind the electric bees swarming inside my head.

'Are you OK?'

'You go away for a minute, leave me alone.' She was crying and it wasn't easy for her to speak. Blood in her mouth made the words sound mushy, like a drunk. 'Give me a chance to freshen up. Go on, shoo.'

I stood up, carefully, feeling shaky, and cautiously started to move back from the rim of the pool to see if there was anyone behind the rocks, or up above us behind the trees. Did they know that we were hurt? I was about to move from the cover of one boulder to another when Sally screamed.

She was on her hands and knees, staring at her reflection in the pool, her breath coming in gasps. 'Oh God, look. Look what they did. Oh goddamnit, Forrest, I'm a mess, I'm just a mess.' She sat back helplessly, looking up at me. 'I look horrible and oh, Christ, it hurts.' Her cheek was starting to bleed again from talking.

I knelt next to her and took her hand. 'Close your eyes and rest for a minute. Your face is going to be fine. I know it looks bad now but you'll be OK. You've got some superficial burns, but it's nothing to worry about.'

'I'm hurt Forrest. I don't think they can fix me.'

'They can fix anything now,' I said. 'They'll probably improve the way you look.'

'Don't bullshit me Forrest. This is bad. This is very bad and I'm scared.'

'I know you're hurt, Sally,' I said. 'We need to get you to a doctor and we need to protect you from the sun. OK?'

'I don't think I can walk.'

'Well I hope you can walk. Those vultures flying overhead don't look all that well fed.'

'Oh Christ, Wahlnut, there's always vultures overhead in Arizona. Those're just dumb ol' turkey buzzards. Should be the Arizona state bird.' She started to smile and winced.

Her legs were purple and swollen from the concussions. I looked at mine and they didn't look much better. There was also a large tender place on my back that felt as if I had been hit by a hundred-mile-an-hour football. 'Let me wrap my wet shirt around your head,' I said. 'It'll keep you cool while I have a look around.'

'It'll keep people from seeing I look like Halloween.' She looked at me, her eyes filling with tears. 'It hurts, Forrest. I know I should be brave, but I'm not brave. I'm scared. You think they are still there?'

'I'll have a look.'

When I started to move back from the edge of the pool she said, 'While you are having your look you might see if you can find our boots and pants.'

The sun was intense, beating straight down and reflecting straight up from the sand. Evers' number one rule for desert survival: Do not barefoot into the desert go. The Arizona desert floor looks, to the untrained eye, like sand, rocks and dirt. It is not. It is composed of thorns, spikes, tacks, rusty nails and used razor blades. Your foot will instantly communicate this awkward fact to you with great clarity the instant you set your naked sole down to search for your lost footwear. After twenty minutes of painful searching, hoping to find them tossed behind a rock or a bush, we had to admit our shoes were gone.

I did find, twenty yards up the hill, on the other side of the pool, behind a clump of trees, the tractor tread of worn hiking boots in the dry dirt. They looked fresh but they could have been a week old. It's hard to tell in the desert. I also found no matches, no tyre tracks, and no shoes and no pants.

We set out barefoot, one tender step at a time, on the trail back to the car. My shirt, damp with another rinse in the pool and splotched with fresh red blood, was wrapped around Sally's head. Sally wore her white shirt but the rest of our clothes were gone. I was naked to the desert sun from head to foot. Sally's feet were tougher than mine, and she had more pain to distract her. Still, she was very careful about where she put each foot. I followed just behind her, trying to make myself as light as possible before putting my pink foot down.

I was trying not to think of what the sick bastard who threw the cherry bombs was going to think of next. Trying not to think that he could be waiting on either side of the trail. Trying not to think how badly Sally was hurt, thinking that maybe a plastic surgeon could perform a miracle, and to cheer us up a little, keep a lid on the panic, I started singing my all-time favourite Country and Western song, the old John Denver anthem: 'Sunshine on my shoulders makes me happy, Sunshine on my penis makes me sad.'

Sally fell. She didn't trip and she didn't fall heavily, she just fell, face first.

'I just have to lie down for a while,' she said, with that mushy voice. 'A day at the beach always makes me sleepy.'

I tried carrying Sally like a child, in my arms, but she was a long ways from childhood and my arms were tired after ten steps. After fifteen steps her bandage, if you could call it that, fell off into the dirt. I put her carefully down, shook the dirt off my shirt and wrapped the cleanest parts of my dirty shirt around her face wounds again. This time she rode piggy-back, arms around my neck, her bruised and burned face next to mine, chin resting on my shoulder.

'Do you know any shortcuts?' I said, feeling the glare of the sun in my face and the pulse in the bruise on my back.

'You in a hurry to get back? I thought we were just having fun.'

'You don't know any shortcuts?'

'This is the shortcut, Wahlnut. Just keep a little more to the left. I'll tell you what. You remember you gave me Evers' law about nothing going according to plan? I'll give you Cavanaugh's law,' she said into my ear, 'Evers' sounding like 'Eversh'. 'It isn't much, but it's true. Like today the water so pretty and clear, making love so nice like we did. Perfect example.'

'What's that?' I said.

'There's always a fly in Paradise,' she said.

'You're kind of a bumpy ride,' she said.

'I thought you liked that.'

'Well I don't mean to complain. This is just swell. But you'll have to forgive me if I mention that for a racing driver you are not exactly streaking across the countryside.'

'I am flat out, Sally. Going as fast as I can go. Road is a little rough.'

'Oh shit. Damn, Forresht, why didn't you tell me? Let me down. Forresht, put me down before you take another step. Your feet look like they've been through a Magimix.'

'You want to wait for the next bus?'

'Wahlnut, put me down. Let me wrap my shirt around your feet while you still have some feet left to wrap.'

I let her down as gently as I could, bottom first, but it wasn't quite gentle enough. 'Oh, owww, dammit, Forresht. How the hell did you find a spiky rock?' I shifted her on to some sand and she started to unbutton her shirt. 'You'll have to help me tear it,' she said. 'I think I'm a little weak for tearing shirts today. Maybe you could start with the arms. Rip them off, use 'em like socks. Then wrap some more shirt around them.'

I tore up the shirt, sliding my feet into the arms and wrapping the extra cloth around them. When I stood up I looked like I was standing in diapers. 'Kind of a comedown from my full-quill Tony Lama ostrich-skin boots,' I said.

'Oh, I don't know. I think I like you better in shirtsleeves. Shirtsleeve shoes could be a real big in Phoenix this year.'

Sally leant forward into my back and I gathered her legs in my arms again. 'Walk carefully now,' she said, 'I always liked that shirt.'

We looked like refugees from a Bible movie, the naked woman with her head in bloody rags riding on the back of the naked, sweating man with his feet in more bloody rags. Thorns and spikes scraped my arms and jabbed my shins.

'No, left, Forresht, left. You're getting off the path.'

'I don't see any path.'

'Over towards that rock. Just left of that rock?'

'Which rock?'

'I thought racing drivers had pretty good eyesight.'

'We do. I can see at least five hundred rocks in that direction not counting pebbles and stones.'

'Can you see how brilliant the colours are? How electric? How dazzling?'

'There's a lot of green and brown.'

'Look. There's a radiance. A light like a halo behind every rock, every needle on every cactus. Orange, and pink.'

'You OK up there, driver?'

'I'm just taking a little nap,' she said.

'You better stay awake, keep us on the road.'

'I got twenty million dollars in a trust fund,' she said in a dreamy, slushy voice, 'and I'll go to sleep any ol' time I fucking feel like it.'

I had to rest three or four times, which involved finding a rock the right height and shape to set Sally on, backing up to it, setting her gently on the rock, and letting it take her weight for a while. Once I tried to wake her and I couldn't. She was unconscious and her forehead was burning. My skin was turning bright pink in the desert sun and I worried about getting lost. But it wasn't that difficult. All I had to find was the road. It was out there in front of me, stretching for miles.

I kept the hills in the distance straight ahead, and after what seemed like several hours but was probably only one, the dirt road was in front of me. Sally was snoring on my back, and I felt such a relief that it took me a little while to realise that I didn't know whether the RentaBuick was to our left or our right.

I guessed left and started uphill up the dirt road and Sally woke up. 'Where the fuck are we going?' she said.

'I think the car is up the hill?'

'What are you going to use for keys, Evers?' she said. 'Didn't it occur to you that when they took your trousers they took your keys? Or do you keep a spare pair tucked away in a secret hidey-hole?'

'Well, I guess we'll have to hitch-hike.'

'Now there is a truly brilliant idea, oak-head. Hitch-hike. You take my breath away, you ol' dazzling intellectual. 'Cept for one tiny little thing, ol' Ironwood. Or maybe you noticed right off the bat that we are not on the interstate. Maybe your little butternut brain has already worked it out from the simplicity of the traffic patterns crisscrossing in front of you that there is about one car every four or five hours.' Her voice was rising, taking on a high falsetto. 'Now, Peanut, you listen to me. You better be careful you don't get run over 'n' squushed like a bug. Don't you go playing in the road now. You know I have to smack you, you go playing in the road.'

Sally started humming, looking up and down the bumpy dirt road as if it were an old friend. 'You stay right here by the creek where I can watch you. You go near that road, Mommy is going to smack you good, you hear? Whyn't you make some nice mudpies for when your Daddy comes home? Keep yourself busy so I don't have to slap your face.'

'There's a car in the distance, Sally,' I said. Just over the hills there was a dust tail rising, coming towards us.

'Momma, you know there hasn't been a car on that road for two whole days. Hold me up, Momma. Let me see if somethin's comin'. I know Daddy's car. Let me see if Daddy's coming back.'

The car that came over the rise was a big white Cadillac convertible with the top down. I stood in the middle of the road and Sally screamed out 'Daddy, Daddy, Daddy, Daddy's coming home.'

Sally waved wildly, one arm around my neck, screaming 'Daddy', as the driver, her little round face framed in blue curls peering under the top of the steering-wheel, her mouth gaping open, both hands on the wheel, the driver kept her foot down, not slowing down at all, and gaping at us turned the wheel just slightly in our direction, forcing me to step back at the last moment to keep from getting hit.

Sally waved and yelled 'Daddy' as the white Cadillac drove past, a little blue fluff of curls barely visible above the back of the red leather seat. The car went over the top of the next hill and out of sight, leaving a cloud of drifting dust and the silence of the desert.

'I guess we don't look like we're her ideal travelling companions,' I said, thinking that if we had any luck the blue haired woman in the Cadillac would report us to the police.

'Daddy,' Sally said in a quiet little-girl voice, her chin resting on my shoulder, 'please, can we go home now?'

I didn't know how far it was to Sally's cabin, but it had to be within a mile or two to the right. I turned and headed down the dirt road, one ragged foot in the dirt at a time. 'We'll be home soon, sweetheart,' I said.

chapter seventeen

Her voice echoed down the big dark caverns. A sweet, promising lure of warmth, and hope and longing. I couldn't make out the words. Then, flinging back the covers, she spoke again and she said, 'Come on you lazy old slug, wake up. OK, Mr Evers, time to get your butt in motion. We're going home this morning.'

I have slept in a mouldy caravan behind a barn in Buckingham, England, in a bed reeking of damp while the spores blackened the formica walls and a woman with stubby hands and soft thighs and a degree in chemistry from Cambridge who wanted to be a racing driver whispered 'Fuck me, fuck me, fuck me,' in my ear. I have slept in a hotel in London so posh they knew my name before I checked in and I have slept in a bed shaped like a boat at the Château de Chandon where Napoleon, the countess whispered in my ear, made love with her ancestors. I have slept in a bed like a funnel where my ex-wife and I clung to the opposite edges like the survivors of a shipwreck clinging to a raft. I have slept in motels in Australia, boatels in Florida, camp sites in Greece, five-star mausoleums in Austria, and I have slept in a Ford Anglia in Portugal, with Mike, my mechanic, his beard glistening with transmission oil, whispering 'Susie, sweetheart,' in my ear. And I have slept in a tatami room in Japan where a Japanese woman undid my kimono as if I were priceless porcelain, and in a hammock on the edge of the Indian ocean while red ants cleaned my toenails, and in a hundred tarmac racing paddocks, under a leaky tarpaulin with the rain pissing down, and in a deep and slippery feather bed in Barcelona in the days before AIDS, with Carmen, she swore her name was, leaning over me in a cloud of perfume, breasts like church bells and a gold crucifix swinging in the opposite direction in between. And strangest of all I slept in a bed with bars at the sides, where a nurse tucked me in and I had troubled dreams from age one to three.

So I am used to sleeping in strange beds. Still, it took just a little while for my slowly opening eyes to take in a crisp white smock that stopped short of my knees and a wall of curtains on a rail around my bed and a six-foot-tall iron-haired woman with a face like George Bush holding my blue blanket in her hand. It took just a little while for my brain to work out that I was in a hospital. In Phoenix.

My head ached, my skin burned and my feet, in gauze booties, felt as if they had been pounded by baseball bats.

'How's Sally?' I said.

When they took us to the hospital, they rolled Sally into the operating theatre while they patched up my feet and swabbed cooling gel on my sunburn.

'You mean Miss Cavanaugh,' the nurse said, correcting me.

'How is she?'

'She's in Tring, on the third floor in E wing. As soon as you check out, I'm sure you can visit her. Can you walk?' The nurse held out a pair of aluminium crutches for me.

Sally was lying on her side with her back to me, facing the window, with the sheet pulled tight around her. I sat on the bed and I put my hand on her shoulder and I said, 'How are you feeling?'

And she said, 'I'm feeling like I'd like you to get out of here and not come back.' She said it quietly.

'Does it hurt?'

'Yeah, it hurts. What hurts is they say they are going to take more tests and if the skin on my temple doesn't heal right away they are going to take some skin off my bottom and put it on the side of my head. Not right away. First they have to let the scar tissue grow in. Then they paste the skin over the scar tissue. Scar tissue never goes away, so they don't replace the scar tissue, they just paste over it. So I'm going to be walking around with my bottom on my head and a lot of scars underneath. Does that answer your question?'

I tried to think of something to say to take the edge off, but all I could come up with was, 'I'm sorry.'

'Well, great. You hang on to that "sorry" Evers, and take it with you, OK? If you knew anything about me, and you don't, you'd know that the last thing I want is pity, yours or anybody's. I don't want to hurt your feelings and I don't want to be rude, racerboy,' she said, rolling over to look at me, the right side of her face padded with a bandage, the left side looking OK, 'but let's get this straight. All you were was a nice fuck.'

Sometimes it's hard to stay cheerful.

I tried anyway. 'You were not so bad yourself,' I said.

'Let me put it another way Evers,' she said, getting up on one elbow, her blue eyes boring holes through mine. 'This is Bobby's trick. I know him, and I know how his mind works, and this is his kind of game. And mine. I really don't care what happens now. I really don't. Except that I am going to blow his head off his shoulders and watch it roll down the street and into the traffic. I'll cheer up after that, feel real good inside. What I'm saying is I don't want you anywhere near him or me from now on. OK?'

'How's the rest of you?' I said, reaching under the covers.

She sat up like a shot. 'God damn you,' she said. 'Get out. Daddy was here and I told him too. Maybe you don't know, it doesn't exactly feature on his official bio. Daddy started out running a wire service in Cicero, Illinois, and after all these years he's still got the connections. And so do I. Which means if I want help I can call up more firepower than World War Two just by picking up the telephone.' She paused for a bit, and then she smiled. 'My right eye won't focus. Isn't that a bitch?' she said.

I kissed her on her good cheek.

The Phoenix Police and Public Safety building at 620 West Washington wears an extra bazooka-proof layer of concrete slabs framing slits for windows. Inside, the interior is friendly enough, if you like brown linoleum. And sunburned members of the public, shuffling along in oversized tennis shoes are welcomed with a friendly 'What can we do for you today, sir?' from a twenty-five-year-old male model in a cop uniform, smiling behind the reception desk at the side of the lobby. He's smiling because he knows that the psychopaths, muggers, drunks, pimps, hookers, stabbers, child molesters, crack addicts, gang-rapers, wife beaters and other sweepings of the Phoenix police vehicles arrive two floors down, at the back, several locked steel doors away. His smile turned to concern, seeing my face. 'You ought to try sun block,' he said, a lot of white teeth showing in a sympathy grimace.

'Does it work for cherry bombs?'

'Oh, you're the guy,' he said, leaning forward, taking a closer look. A big blonde face showing zero. No more PR, showing the results of intensive training in the sensitive handling of the public. Now he was just a cop having a look. 'You're the guy was out in the desert with Cavanaugh's daughter.'

'Can you tell me who's working on the case?'

'If you mean who's in charge, that'd be Clarence Harmon. I think he might be in if you want to talk to him.'

Harmon sat in a small office three floors up with more industrial strength brown lino on the floor, his desk facing a blank wall painted a soft blue. A pretty woman in a red dress smiled at him from a picture frame holding down a stack of papers that curled at the edges. The other two desks pushed against two other walls were empty and I sat on one.

'How are your feet?' he said. He was about thirty-five, still showing acne scars and a teenager's nervous habit of chewing his cheek. He kept looking past me, out of the smoked-glass window.

'They feel like I'm walking on broken beer bottles but they're fine.'

He nodded, serious. 'So what can I do for you?'

'I was hoping you might tell me who did it.'

He looked at me, impatient, waving his hand in the air like he was clearing away the flies. 'I'll tell you Evers, I don't like seeing the public in here because it interferes with my work. But it is the law and I adhere to the law. But that doesn't mean I have to tell you anything. I mean if I could, I wouldn't, because if you start telling the public anything sooner or later some asshole is going to sue you for something or some assistant DA is going to have you transferred to Dogpatch because you screwed up his case because you told some member of the public something. But even if I wanted to, I can't tell you anything because I don't know a goddamn thing except old man Cavanaugh rings me every hour to ask me if we found anything yet.'

'What do you tell him?'

'What I'd like to tell him is that my case load includes about twenty Mexican kids who cut each other up last night and it looks like we might have our first gang war in Phoenix for a long time. And that promises to be exciting because every asshole with two legs can get a gun in Phoenix. Used to be they'd go out an' play some fucked up version of John Wayne. Now they got automatic weapons, shotguns and grenades at four hundred dollars a pop and they want to play Rambo. And to keep that comedy burning bright there is a new pipeline that has just opened up and it is spraying crack all over our schools. Which may or may not be connected to an unknown arsonist who set fire to an elementary school last night. Meanwhile we have the more classical domestic shit like the wife stabbed her husband sixteen times in the chest in Deer Valley last night but didn't kill him, and there are four follow-ups I gotta do today on Barnes. So I would like to tell Mr Cavanaugh I would like to think that this is a democratic system where I have the staff and the time to deal with each of these violent acts against the public peace with the care and concern that they deserve and not waste my time talking to a rich old fart on the phone who's shaking his dick in the air because his daughter got her face burned in a fireworks accident.

'I'd like to tell him we have extremely rich and dirt poor and none of them like cops but every goddamn one of them looks to us to keep this city from coming apart. But I can't tell him that, I have to listen to him and I have to talk to you because if I don't I'm going to have to listen to a lot of old farts waving their dicks at me and threatening to bust my ass down to Communications in the goddamn basement.'

'It wasn't an accident.'

'OK, it wasn't an accident. There's still nothing to tell. There was a rainstorm and by the time I got out there the only tracks we could make out were the local cops who walked in behind their flashlights last night and stepped all over everything.'

'Nothing?'

'Well, I can tell you they weren't cherry bombs, they were

what the kids call a blockbuster. About four times the power of a cherry bomb. They make them out of black powder.'

'You don't know who manufactured them?'

'I can give you the chemistry of the powder if you're interested, which is sodium, charcoal and potassium nitrate, and I have an analysis of the paper. But no, no manufacturer. Most fireworks are made by unregistered independent small-time operators all over the country, Mexico and the Far East. They could have come from Iowa or Alabama or Camfucking-bodia. You ever see a fireworks factory?'

I shook my head no.

'They are little one-man shacks about fifty yards apart scattered around an open field. So if one of them blows up only one man gets hurt.'

'Or woman.'

'Or woman. How is she?'

'She doesn't want to see anybody.'

'She's gonna get her wish. That nice lady told the officer investigating her case, meaning me, to fuck off. Kind of dampens my enthusiasm. Have you thought of anybody else it might be besides Bobby Roberts since you spoke to, whozzis, Detective Kelly?'

'It has to be Bobby Roberts.'

'So she said.'

'Did you know that she and Bobby were engaged?'

'That was years ago. What I heard was her Daddy broke it up by setting up Roberts with a hooker and telling her about it.'

'You don't think there's any connection between Roberts and Barnes?'

'Sure there's a connection. There's always a fucking connection. I've been talking to Roberts about it. But if it was Roberts flinging the fireworks at you he has a hell of an arm. Roberts wasn't even in Phoenix when you were attacked, he was in San Diego. He has his boarding passes, credit card voucher for lunch at an outpatient alcohol clinic and witnesses including doctors and nurses at the clinic. Verified by the San Diego police. You want to do something, Evers, talk to somebody who might have some answers. Talk to Cavanaugh. See if he has any thoughts on who wants to get at him through his daughter. See if you can get him to go a whole hour without calling me. And if you think of something you think I ought to know, take one of my cards,' he pointed at his desk without looking at it. 'You can reach me at that number, any time. Just don't waste my time.'

Then he stopped looking out of the window and watched me take one of his cards. 'When are you going back to London?' he said.

Judith Behrman said come on over, she'd be glad to see me. She said she had something to tell me. When I got off the elevator on the top floor of her building, Judith was standing at one of the floor-to-ceiling windows that ringed the room, a portable phone tucked between her shoulder and her ear, and a sheaf of notes in her hand. Behind her there was the blue sky and the flat landscape of Phoenix, punctuated by lumps of rock here and there, dwarfing the isolated skyscrapers that stuck up out of the desert floor from time to time, looking like scale models of the real thing.

When Judith got off the phone she spread the sheaf of papers on her desk. 'OK,' she said, rolling her shoulders, getting into it. For a soft and cuddly looking woman, her manner was as cuddly as a thumb-tack. 'Here's a map of your original property and here's an overlay of what you have now,' she said, laying a clear plastic outline of one map over half another. 'What used to be around half of your land is now held by Skyways Development Trust Co., which I think you already know. Skyways Development Trust is a wholly-owned subsidiary of Darval, a wholly-owned subsidiary of Empire.'

'Shells within shells.'

'Within shells. Now the only thing I can find that gives us any kind of a handle is that when Simon, Roberts and Phillips, the lawyers for Skyways Development Trust, took out an abeyance for commercial development on what was your land, they never filed. So technically you may be able to prevent or delay commercial development if you are willing to initiate litigation against a large and wealthy firm with its own legal staff on the basis of a minor technicality. Although I wouldn't tip your hand before they started construction because it may be possible they could fix it prior. But once they start construction you could go after them saying their deed doesn't have a commercial abeyance filed with it and by the time they come back to you on that you might have the greenies on your side.'

'You don't make it sound very promising, Judith.'

'Well it promises spending a lot of money which I would be happy to take. And it promises to take a lot of time. Which I'm happy to spend at your expense.'

'That's my only option?'

'Litigation in this town is the last thing you ought to consider, Mr Evers, but I mentioned it first because it is what I do. I hear Cavanaugh bought heavily into commercial property just before the Savings and Loan thing hit along with the recession. So he may be over-extended there.'

'What kind of commercial property?'

'Office buildings like this one. I can't be sure about it but I think he is the owner of the corporation that owns this one. I don't know what their financial structure is, or how much debt they carry, but I'd guess they are not delighted about paying out a hundred and forty-three thousand dollars in Federal, state and local taxes every quarter on an empty building. What I'm saying is, I think he owns at least a half a dozen of these, maybe more, and you might just wave that neglecting to file an abeyance at him and get a deal out of him. Although if you are going to make a deal with Cavanaugh you better have zippers on your pockets.'

'From what I've seen of Merrill Cavanaugh he's not an easy man to deal with.'

'Well from your point of view making a deal with him might be more attractive than going before a judge who had dinner with Cavanaugh the night before.'

Cavanaugh's house was off Camelback in the vast open flat suburban tracts of north-central Phoenix. It was a one-storey ranch, plain as a fence, larger than most and painted a dark weathered green, low under the trees as if it had always been there; no lawn, pine needles on the roof, old wooden chairs on the porch.

A thin old man in an old, faded cowboy shirt and a short, dark, butler's apron opened the door, chewing on a toothpick. I followed him down a long gloomy hallway into a game room, where the game was staring down from the walls with little brass plaques to commemorate where and when they had been shot. The room was large, cool and dark with a polished oak floor and it smelled of cedar and burned out fires from the fireplace.

'How's my daughter?' Cavanaugh said. He was looking down at me, sitting on a bronco machine like they have in Dallas bars, with a saddle strapped over a leather midsection and a jolting power drive underneath with enough kick to send a movie star's career into obscurity.

'She told me you'd been to see her.'

'I've been to see her but she won't tell me anything. I thought maybe she told you something she didn't tell me.' Cavanaugh had a bottle of Modelo Negro in his hand. Drinking alone in the afternoon was not a good sign, but he looked in good shape for seventy, a little tubby in his flannel shirt and tight jeans, but solid. His shirtsleeves were rolled up and he had the forearms of a steelworker. Blue veins like grapevines on the back of his hands.

'You ride that machine?' I said.

'We used to throw some pretty good drunks and I could usually stay on it longer than most. For a little while there they were calling me "Travolta" just to piss me off.' He took a swig of beer. 'Sonofabitch is broke now and I can't get anybody to come and fix it. Trouble with all these damn toys, all the goddamn airplanes and heatpumps for the pool and helicopter, trouble is the stuff is always breaking down.' He took another swig of beer, remembering something. 'It always breaks down, and the only guy who can fix it, the guy we used to call the handyman, is called a goddamn technical service representative and you can't get ahold of him because he is on his goddamn three quarter of a million dollar boat down in the Bahamas, tryin' to get somebody to fix his boat for him so he can make a little money on the side runnin' dope. These days everybody's trying to make a little extra on the side to pay his bills. You want a rule of life, Evers, you write this down: everything breaks. Every goddamn thing breaks. You love your daughter to death and give her everything she needs, everything she wants and everything you can think of to make her happy and it doesn't matter because she breaks. She gets broken and who

125

is going to fix her? What the hell were you doing out there anyway, Evers? You were fucking her werencha?' His snapping turtle face held no expression at all. Little faded blue eyes peering out behind an old man's folded lids.

'What she said was that she didn't want to see me. She didn't want to see anybody. She said she didn't want to see you either.'

'Maybe she didn't want to but she did. And I agree with her, I don't think seeing you,' he said, climbing down out of the saddle pointing his bottle at me, 'is a good idea at all. Not at all.' He walked over to an old and worn blue leather chair, settling down into the sweet spot, then looking out the window, softening his tone, the country gentleman in his den. 'Sit down, sit down, make yourself at home. Don't misunderstand me, Evers. You may find this hard to believe but I know a little about you and I like you. I recognise a magnum ambition when I see one. And I like ambition. I like to encourage ambition when I can. Trouble with you is, ambition doesn't seem to be doing you any good does it? I mean you don't seem to be getting anywhere. You rolled Bobby's Range Rover so it looks like chewed gum and got him good and pissed off at you and you got my daughter's face blown off. Now what was it you wanted me to do for you, son?'

chapter eighteen

'Before you do anything for me,' I said, swinging up into the bronco saddle, 'there's something you might want to do for Sally. I think she's suffering from depression and it might not be a bad idea to have a psychiatrist have a look at her.'

'I appreciate your concern, Evers. It's kinda touching you want to get a psychiatrist for my daughter. Just because she tossed you out doesn't mean she's mentally disturbed. Probably a sign of good sense. Sounds to me like you don't know her real well so let me tell you a little something about Sally. A trick-cyclist could take a look at her, but if he says "boo" she'll tear his head off.' He emptied his bottle and set it carefully down on the oak floor.

'What you saw this morning, Evers, that is her normal state of mind. Absolutely normal. You may have previously seen her doin' her honey act and thought that was her normal state. It's not. All that sweetness and smiles is just how she goes when she wants some sucker to get stuck on her. Nothing personal, you understand. She's been hard on men since Bobby. She's still kinda bitter about that. Course, I don't blame her for being disappointed in Bobby. I'm kinda disappointed in him myself. What else?'

'If that's her normal state of mind, Cavanaugh, then she definitely needs psychiatric help.'

'Call me Merrill if you would, please. Anything else?'

'Sure. How about the land you stole from me, Merrill. I'd like it back.'

'I'm sure you would, Forrest. But first you have to understand, nobody stole that land. That land was acquired entirely legally under eminent domain and fair market-purchase price. And even if I wanted to, there is nothing that I could do to get it back for you. That land is owned, legally owned, by a public corporation, not by me. I have a busy day today, Mr Evers. Are we running out of topics?'

'I thought you wanted to talk about property. "Bring out your papers," you said, "and we'll talk about your land." Well, let's talk about my land for another minute or two, Merrill. You mind telling me if you have any plans for it?'

'Ah, well now, we are making progress. I don't mind talking about my plans. I'm happy to tell you about plans for that land and the rest of Phoenix.' He gave me a lipless smile and settled back in his blue leather chair, spreading his hands over the ends of the arms. President Cavanaugh.

'Phoenix is the eleventh largest city in America and it doesn't have a port. It is not on the sea and it is not on a railroad and if it wasn't here there wouldn't be a road to it either. Except for some computer and radio stuff, we don't manufacture enough to fill the hole in a doughnut. And if we didn't suck the Salt River dry and siphon off a lot of the Colorado, Phoenix wouldn't exist at all. What I'm telling you is Phoenix doesn't have a reason to exist so we have to invent one. Otherwise we'll turn into another half-empty shopping centre off the interstate. Now I suggest you listen carefully because I am about to tell you what is going to make Phoenix a world-class city in the twenty-first century.'

'I'm all ears.'

'Don't be a smartass. Let me ask you this. Do you see the world getting any better? Or easier?'

'Not,' I said shifting my weight on the saddle, 'from where I sit.'

Cavanaugh pushed himself out of his chair and started pacing, head down, onstage, warming up. 'The harder the world gets, Evers, the more people need refreshment, and I am not talking about Pepsi-Cola. I am talking about a place where you can let go, relax, have a ball, charge your batteries, refresh your soul and feel good about it. I'm talking about the simple pleasures of the warm sun on your back, swimming in clear water, and breathing clean, clear air. I'm talking about growing stronger, being rested and ready to face the dim and repetitious grind most people call life. I am talking about more than simple recreation. I am talking about nothing less than Re-Creation.'

'Re-Creation,' I said.

'That's right. Like recreation only it is two words. Two words to mark down, Evers, Re-Creation. As you probably know, that's how Phoenix got its name in the first place. It was an Indian city, maybe as big as sixty maybe even a hundred thousand people. Fifteen hundred years before the birth of Christ they were gone, vanished and nobody knows what in hell happened to them. City was abandoned until a prospector in 1867, name of Swilling, fell into a dry ditch and said, hey, wait a damn minute, this isn't a ditch, this is a canal. This could be a city. He got a bunch of miners to dig out the canals and the place was reborn. Re-Creation. Rebirth. The history of Phoenix is Re-Creation and the future of Phoenix is Re-Creation. I am talking beyond New Age, beyond the next decade. I want Phoenix to be the new world centre for mental, physical and spiritual Re-Creation. People will come to Phoenix to be refreshed and restored, to feel brand new again, and to have the time of their lives while they do it. Excuse me while I help myself to another beer. You sure you won't have one?'

I said no thanks and he got up to get another beer from a full-size refrigerator next to the bookshelf.

'This year a million people will come to Phoenix for the sun and the resorts and let me tell you they are just the first wave. I am going to turn this town into the richest playground on earth. Phoenix is going to make Las Vegas look like a sleazy little cow town.'

He closed his eyes, dreaming his dream. 'Some men build houses, some build companies, I am going to build a city like you have never seen before. You asked about that piece of desert your mother used to own. Take that as just one example. What's the biggest race in the world? The Indianapolis 500. Well I love racing and I always kind of liked Indy, but that track was built in 1909. And when it was built, the fastest cars in the world raced flat out around it. Nowadays they got a million rules at Indy that tell you what you can't do with your Indycar.

'This is America, the West. Think big. I've looked into it,

and Jesus Christ, if a strangled little small-block can drag an Indycar at two hundred and thirty miles an hour around Indy think what we could do if we did away with all those restrictions. Let 'em run full boost. Let 'em run any damn wing they want. Let 'em run any damn engine they care to bring to the track.

'I'm talking about real spectacle, real sport, Forrest. Suppose we built a track five miles around and no limits. Let 'em go three hundred miles an hour. You ever see four cars side by side coming into a turn at three hundred miles an hour? Dangerous? You bet your ass it'd be dangerous. You think I'd like to put the danger back in racing? Goddamn right I would. That's part of the thrill, part of the spectacle. You're a driver, you tell me, has danger ever held you back? Hell no.'

'There were plenty of times danger held me back.'

He ignored me. 'We are going to have the biggest and the fastest motor-racing track in the world and that's just the beginning. We are gonna have the Cowboy Arizona Derby on another track in the middle of downtown that'll make the Churchill Downs look like a dog track. We will be the conference centre for the new world. A living example of a city sustaining itself without pollution, crime or all the other crap that comes with an industrial city. We will have all the banking, finance, insurance, legal, construction and maintenance industries that it will take to build and sustain the Re-Creation centre of the world. And I am building the buildings now to house and service those industries.'

'I've seen them,' I said. 'And they are empty.'

'Course they're empty. If you are going to cross the river before the bridge is built you got to jump, take the leap. Take another example, this Formula One team we were talking about. As far as I am concerned, let's do it. Let's build a Phoenix Formula One team, show the world we are world class in high-tech recreation. Tell the world that Phoenix is Re-Creation city, a city designed for the refreshment of the Human Body and the Human Spirit. What do you think?'

'I think building a city is probably easier than building a successful Formula One team.'

'What's the problem?'

'Everything in Formula One is a problem. The cars are fragile.

They need non-stop intensive care from a team of aerodynamic, electrical and computer physicists. The drivers take them out and smash them against the wall. The engines cost around seventy to a hundred and fifty thousand dollars and they come with no guarantee. A Formula One team will eat a million dollars a week if you want to be competitive and two million a week if you are serious about winning. They need drivers and if you think I am an edgy, egotistical, self-centred bastard, I am told I am a sweetie compared to most drivers. A Formula One team needs major sponsorship from several international corporations all of who have to have their hand held. It needs the backing of a major automobile manufacturer like Renault, Ford, Falcon or Honda. And I could go on about wind tunnels and autoclaves, and public relations. But let me put it this way. You would probably get more warmth and satisfaction raking your money into a big pile and setting fire to it. Besides except for tyres, the technology isn't here, it's in Europe and Japan. So you'd have to base your Phoenix team in Europe.'

Cavanaugh held up his hand to stop me. 'Let me just make a little guess here. We are talking about a hundred million dollars and in my book that is a substantial business. Somebody spends fifty to a hundred million dollars, they are not giving the money away. The only reason you spend a hundred million dollars is to make another hundred million dollars. Correct me if I am wrong but I have done my homework and it is my impression that Williams and McLaren make a hell of a good profit. What I am telling you Evers is that the money is not a problem.

'Put the figures down so I can see them, then we can get started. I understand the technology is not here. Hell, that doesn't stop Indy cars. They're all made in England. I am not talking about a little backwater, hope to make it past pre-qualifying and getting into the race. I am talking about winning now. See, I was talking about calling a team Darvol just to get out on the track. But my vision has expanded since I last spoke with you. I want to win the World Championship and I want to do it with the Phoenix Formula One Team. And I fully appreciate that you cannot do that in one season. OK, you will have to look abroad for the talent and the technology. Do it. It will take time and money, I hear you. But it is also going to take time and money to rebuild Phoenix as the Re-Creation Centre of the World, to attract the Disneys of the future to build their businesses here and to establish our reputation. My son, you have to start somewhere and the time to start is now. If you don't want to start now, I doubt I am going to have much trouble finding somebody else in Formula One racing who would think this is the opportunity of a LIFETIME. Christ, you work this racing thing right, you can make enough money to buy your land back ten times.'

'I thought you were planning to build the world's biggest and fastest race track on that property.'

'Isn't that a great idea? No reason you couldn't supervise that too. Trouble with you people in Europe is you live in those little bitty countries and it takes a while for you to learn to think big.'

'Caesar, Alexander the Great, Napoleon, Hitler . . .'

'Yeah, all right. I'll grant you America hasn't cornered the market in megalomaniacs. I'm not talking about ruling the world, I just want to make this city WORK. And Re-Creation is one sensaaational idea. It's Green. Provides employment. I am talking about delight. Making people happy. Go back in history and you tell me when the world ever been more in need of Re-Creation? When has the world ever needed a chance sit back and consider the ways we can keep from devouring ourselves and our planet. When has the world ever needed Re-Creation more than it needs it now?'

'You think a Formula One team is going to help save the world?'

'Don't fool with me. I think a Formula One team could be a small but important piece of a large puzzle that I am trying to put together with a lot of awkward pieces. I think an American Formula One team, properly run, would be an international focal point. It could be the best international advertising money could buy. And it will make money. Why don't you give it some thought, and put your ideas down on paper?'

'You're serious about this?'

Cavanaugh heaved himself up out of his chair and came over to me, putting his face in front of mine. Little blue veins crisscrossed little red and purple veins on his nose. 'You're damn right I'm serious about this. Come on, let me pour you a drink, if I may. There's something else I want to talk to you about.' Then he picked up what looked like a TV remote control and turned on the bronco machine.

chapter nineteen

The saddle gave me a slow and sexy squirm between my legs and then jack-hammered my backbone sending me a couple of feet up in the air. I landed hard on my shoulder on the polished oak floor.

'You got to hold on to the handle,' he said. 'Hold on tight.'

'I thought you said the machine was broken.'

'It is. It only runs at full speed. You want to try it again?'

'What else do you do for fun, pound your nuts with a hammer?'

'Just takes a little while to get the hang of it, son. Why don't you give it another try?'

'I'd be happy to do that, Merrill, if you don't mind doing a demo first. Show me how it's done.'

'Glad to,' he said, laying his belly against the leather body of the thing, hauling himself up and settling into the saddle. 'Like I said you got to hold on tight. Don't fight it and don't try to predict it 'cause it'll fool you. You think it's about to go one way and it goes another. You have to ride it, go with it. Turn the sonofabitch on. Just press the button. You want to bet a hundred dollars I can stay on this?'

'For how long?'

'Ten seconds.'

'That's not any time at all for the man they call Travolta. Make it twenty-five.'

'You didn't stay on it for one damn second. Make it fifteen if you have your heart set on doing permanent damage to an old man.'

'Fifteen seconds Merrill,' I said. 'As soon as I figure out how to work this thing.'

I picked up the remote, pressed the button and the machine

began to bump and grind, turning and bucking. Merrill shook, bounced, jiggled and swayed, his head shaking like a grizzled puppet, his wide, lipless mouth set in a straight line. And he made it look easy, keeping his knees up and his left hand high as if he was waving to a crowd, moving with the machine. After fifteen seconds I stopped the machine and he slid off the saddle, sweating and breathing hard.

'You owe me a hundred dollars,' he said, a big grin moving his ears back a notch. 'You want to try to win it back?'

'How long do I have to stay on?'

'Considering what a rude bastard you are I oughta say ninety seconds. But I'm such a sweet-hearted ol' pussycat I suppose I could just settle for ten. Since you were not exactly born on a horse? Are you game?'

I hesitated and he said, 'You can have as many tries as you like.'

'Ten seconds then,' I said. It didn't sound like much.

I pulled myself up into the saddle and locked my hand around the handle that was wrapped with worn friction tape, still warm and damp with sweat from Cavanaugh's ride.

The machine didn't buck as hard as a Formula One car. On the other hand, you aren't strapped in with a four-point safety harness either.

Still, it wasn't difficult. You keep your knees up to keep your weight centred. You lock your hand on to the handle and pull down hard so the machine can't bounce you and you ride with it, not anticipating the machine but sensing in the first microsecond of its move the force and direction of the move, letting the energy flow up through your body and out your arm. Nothing to it if you don't count fifteen falls, scraped knees and elbows, a strained shoulder, a sore neck, a nasty lump on the back of my head, a sore tailbone and a mildly sprained wrist. I was beginning to have my doubts and for all I know Cavanaugh turned the machine down a notch or two but I finally stayed on for ten whole bone-bruising seconds.

'You're a stubborn sonofabitch,' he said, walking over to make himself a drink from a wet bar built into the bookcase.

'Just having fun,' I said, leaning against the machine, breathing hard, hurting, wondering if I was bleeding.

'What do you want to drink?'

'Glass of water.'

'You want a fuckin' parasol in it? Tell you the truth I'm relieved you finally stuck on, Forrest, I was getting worried about you.' He turned toward me swirling a whisky and soda in a big crystal glass. 'How the hell did you get the name Forrest?'

'My mother thought it sounded English.'

'She would. Well, what do you think of my idea?'

'Which one? Your city, your racing team or your race track?'

'Take your pick.'

'I think you are barking mad, Merrill. Maybe you know what you're doing putting up empty office buildings. But you don't have a clue what it takes to run a Formula One team or the politics of getting approval and sanction from FISA or from Indy for that Roman Circus you want to call a race track. The other thing is, I don't know why you'd choose me to run it. There must be fifty people who would know more about it and do it better.'

'Maybe, but I think you'll do fine. I flatter myself that I am an excellent judge of character, Forrest, with the possible exception maybe of Bobby. And you just showed me what I already knew. Which is that you could do anything you put your mind to.'

'I can't fly. And I can't drive a Formula One car.'

'Oh, horse-shit,' he said. 'Look at you. You got your tail between your legs because you can't be a racing driver. Well isn't that too God damn bad. Feeling sorry for yourself. Pathetic. You underestimate yourself, Evers. And you under-estimate me. I have a small staff and I have some power. Which in this town means money. I do my homework and I can tell you exactly what it costs to run a Formula One team. I can tell you which judge to call, state and federal, and which state and federal legislator to have supper with when I want something done. I know your phone number and your bank balance. I know what you have done for most of the time since you have been here. And, as I say, I am an astute judge of character. You know what the buzzword in business is this week. "Compression." Which is a fancy way of saying go faster. Do more in less time. We got a whole generation of managers who think the secret of success in business is cutting costs. Forget cost cutting. Money is time. And the sooner you get to market the sooner you start making money and the longer your lead over the competition. What's a racing driver good at? Speed. How does he go fast? By taking existing time and chopping it up into tiny little pieces. When you are driving a race car you are making more decisions in ten seconds than most people make in a month. So don't tell me I don't know what I am doing. And don't tell me you are not right for the job. You are perfect for it.'

He came over to me, his red face in mine. 'Let me tell you what will enrage you about growing old,' he said. 'ENRAGE YOU! Slowing down. Just as the world is picking up speed you are losing it.' He finished his drink and threw the glass into the fireplace, smashing it.

'NOW,' he said, 'I did mention that I have a busy day and if you like we can start slow and take this one lap at a time. So just tell me, would you be willing to take on the task of starting the Phoenix Formula One team? I just have two requirements. Paint the cars yellow and orange, make 'em look sunny. And the other thing is, get them across the finish line first. Put together some facts and figures with a projection and a time frame. Something solid, meat and potatoes. Like what it will take to get started and how long it would be before we can put cars on the track.'

'I can do that,' I said. 'But there is one more topic we ought to cover.'

'And that is?'

'If you are so well informed,' I said, 'maybe you could tell me who the bastard was who had Bill Barnes killed.'

'Maybe I could,' he said. 'But you just might be overestimating me. Is that it or have you got anything else?'

'How do I know you are serious?'

He pulled his wallet out of his back pocket. 'I prefer an informal way of doing business, Evers. It saves me a lot of time and I never have to have lunch with assholes. Now I have formed the Phoenix Formula One Racing Team Corporation, legally incorporated in Maricopa County in the state of Arizona with total assets right now of five million dollars lying in an interest bearing account, one-oh-seven six-five-one-four nine-nine-eight, which you may access by registering your signature with the Sun Valley National Bank on Central Avenue a few blocks up from Van Buren. Right now the Phoenix Formula One racing team has this house listed as its corporate headquarters. But I reckon you will want to set up a temporary headquarters. That five million is seed money and although I don't give a damn how you spend that money apart from wisely, my accountants will. I am the chairman of the corporation and you are the chief executive officer. Now do you have any questions? Or are you going to allow an old man to get on with his serious business?'

chapter twenty

My feet were much better, thank you. They didn't like being walked on and when I lay down on my prairie-size bed at the Biltmore, they gave off a dull throb. They were a day or two away from dancing, but the green balm the hospital had given me was magic. The rest of me, the lump on the back of my head, the sore and twisted shoulder, the bruised coccyx, and the scrapes, floor burns, and the fading bruises from the cherry bombs on the rest of me didn't hurt at all. For I had been covered with balm. Balm so soothing I was tempted to forget about Barnes.

The Sun Valley National Bank had been glad to see me. They took my signature on record and issued me a large desk-top chequebook. 'These are just temporary, of course. If you would like your cheques imprinted with your corporate logo, we'll be glad to do that for you. Take about a week.'

I had five million dollars. Seed money he called it. As if it was loose change. Maybe it was.

I rang Bill Platt, General Manager of Motor Sport at Falcon Motors in Detroit. He had been Vice-President of Corporate Affairs, and he knew how to work the press and how the corporate cookie crumbled. Among the big Detroit manufacturers, Falcon was the only one that had taken on the world of international racing head on. Others, like GM and Chrysler, had their programmes, but they weren't anywhere near Falcon's commitment. Falcon knew what Formula One could do for their image around the world. They also knew what gaping holes it could punch in their balance sheet.

'Hello, Forrest.' His voice was flat, noncommittal. It had taken me an hour on the phone in my room to get through the secretaries, meetings and the vast indifference a large corporation uses to protect itself from outsiders.

'I want you to listen for two minutes,' I said.

'Make it one. It's six thirty, I still got to take a couple of meetings, and I'm tired of coming home to little shrivelled things on my plate.'

'All right, I'll make it ten seconds. We're starting an American Formula One team and I think Falcon should supply the engines. How soon can I get on your calendar for a formal presentation?'

'Who's "we"?'

'Myself and a Phoenix investor, Merrill Cavanaugh.'

'What kind of sponsors you got on board?'

'The best,' I said.

There was a pause. 'I think if you had any sponsors you'd name 'em. Who's designing the chassis? Who you got for drivers. Or is this your first call?'

'This is my first call.'

'How long will it take you to put together a half-hour presentation?'

'Seven working days,' I said, guessing.

'That's not long enough. Come see me in two weeks from today. Eleven fifteen in my office.'

'We'll come singing and dancing.'

'Do us both a favour, Evers. If you don't have a major sponsor, the drivers and a designer hooked up by then, save the plane fare.'

I had a slow supper in the hotel restaurant and after midnight I rang Bernie Ecclestone at the FOCA offices in Princes Gate in London and he said it was a good idea if I could make it work. Come back to me when you've got it together, he said. I rang the Fédération International de Sport Automobile in Paris and they outlined the procedures required for filing team accreditation through the ASL in the US. I rang four Formula One designers in Britain and Jack Corrigan in France, a young designer I knew was having a hard time with Team Sauvage. The team had plenty of money from the French government, but if the rumours were right, Team Sauvage were too broke to pay their designer. He said sure, if we could get it to happen. The other four said it would take serious money, meaning over a million a year. I rang drivers, mechanics, aerodynamicists, journalists, I rang everybody I could think of and then I lay back on my bed and I smiled. It could work.

If I didn't worry about where the money came from.

If I forgot about Barnes.

Then I rang Ken Arundell at his home in Wiltshire. There was the chill of the English Country House in his voice. 'How have you been, it is so nice of you to call,' he said. There was a pause. 'It's nearly a year now, isn't it. I have been, uhm, quite concerned about you.'

Just dialling his number filled me with guilt. I had destroyed both of his cars and his career as the last private entrant in Formula One racing. He couldn't have been glad to hear from me. At the same time, he couldn't have been more of a gentleman. Probably the last one in Britain.

I told him a little about the Phoenix team and he stopped me. 'Well, yes, of course I miss Formula One terribly. But I don't think I should manage an American team. I'm not very American.'

At six foot seven in a well-worn Savile Row pin-stripe suit, or a yellow woolly jumper and baggy flannels at the weekend, and an accent that rang of stately homes and echoed of Empire and noblesse oblige, Ken was as American as Buckingham Palace. 'The team will be based in Britain,' I said.

'Where in Britain?'

'You tell me.'

'And you have money? Money is rather important, you know.'

'The man behind this claims he is a bottomless pit of money. He has put five million dollars up for openers.'

'Yes. Well. I've found that men who describe themselves as a bottomless pit of money are usually right. Although not about the money.' This was followed by the terrible wheezing sound that meant that he was laughing.

'But you're interested.'

'Oh yes. I'm very interested. Who were you thinking of for drivers? Not yourself were you?'

'No, not myself.'

'Good.'

'Ken, this is early days. I'm just sounding people out. Don't count on anything.'

'Oh good heavens, no, Evers. I certainly won't count on anything.'

At 2 a.m. I couldn't sleep. Thinking it was probably not the best idea in the world, I put on my sneakers and drove to the hospital. The nurse behind the desk at the main entrance looked up from a late-night movie. 'Dr Evers,' I said. 'I'll be with Miss Cavanaugh in Tring.'

chapter twenty-one

I pulled off my running shoes that looked like Mexican architecture, slipped off my belt, jeans, shorts and my shirt and placed them silently on the windowsill, naked in the semi-darkness of the room except for the gauze booties on my feet.

Sally was breathing evenly with a little snore, the air going in and going out. She had a smaller bandage on the right side of her face which seemed like a good sign. I put my hand on her cool forehead and her eyes fluttered open.

'Who?' she said, her voice creaky with sleep, unafraid.

'Doctor Evers,' I said. 'I've come to take your temperature.'

'I told you to go away.'

'I did. Now I'm back.'

'Why aren't you wearing any clothes? You look ridiculous.'

'I couldn't sleep. How are you?'

'I'm scared.'

I sat down on the side of her bed. 'What did the other doctors say?'

'They said it probably won't show much. That it'll probably be covered when my hair grows back. They said that my optical nerve has been compressed, like bruised. And, uh, they said if I'm OK tomorrow, no fever and my headache is gone, they said I could go home tomorrow afternoon.' She looked at me for a moment and thought of something. 'For God's sake, Forrest, somebody'll see you.'

'It's a risk I'll have to take.'

'They'll think you are a pervert.'

'I am a pervert. I could be in my nice big bed at the Biltmore, sleeping with my jammies on. I missed you,' I said, bending down and kissing her between the eyes.

She pulled back. 'Cut it out. Believe it or not, Forrest, I don't feel very sexy. Do you get off on sex with wounded women?'

'This could be a first. I thought you might like some company.'

'Forrest, I don't want to see anybody. I don't have anything to talk about.' She turned away.

'How'd your day go?' I said.

She rolled back to face me again, not angry, just tired. 'It didn't go at all. What I did was this, lie in bed. Except for the brain scan it was a normal lying around pretending to have a coma day. What did you do?'

'I saw your father. He says you are a monster.'

'He's always saying that. It's his way of trying to keep men away from me. I think it encourages them. Like challenging the young bull to take on Papa bull.' Sally punched the pillow into shape and pushed it underneath her, leaning on her elbow, looking up at me. 'You look a mess. Did he beat you up?'

'Now that you mention it, I guess he did.'

'What'd he do? Sucker you on to that stupid bronco machine. or did you go for one of the real ones?'

'What real ones? I didn't see any horses.'

'He keeps a couple of nasty old broncs in a corral out back. If he really wants to intimidate somebody he gets them into thinking that their balls are at stake if they can't ride a homicidal maniac of a horse. But last winter one of them horses kicked some fool from the State Highway Department upside the head, fractured his skull and Barnes wrote up a story in the *Sun* about it raising questions about what Daddy was up to with the Highway Department. So he doesn't like to use the real ones if he can help it, but he likes having them around. He says it makes him feel like an old cowpoke. He's got that big ol' ranch east of Scottsdale but he hardly ever goes there any more. I guess he's more interested in makin' his deals than running after some ol' cows.'

'Is it true, that story about Bobby? That he set Bobby up with a hooker so you'd find them together?'

'Yeah, it's true,' she sighed. A story she had been through a million times. 'He told me he was going to do it. And I said fine, go ahead. "I know Bobby," I said. "He'd never do a thing like that." '

'You knew Bobby pretty well?'

'Oh God, did I know Bobby. I knew Bobby since I was six. One day Daddy brought him home, this beautiful twelve-year-old boy with blonde hair, and I was just amazed. I thought he was a present just for me. Daddy kind of adopted him for a while. Bobby was home for a couple of years and I thought he was just swell, you know. Kind of like having this movie star in the same house with you. Then Daddy sent him away to school on the east coast and I went to school in Texas, and I didn't see him much for years.

'Then, when I was in college and he came back to Phoenix he started asking me out. I thought he was a dream come true, Forrest, I really did. When we were engaged, he was different than he is now, you know? I mean he was thoughtful and sweet and he was just out of law school and starting out with his own practice, and I was just a kid in college over in Tempe and he was like an older brother except he wasn't and he was really sexy. I thought, That's it. He is *the* one. I loved him silly, Forrest, I really did. Then Merrill got to him, somehow. After that thing happened with the hooker Bobby just took off for San Diego and I didn't see him for a couple of years. I don't know, but I think Daddy gave Bobby a lot of money to go away.' Sally looked over her shoulder towards the open door. She went 'Shhhhhh.'

There was the squeaking of rubber soles in the corridor and a six-foot-tall nurse with wide shoulders loomed in the doorway. 'Are you all right, Miss Cavanaugh?' he said.

Sally sat up, holding the blanket, hiding me except for my head. 'Sure. Absolutely perfect in every way. Goodnight now.'

The nurse started to come into the room, shining a flashlight on us. 'I heard voices.'

'Doctor Evers is with me.'

'Good evening,' I said with a smile and my best, posh, Harley Street tones. My British accent wouldn't fool a Brit, but I can pass in Arizona.

He stopped, doubtful. 'There aren't any doctors on the floor tonight.'

'Doctor Evers is my personal physician,' Sally said. 'What's the point of a private room if I can't have my personal physician?'

'I'm sorry, but hospital regulations . . . '

'Look,' Sally said, 'I'm fine. I'm being discharged this afternoon, and I want Doctor Evers here. I need him here.'

I stood up and walked around the bed. 'Nurse, I'm sure you'll understand I have a personal interest in my patient and it is important that we not be interrupted.'

'My goodness gracious,' the nurse said, shining his flashlight on me.

'As you see, Doctor Evers is fully qualified,' Sally said, looking at me. 'How would you feel about two hundred dollars?'

'I wouldn't feel good about it at all. We're talking about my job here,' the nurse said.

'Five hundred,' Sally said.

He looked at his clipboard. 'Well, your temp is normal and your pressure is OK. But you've had a blow on the head and you don't want to get too carried away or you might just burst something like a little blood vessel inside your skull and turn yourself into a drooling veggie. You talking cash?'

'Cash,' Sally said. 'Doctor Evers will see you on his way out.'

'Keep the noise down,' the nurse said, closing the door.

It was dark for a moment then Sally switched on the nightlight by her bed. She burst out laughing. 'Goddammit Wahlnut, if you aren't the silliest looking man I ever did see. Look at you,' she said, hooting, 'that big hard-on and those little baby booties. You look like somebody left you in the crib too long.'

'I've got a lot of patients to see this morning, Miss Cavanaugh . . . ' I said, still in the tones of the terrrribly Brrritish quack.

'You come on in here, Wahlnut,' she said, still laughing holding the covers up, inviting me in. 'I don't think it's a real good idea for me to be foolin' around, but I sure could use a hug. You be careful, now,' she said as I got in the narrow bed. 'I feel fragile, like I'm broken in places I don't know about yet.'

I gave her a cautious hug, pulling her gently to me and we lay side by side, Sally's dark blue eyes inches away, peering in the soul windows.

'I'm sorry I was so nasty to you this morning, Wahlnut,' she said. 'I was afraid. I'm still afraid.'

'Where does it hurt the most?' I said.

'Here,' she said, taking my hand and putting it on her temple where the bandage was, 'and here,' down between her breasts, 'and here,' down to the soft round mound of her tummy, 'I feel all upset.'

'The healing hand of Doctor Evers.'

'I can feel it. Feels nice and warm. You know I'm gonna be as ugly as an ol' prune, Wahlnut.'

'When you die and they bury you under the ground,' I said, 'that's when you get ugly. Until then, I think you're going to look OK.'

She closed her eyes, resting. 'For a while I thought I was going to die. I thought that something bad, like a haemorrhage, was happening, just like the nurse said, that I was bleeding inside my skull and that I was going to die. I had the worst headache. And they wouldn't even give me aspirin. I know you're trying to cheer me up but I still can't focus out of my right eye. If I close my left eye you go all blurry. Are you OK? What are those dumb things on your feet?'

'It's a new kind of hospital condom. You keep them on your feet to keep them pre-stretched.'

'Come on, Wahlnut, stop foolin' around. How are you?'

'I'm sore and tired, and glad to be here,' I said. 'Ouch.' Sally's hand was trailing across my back.

'You got a lot of lumpy places, Wahlnut. Is that from the fireworks or is that Daddy's bronco did that one?'

'I forget which. Maybe both.' I gave her a kiss on that wide, soft mouth of hers, just testing the water. The water was fine. 'Until you asked me if your father had beaten me up, I hadn't realised that he had. It was kind of subtle for a mugging.'

'What'd he say?'

'He gave me a long speech about rebuilding Phoenix as the Re-Creation city of the future.'

'Yeah, he tells that one a lot. He's got several of those. There's "Phoenix, Financial Hub of the Twenty-first Century," there's "Phoenix, Urban Game Park," and another one of his favourites is "Phoenix, SunPower City of the Future". What was he leading up to?'

'He kind of laid out the candy store in front of me and said take what you like. I picked the American Formula One team. It's a little bizarre but I know in my bones it could work. It's what I came here to tell you about.'

Sally put her hands behind my head and pulled us together and gave me a long and slow kiss, the kind of saxophone kiss that begins warm and slow and then you lose yourself in the connection. The kind of kiss that goes on for a while, warms your whole body, makes you glad to be alive and goes on for a little while longer and then it isn't nearly long enough because you are hooked. As hooked as a teenage kiss-addict.

I started to pull her towards me again and Sally pulled back. 'You better be careful of him, Wahlnut. He's an old poker player. He'll show you one hand and he'll play another.'

'Where's his money come from?'

'That's a hell of a question. No wonder people throw rocks at you. Where does any money come from? It comes from money. He's always had it ever since I can remember. Plenty of it. What do you want to know for?'

'He gave me five million dollars in cash to start a Formula One team.'

'Well, isn't that a damn shame. Wouldn't you like something to do for a change, Wahlnut? Instead of creeping around hospitals at night with a hard-on and baby booties?'

'Something is off the wall about it. It's not the money itself, I'm glad to have it. Glad to have the chance. What bothers me is that people who have money like to have their money working for them. They don't have five million lying around in loose change.'

'Daddy does.'

'Well, I hope your Daddy does. That day when I rolled Bobby's Range Rover, when I was riding in a taxi back from Cave Creek to the hotel, I asked the cab driver who was putting up all those office buildings when the ones that were already up were empty. And he said, "Must be folks with more money than brains." I don't know how much money your Daddy has, but I'll bet he doesn't have more money than brains.'

'Well if you want financial advice about the future of Phoenix, Wahlnut, you sure don't mess around do you? You go straight to the top, ask a damn cab driver.' Dryyyhhvvvuuuhhhh, she pronounced it. Her eyes were closing, sleepy.

'How come Bobby is always going to San Diego?'

Her eyes were closed now, her voice a little distant. 'Oh phooey, you old oakhead, everybody in Phoenix goes to San

Diego. They go in the summer to the beach cause it's cooler. They even got a word for 'em. They call 'em Zonies. Daddy used to take me all the time.'

'In the summer?'

'Not just in the summer.' Her breathing slowed, became deeper and after a while she was back to the soft little snore that had greeted me when I'd walked into her room. Breathing in and breathing out.

My arm was going to sleep and I shifted towards her. I put my arm over her while she slept, curled against me. And I thought of what she had said the day before, when we had gone to the pool in the desert, that we shared the same skin and had the same bones and I felt the connection and it felt like a kind of loss and it felt like love.

When the light started leaking in around the window blinds I got up quietly, put on my clothes and left. Over my shoulder, as I closed the door, she looked as small and as innocent as a girl who was sleeping in her own room at home, dreaming until her mother would come in and wake her up for school.

The nurse stopped me on the way out and I wrote him a cheque for five hundred dollars. 'Come back any time, Dr Evers,' he said.

When I got back to my room at the Arizona Biltmore, there was a short, wiry man in a yellow T-shirt and blue shorts, no socks and NIKE Air Pumps standing outside my door. He was maybe fifty-five or sixty and he looked as if he lived without water. A desert rat. He went, 'Mr Evers?'

I nodded yes.

He handed me an envelope and he said, 'You have been served, Mr Evers.' And he turned and walked quickly away down the hall, his Air Pumps going squish, squish, squish in the orange carpet.

The envelope was a lawsuit from Bobby Roberts for fifteen million six hundred and seventy-five thousand dollars claiming neck injury and other grievous bodily harm, slanderous public insult to his character and to his professional and corporate reputation, reckless assault with criminal intent – and the list went on and on for two raging pages of itemised offences against Mr Roberts followed by six more pages of uncon-ditional legal meatchopper.

Among the many itemized charges one caught my eye, citing the loss of his car as causing him to lose important business, stating that he had been compelled to rent a Mercedes 500 SL and was charging it to me at three hundred and seventy-five dollars a day plus sixty-five per cent for professional services for the time he spent in the car. Another little gem listed an unpaid bill of four thousand five hundred dollars. This was charged to me for legal consultation on the afternoon we'd spent together, the afternoon when we went driving backwards. Even counting the time Bobby spent driving home, the whole round trip was a half-hour short of two hours. Still give him the benefit of the doubt. Make it two hours, total four thousand five hundred dollars. At two thousand two hundred and fifty dollars an hour good ol' 'sick, sore, lame, and disabled' Bobby Roberts was rating his legal advice almost high enough to qualify as a rookie Formula One driver. Time to offer my condolences and humble apologies to the injured party, I decided, feeling cheerful. Time to see who the real Bobby Roberts really was.

chapter twenty-two

Heigh Ho, heigh ho, it's off to the Dealer we go.

To the NCD as they say in the trade, the New Car Dealer. The direct descendant of the New Camel Dealers of Jerusalem, Bethlehem and Chaldea before Jesus was born. Have we got a deal for you, Mr Wiseman. One hump or two?

Arkwright, Lawson and Honeypepper, their display ad in the yellow pages said, were 'specialists in the purveyance and care of fine imported classic automotive investments. Appointed agents for Rolls Royce, Jaguar and Range Rover'. 21003 East Camelback.

My feet sank into camel beige carpet on the showroom floor and overhead a ballroom chandelier blazed away at nine thirty in the morning, indicating high class. Heavy air-conditioning kept the air slightly chilled and stirred with a whiff of lavender. Another aid, no doubt, to brisk sales.

The NCD of today has moved up a notch from the fly-blown sand lots in Babylon and Chaldea, but the retailing of four-wheeled double-humpers hasn't changed at all. Show a glimmer of interest in any of the beasts and the man whose shot you are, who has been gnawing his nails waiting his turn on the rota list, is in front of you, between you and the car. About six-foot seven, skullfuzz razor-cut, dark-blue pin-stripe suit, rep silk tie and the look of the starving wolf in his eyes.

'Very fine automobile, sir,' he says in the hushed and reverential tones of an usher at a funeral.

I am interested in a Range Rover they have mounted on a slowly rotating turntable. Not a perfect replica of Bobby's car, it is dark metallic green instead of silver and the seats are tan leather instead of black, and there is no roll-bar or array of lights. But it is a convertible and it is close enough. 'Very fine automobile,' I agree. 'Had it long?'

'Mr Uhmm?'

'Evers, Forrest Evers.'

'Russell Belgium,' he said, giving my hand a firm, sincere shake. 'It just came in, Mr Evers. We don't seem to be able to keep a drophead conversion in our showroom for more than a few days.'

I looked at the invoice sticker on the window. Arkwright, Lawson and Honeypepper had taken delivery in October. Since then the big spenders who winter in Phoenix had come, played golf, cruised the streets in their Cadillac Sevilles, Mercedes and Japanese discount Mercedes and gone home. So Arkwright etc were already out five months' carrying charges on the wholesale price plus insurance, prep. and overheads, and they were still stuck with the beast. They would be glad to deal rather than putting the car up for wholesale auction and taking a loss.

'It's a pretty colour,' I said. 'What is the best you can do on it?'

'With leather, air, Turbo-Technics Twin Turbos and uprated suspension, six-speaker Bose 120-watt FM and CD with pre-amp, auto-seek and digital signal phase locked loop, ABS, town and country accessory group, wide track mags and 220 x 70 Eagle radials, and, of course, the Crayford Drophead Conversion, your investment would be seventy-six thousand seven hundred and ninety-five dollars with warranty, undercoat, silicone seal, preparation and delivery including Federal, state and local taxes.'

His face shifted down to a lower, more personal gear. 'Unfortunately, Mr Evers, I'm afraid that the level of service that we provide for our clients doesn't allow us the luxury of discounting,' he said, ending with a sorrowful smile for the imperfect world we live in.

'Yes, of course,' I said. 'Silly me. And how much more would a roll-bar with a full set of Baja night lights screwed on top add to my investment?'

Belgium leafed through a price list he had in his vest pocket. 'That would add, let's see,' he said, reaching for his calculator, 'three thousand five hundred and seventy-eight dollars seventy-five cents plus tax for the roll-bar and two Cibie 2100-watt laser beams and four Cibie wide angle dual prism Titan Halogen Sun Guns which are, as I am sure you are aware, the state of the art.'

'Would that be installed?'

'That would be installed, Mr Evers.'

'Well, then, Russell, if you could do that and have the car ready for collection by noon, then I would be happy to write you a cheque for sixty-six thousand seven hundred and ninety-five dollars.'

'No trade in?'

'No trade in.'

'And no financing?'

'No financing,' I said. Normally a dealer would be glad to carry financing on a sale and make the extra percentage on the interest. But in hard times cash is gold.

'I'm afraid we would need three to five working days for your cheque to clear, Mr Evers.'

'The cheque is drawn on my account at the Sun Valley National Bank on Central and backed by Merrill Cavanaugh.'

'Backed by Merrill Cavanaugh,' he said, nodding wisely as if I had chosen the perfect wine to go with the fish.

'I'll ring the Sun Valley, if you like,' I said, 'and ask them to cash my cheque for you this morning. Or I could have them deliver the cash to you if you prefer.'

'If you would ring them that would help,' he said. 'You are asking for a substantial downward adjustment. I think we can do it but I'll have to check with my supervisor.'

'By all means,' I said, writing out the cheque. 'And would you be good enough, when you speak with your supervisor, Mr Belgium, to mention that if he or she adds a dollar to the price I shall shop elsewhere. I'll pick up the car at noon.'

'Ring the bank and if they'll cash your cheque this morning we'll have the papers and the car ready for you on the stroke of twelve,' he said happily, taking my cheque. 'A pleasure doing business with you, Mr Evers.'

'And with you, Mr Belgium.'

With a couple of hours to spare I drove to old downtown Phoenix, where they have spent several hundred million dollars on a facelift and a municipal centre where millions do not go.

Downtown Phoenix is an old and respectable lady in bright new clothes, mourning the death of the creatures we used to call pedestrians. Across the street from the old San Carlos Hotel (recently refurbished, single rooms from sixty-five dollars) the Empire Tower rises thirty-five storeys of shining aluminium and mirror glass into the blue sky. The building wasn't quite finished. There was no carpet on the concrete on the ground floor and wires hung unconnected from the ceiling and the walls. The directory listed just one occupant, Empire Development Corporation, and it was not on the top floor but on the ground. Behind the elevators a steel fire door, painted in red lead primer, had an Empire decal stuck on it at an angle as if someone had just slapped it on. There was a digital punch-pad security lock next to the door, and not knowing the code, I knocked.

Nothing.

I knocked again and there was more nothing unless you count the sound of cool air moving through the air-conditioning ducts. Overhead, thirty-five storeys of empty office space waited for the future. I pounded on the door, putting some force into it, and a moment later the door handle turned and a man was opening the door, standing in the doorway. 'What?' he said. He was round faced, balding, about thirty-five and had the tense and impatient look of a man who has fallen behind in his work.

'I'm looking for the head office,' I said, adding, 'of Empire.' Over his shoulder there must have been twenty people at computer stations, working at keyboards, talking on the phone, sending faxes, making copies, drinking coffee out of paper cups and looking at building plans laid out on a large central table. It wasn't a suite of corporate offices, it was the engine room. But for what? It could have been a tax assessor's office, except that there was nothing on the walls, and no pictures that I could see of husbands, wives, kids or boyfriends on the trestle tables. There was a fortune in electronic equipment but it looked as if all you had to do was pull the plugs and carry out the computers and peripherals and the room would be empty within an hour without a trace of anybody or anything ever having been in there.

'What're you, a tourist,' he said starting to shut the door. I kept the door open by taking a step forward, so he couldn't shut it without pushing me out of the way. 'Fuck off,' he said.

I was thinking it was a tiny office for a multibillion-dollar operation, but maybe it was just one of several. Doing what? I wondered. Putting up more office buildings? I said, 'I am an associate of Merrill Cavanaugh.'

'Half of Phoenix,' he said, 'is a Goddamn associate of Merrill Cavanaugh. If you want a tour, get him to take you around. Otherwise, I can't let you in. Can Not. Is that clear enough? So I am *not* going to let you in and if you don't step back and let me shut the door the next step is I call the police and they give you a bad time for trespassing, OK?'

I stepped back and he shut the door. And as he shut it, one of the women at the large trestle table held up the plan that they were looking at to examine some detail and I could just make out, in that fraction of a second before the door slammed shut, the words 'San Di' across the top of the map or blueprint or whatever it was.

'Roberts and Associates, good morning,' she said with a telephone smile. 'Whom may I say is calling?'

'Hello, Yvonne. Forrest Evers. How've you been?'

'I'm sorry, Mr Evers. Miss Eikelberry is no longer with the firm. May I be of assistance?'

'Is Bobby in?'

'Mr Roberts is out of the office today. Would you care to leave a message?'

'I'd like a word in Bobby's ear. His car is ready for delivery.'

'I see. I could give you his mobile and you could see if he picks up.' There was a brief pause while she found the number. 'Oh-eight-nine-seven, four-five-four-three-five nine-eight-seven-seven-two,' she said.

'Thank you. Did you know that Yvonne said that she had reason to believe that Bobby is a turd?'

'I'm afraid I have not met Ms Eikelberry.' There was another brief pause, then there was a giggle. 'But I have heard that opinion.'

On the phone, Bobby went, 'Jesus Christ, Forrest! It's good to hear from you. I was hoping you'd call me. I hear you got my message this morning. Yeah great, I'm convalescing. The doctors say it could be a month maybe two before I'm able to resume the pressures of my daily duties. You want to settle out of court for ten or is this just a social call?'

'I would like to come see you, Bobby. Merrill and I have a little proposition you might be interested in.'

'Merrill? Well sure, come on out. No hard feelings. I'm just going to peel your skin with a dull knife and nail your ass to my flagpole. Fly it in the wind to show folks what happens when you fuck with me. But if you got something going with Merrill in the mean time, I'll be glad to listen.'

Bobby's house was high on the south side of Echo Canyon, on Wonderview Drive, overlooking the Phoenician Golf Course, Scottsdale and a hundred and fifty miles of Arizona in the distance. He was standing high overhead, a tiny figure looking down at me from the terrace by his swimming-pool, waving as I pulled into the parking lot alongside his rented Mercedes coupe. 'Good to see you, Forrest,' he shouted down. 'What can I get you to drink?'

A glass elevator brought me up the side of the rock face where Bobby was waiting for me, his hair and swimsuit dripping, drops of water on his wide, tanned shoulders, a gin and tonic in his hand. He looked in good shape for a man in his middle thirties. 'I've decided to take a little holiday,' he said, 'devote myself full time to your case,' his voice rising like a question. He looked thoughtfully into his drink, swirling the ice-cubes. 'You got yourself a lawyer yet, Evers? I can recommend a good firm, or what the hell, five good firms if you like. I'd pick one with a light case-load and a lot of free time right now because they are going to need it. Now what would you like to drink?'

It was a wide, deep pool and the water sparkled blue under the hot noon sun. 'I'll take a glass of water and a swim,' I said. 'You have a spare suit?'

'Sorry, we don't carry 'em. But if you want to go skinny-dipping be my guest. There's nobody here but you and me and Rosita up at the house and she's used to looking the other way. I hear you like skinny-dipping.'

'Only with friends,' I said.

I got myself a glass of water and came back to the edge of the terrace where Bobby was staring out over the valley.

'You're not going swimming?'

'Another time,' I said, leaning on the railing, looking out over the distance.

'Suit yourself.'

'I hear you fired Yvonne.'

'Oh, Christ. Yeah, I had to. Gave her six months' pay and sent her out the door. I couldn't have her weeping around the place, fucking up the files.'

'I met her.'

'You did, huh? Nice kid. It was my own damn fault. I mean she is a sweet little thing and I kinda like her. But I don't know why I never learn my lesson. You know,' he said, straightening up, looking back at his house looming over us, 'I have all this' – he waved his arm to include his pool, house, and Scottsdale – 'and there are times when it makes me so damn lonely I can't see straight. And then I run into some woman and I think Goddamnit this is it. This is fate that she is on the next bar-stool at the club or waltzing into my office looking for advice or a job. And something tells me she is the one. This is the woman who hangs the moon and gives the sun a shine. And I become her greatest all-time enthusiast. Everything she does and says is cute and smart and fresh. And we screw like rabbits and we do everything together except communicate and one morning I wake up and I just don't want to deal with her shit any more.'

He took a long sip of his drink, looking out over the desert towards Tucson. 'And she never knows what's happened. I went to a shrink once and she said it was because I was adopted, a defence mechanism. She said I am compelled to abandon the lady before she leaves me on a doorstep. Which is a pretty good theory but I think it's about eighty-eight per cent bullshit, you know what I mean? 'Cause there was one woman I really cared about. Maybe Sally told you we practically grew up together and I never felt so close to anybody in my life, like having a sister only she was available and *god damnit* she was beautiful. Jesus, you should have seen her when she was twenty-one. I've never seen another woman so gorgeous. And I suppose you know that it does not endear you to me that you are seeing her. She's far too good for some old has-been racing driver.'

'You think she's better off with a bent lawyer?'

He looked at me for a moment and decided to leave it. 'Oh, I don't imagine in my wildest dreams Sally and I'll ever get together again. All we can do now is fight. Damn woman wouldn't forgive a dog for barking. She ever tell you what happened? How I was set up?'

'She mentioned it, but she didn't tell me about it.'

'I never had a chance,' he said draining his drink and flinging the ice-cubes over the side to fall for a few seconds before shattering in silence on the parking lot. 'You sure I can't get you something besides that awful stuff you're drinking?'

When he came back from the bar he was saying, 'First office I ever had. Fresh out of law school and Merrill got me a job with this firm that specialised in divorce disputes. Divorce is the national sport in Phoenix and it's good money if you know anything about human nature. So I'd done a few cases and I am sitting in my office on my behind thinking that I know something when a Mrs Hayward walks in without an appointment and shuts the door. She is crying a little bit. Not much, just a little, being brave. She is about my age, about twenty-six, and she has long straight red hair down to her shoulders and she has green eyes and translucent skin and fine delicate features.' Bobby waved his hands around his face to give me the idea. 'And nature has been bountiful to Mrs Hayward. Nature has given her the figure of God I don't know what, but she had delicate hands and delicate ankles and the most astounding tits I have ever seen roaming loose under a woman's dress and she bent over my desk and her green eyes looked into mine and I could smell her perfume and she said, 'Oh, Mr Roberts, I am so ashamed.'

Bobby stretched and sighed and took a sip of his fresh gin and tonic, and smiled at me like an old friend. 'Well I was twenty-six and horny as a bull in a ring and I didn't know any better. I didn't know anything at all. She said her husband was older than she was and travelled all the time and she was at her wits' end. She just didn't know what to do, she thought maybe she ought to consider a divorce even though she liked the man. She said she didn't expect me to understand, that a

158

man couldn't understand what she was going through, and my dick is jumping up and down and saying, "I understand. I do, I do."

'And she asked me to come over to the window with her and she pointed over towards Scottsdale and she said her house was over there and she didn't want to go back there because it was empty and she was so lonely because she didn't know a soul in Phoenix. Her breast was pressing against my arm and she put her hand on my chest and I remember I was wearing a damn necktie and she said she'd never asked a man before. And then she took my hand and cupped it around the end of her breast, just that flimsy dress, no brassière and oh, God, I never had a chance. She kept saying, "Please, please, fuck me please," and I thought I was the luckiest man in the world when she lay down on that new blue carpet with knees up and wide apart and held out her arms to me, I mean she was breathtaking and I had just entered her as she had raised her pelvis all pink and slippery up to meet me and we had fallen back down to the carpet, just finding the rhythm, a little slow, a little quick, the way you do, and she kept saying, "Please fuck me, please," in my ear so I never heard anything. I never heard the door open and I didn't look up until I felt this kick in my side, the women were wearing those needle-nose shoes then and Sally was kicking me in my ribs and my chest as I tried to get up and she was screaming at me, "You bastard, you fucking bastard."

'And I remember thinking that it was almost a joke because I thought I probably am a bastard not knowing who my folks were and I certainly was fucking. But of course it wasn't what you'd call at all funny and Sally was gone before I could say a word although God knows what I would have said.'

'Did you call her, talk to her?'

'Hell, yes. She was living at home and every time I called, all I got was Merrill, saying he was sorry, she didn't want to talk to me. The next thing I know she has gone to Rome, for Christ's sake, for six months or a year and Merrill is saying maybe the best thing for me, since my reputation among the divorce-court circuit is not exactly soaring with the story going around about my diddling the lady in my office and he's saying he's got some business in San Diego, and if I'll let him finance me, get me an office and my own firm, he's got more than enough business to keep me busy full time.'

'Did you know he set you up?'

'Not for, I don't know, four, five years maybe. Sally told me on the phone to stick the knife in one time when I was trying to make peace, asking her to dinner.' Bobby folded his arms across his chest and his eyes took on a cutting edge.

'So tell me Evers, what's on your mind? You said you and Merrill were cookin' something up. Or did you come out here to find out about my love life, if you can call it that?'

'Well, it's about that Range Rover down there.'

'I was wondering about that. It looks a lot like mine. You going to take it out for a roll this afternoon?'

'It is yours.'

He held his hands out, palms out, mock surrender. 'Hang on. You offering me a fifty-thousand dollar car to make a fifteen-million-dollar lawsuit go away? I don't know what you've been stuffin' up your nose, Forrest, but this is the major league now. Big time. You can't play this game with Dinky toys.'

'That's a company car, Bobby. I'll get to that in a minute. First let's talk about that lawsuit. There are several witnesses, state legislators among them, who saw you drunk at Brownies before we left. Yvonne, I have the impression, would be happy to testify to the value of your word. And if I say you jerked the wheel, who do you think they are going to believe? They might believe you, Bobby, but I wouldn't bet on it. Either way, you are not going to come out of this looking like a prince.'

Bobby's eyes looked at me over the bottom of his glass as he drained his drink, not saying anything.

'That Range Rover,' I said, 'is a company car. The car of the vice-chairman and chief financial officer and legal counsel of the Phoenix Formula One team, with special responsibility for marketing, advertising and public relations.' What the hell, throw it all in, I thought. Let him pick what he wants.

'Now you can mess around with an embarrassing lawsuit if you want, Bobby, and think it is big league. But just try stretching your mind to sixteen countries on five continents. The players are the largest corporations on Earth and the audience totals out at around four billion. And if you can't make, personally make, ten million dollars out of that in two years then I will buy you a dozen of those Dinky toys,' I said, gesturing to the Range Rover beneath us.

'Who is setting this up,' he said, 'Merrill?'

'Merrill has put up five million for openers. I'm running it.'

Bobby threw his ice-cubes over the side again to arc out in the blue sky, brilliant as diamonds catching the sun, falling and shattering where the ice from his first glass had evaporated without a trace.

He turned back towards me and shrugged.

I tossed him the keys. 'Think it over,' I said. 'We have a meeting with Falcon in Detroit in two weeks and I'd like an answer in the morning.'

'I think we should have another drink,' Bobby said, smiling that engaging, good-buddy smile of his.

Later, in his living-room, with the lights of Scottsdale and Phoenix beginning to blink in the distance as the sky went from deep blue to purple, Bobby was leaning forward, fresh gin and tonic in his hand, making the effort to keep from sinking into a black leather sectional by the empty stone fireplace, saying, 'Like the PR. I'd be good at the PR. I've got the connections.'

Sally's house was set against the south-west slope of Camelback, its back turned on Bobby's house on the other side of the mountain.

Down below, along the edges of the Arizona Biltmore golf course, lesser millionaires had built their big white versions of grandeur. Inspired by the Hollywood of their childhood with big white columns out front and rooms large enough to have their own personal echo, they were houses designed to be deeply impressive, monuments to a lotta money. From the slope of the mountain, in the afterglow of the sunset, they looked like a carefully arranged row of doll's houses, as if they had empty backs and in the dark a child would reach in and rearrange the furniture and the lives inside.

Sally's house was smaller, on a different scale, an aluminium and glass series of boxes, one set on the other, just big enough for one woman and a friend. The living-room and the terrace overlooked her pool which, with the city spread out below, made a breathtaking view. A stream came trickling down the rocks to fall into the pool and the plexiglass diving-board looked like solid crystal over the blue water. She led me through her kitchen with the stainless-steel pots on hooks over the stainless-steel professional range and through the dining-room with its plain pine table and plain pine chairs into her bedroom where she tossed off her swishy little blue silk robe and let it fall on the carpet as she bounced into bed wearing nothing and held the covers back. The night-light by the bathroom door gave off just enough light to see the carpet and the duvet and the walls were contrasting shades of grey and pale blue. And the end of the room was a wall of curved glass, invisible, looking south to the city, looking like a model for the city of the future, silent, twinkling, surrounded by the darkness of the desert and the mountains with Sally's bed floating motionless above.

'Come on,' she said, holding back the covers.

We made a strange couple, Sally shouting out, 'You shit, you bastard,' and kicking hard and missing and kicking again and stubbing her toe on my shin when I told her I had seen Bobby, and telling me again that I was to stay the hell away from that bastard, and then wanting to know how he looked, and what he said and if he was drinking too much. And when I said that I thought Bobby and Merrill had something to do with Barnes' murder, that Barnes had been on to something that Bobby and Merrill were doing together, she said that was a typically stupid, arrogant and ignorant thing to say. She wouldn't be surprised, she said, at anything Bobby did. But her Daddy, she knew, was far too big a man to mess with that kind of stuff. 'You got anything on my Daddy,' she said, 'I want to know about it. Because I know it isn't true.'

And then, later, when we were quiet, the two of us eased in and out of sleep, floating over the city and the desert with Sally curved against me, her back against my chest and her soft bottom nestled in my lap and my arm over her and my hand cupping her breast. Not lovers, you understand, just good friends.

chapter twenty-three

Sally's aquamarine and blue silk scarf blocked the window except for a halo of light-blue sky over her head. In the morning she had stood in front of her bedroom mirror and carefully wrapped the silk, half hiding her face, doing it over and over until it looked casual. It was worth the effort. She looked like she had just stepped out of the summer of 1949; a star of the silver screen, flying in to the Coast on a Lockheed Constellation, wrapped in glamour. Semi-incognito.

'There's the old pile,' she said, 'on the end of the peninsula, just back from the cliffs with the red-tile roof.'

I bent forward and looked past her through the scratched and frosted window. 'They all have red-tile roofs.'

'The big one, Wahlnut. At the end. With the big pool in the back.' I thought I saw it, a white stucco wedding-cake with a red roof at the edge of the Pacific, but the wing rose as the plane levelled out, on the glide path skirting the fifteen-mile-long southern perimeter of the US Naval Air Station Miramar on the north edge of San Diego.

We landed at Lindbergh Field, San Diego International Airport, next to the US Naval Training Center and the Fleet Anti-Submarine Warfare School, across the bay from the US Naval Air Station on North Island with the US Naval Amphibious Base at the tip of the island facing the main US Naval Base in San Diego. Which is just north of the US Naval Communication Station, Imperial Beach, and the nearby Outlying Landing Field Imperial Beach (US Navy), and west of Brown Field with its US Naval Space Surveillance Station. Not forgetting the three miles of US Navy Recreation Center and Golf Course to the north and the eighty-some square miles of the US Naval Air Station Miramar sitting on top of San Diego.

If you were paranoid you could get the feeling that San Diego is a cluster of navy bases with a city stuck between the fences. Plus, of course, a zoo.

The air was softer than Phoenix and moist as the fog was lifting. We rented a white Chevrolet Caprice Classic that Sally christened Moby the Great White Whale, a rolling boudoir with ersatz wood, red velvet upholstery, red fuzz balls on the carpet and a whale of a ride. 'Just what is it you are looking for, Mr Ahab,' Sally said.

'Hang on to your harpoon,' I said, 'I'll know it when I see it.' I grinned, but Sally turned out the window, looking the other way.

'Forrest,' she said, turning back to me and fixing me with those deep blue eyes, 'there are times when you act like a little boy, playing a game. You think it's a hoot you are going to find out something nasty about my father. And I'll help you because I'm happy to rid you of your delusions. I know my Daddy and I know he fights hard but he fights fair. Let me ask you a question. Don't you think you are over-reacting to falling off a damn toy bull?'

We took a detour along the waterfront and through downtown San Diego and as we drove along the water, the sun came out from behind the mist with Phoenix's brain-frying intensity. If you stood under it long enough, you too could become sand.

Skeletons of what was going to be a row of tall and expensive hotels barricaded the edge of the north bay, and just a few blocks inland an island of glossy new and empty office buildings rose thirty storeys high in the midst of San Diego's crumbling Victorian downtown. Office workers in their shirtsleeves and blouses were sunning themselves on their lunch hour. And ragged men with long hair moved in and out of the shadows like schools of homeless fish, pushing shopping carts loaded with bundles of their next-cleanest dirty shirts, soiled pants and spare split-open shoes, looking for a place to hide from the Chicano gangs and their AK-47s at night.

'It's been years,' Sally said, brightening up as we left the downtown traffic jams behind us and headed west on the Pacific Avenue for the ocean. 'We came here all the time when I was a kid, but I never even think about it now. Except to call Daddy when he's out at the house here. When was the last time, let me think, must be ten, no less than ten, six years ago, since I was here, after Bobby came back to Phoenix? I went with a bunch of friends and threw a party that went on for four days. Then I left and never came back. I just never thought about it, you know, like a movie on TV that you kinda half watch and then when it ends you forget all about it five minutes later. Did you hear that San Diego is like Spain if Walt Disney did Spain?'

No, I hadn't heard that.

'Well it's not true,' Sally said. 'But there's some truth in it.'

We drove out to Sunset Cliffs Boulevard, turned left, and miles later, at the end, drove in through the open rusting gates, the gravel crunching under the tyres and the car rocking and bumping over the potholes. It was a house built to impress, a red-tile roof with its gables and turrets falling down low like the brim of a hat to cover a wide porch that wrapped all the way around the white stucco house and kept the hot sun from shining directly inside.

'A sea captain built it,' Sally said happily as we climbed up the steps and on to the wooden porch, 'around 1910, and there's a lot of lovely panelling from the captains' cabins from ships they were breaking up in the shipyards.' She unlocked the door and the house looked as if it couldn't have changed much since it was built. In the gloom, polished mahogany, cherry and oak gleamed on the walls and Yankee clippers and old coasters battled typhoons in gilt frames over the stone fireplaces. In the front of the house a great window opened out on to the Pacific so you could see the ships coming in and out of the north. Sally went from room to room, turning on the lights and the house still kept its air of comfortable darkness, with pools of light from converted oil lamps. We could hear the surf rolling in on the shore below and the house felt solid and secure, like a well-built sailing ship, ready to ride out a force-ten gale from its mooring high on the cliff.

'Wahlnut,' Sally called down from upstairs where she was slamming doors and opening windows, shaking the house out of its sleep. 'See if Ernesto left us anything to eat in the refrigerator. I could eat a damn horse.'

The kitchen was off a formal dining-room, through heavy swinging doors. A nice old kitchen, even under the glare of the fluorescent lights, with a chopping block and large and scrubbed wooden table in the middle and big porcelain sinks and wooden counters. A kitchen for a full-time professional staff. Old-fashioned oak doors with brass hinges and heavy brass pull-handles opened into an empty walk-in meat locker, an empty musty-smelling refrigerator and another refrigerator with a bowl of freshly baked chocolate chip cookies, two cartons of milk, a tossed salad under a film of Saranwrap, a quiche, a roasted chicken, several cheeses, three bottles of white wine and two of Evian.

'Well come on,' Sally said, peering over my shoulder. 'Don't just stand there like a dummy, let's eat.'

We took the food out and put it on the kitchen table, Sally finding silverware in the drawers and china on the shelves. When we sat down she tore off a chicken leg and handed it to me. She tore one off for herself, took a bite, and looked around the kitchen, remembering. 'When I was about knee-high to a duck, I used to love coming in here, Wahlnut. Ernesto and his wife, Carmella, would give me tastes of what they were cooking and let me help them get supper ready. Or more like it, I guess, they let me think I was helping.'

'You always had servants?'

'We always had help, if that's what you mean. You want to get high minded and all liberal there were fifty people waiting for every job we had. And Ernesto and Carmella have a rent-free apartment in the house and they get their Medicaid paid.'

'You're a little touchy.'

'Yeah, I'm a little touchy. I got up at the crack of dawn a week after I got out of the hospital from having my face half blown off to go to some place I don't want to go with some man I don't know, about to do I don't know what. And my eye still won't focus. What the hell are we doing here, anyway?'

'I want to see what your father does when he is here.'

'Why don't you just pick up the phone and ask him? Besides I told you what he does. Same thing he does everywhere. Talks on the phone, gets people over, gives 'em drink, charms the pants off 'em or scares the shit out of them.'

'Or both.'

'You bet your ass, both. Now come on and 'fess up. What are we up to? I can't help you if I don't know what direction you're headed.'

'I want to know where your father's money comes from. I want to know what Barnes was looking for in San Diego.'

'Well in my experience Daddy carries most of his money in his back pocket in his wallet. But sometimes he's got some loose change in his right pocket. Anybody ever tell you not to look a gift horse in the mouth?'

'He's my partner. Could we have a look at where Big Daddy does his phoning, charming and his scaring?'

'Not before I finish this chicken.'

Cavanaugh's office was on the top floor, where the servants had lived before the war. He'd had the walls knocked out and it was a light and airy space with views over the ocean, the harbour and the city. To the north-east, a cargo jet was landing at Miramar Naval Air Station. To the east, a fighter was taking off from the North Island Naval Air Station in the harbour. And out over the blue sea, a white gull circled, turning his head left and right, looking for a floating scrap of food.

There were two desktop PCs, a modem, a fax, a printer, a copier, an answering machine and two phones; a normal home office these days. The phones were on a large old oak roll-top desk, with a dozen cubby holes stuffed with papers, and the desk itself was strewn with newspapers, faxes, notepads, pencils, pens and print-outs of weather forecasts.

'I don't expect my Daddy is going to feel good about your rummaging around his desk.'

'Are you going to tell him?' A newspaper looked interesting. It was dated March 17, a week before.

'Course I'm not going to tell him. But I'm not going to feel good about it either. I mean fine, you just poke around until you find out there is nothing for you to find out. I'll just stand here and fidget.'

'I just need a couple of minutes,' I said, picking up the paper. The *San Diego Courier* was open to the shipping page. There was a smudge on the page, where he had held it with his thumb, and just above that the details of the *Commander Melvin Forbes*, USN cargo supply ship CS6385-C, docking at pier 17 at the San Diego North Harbor Naval base, Wednesday, March 24, at 5 p.m. Today. It wouldn't hurt to look, I thought.

'Is your father short-sighted?'

'Some.'

'He holds his newspaper like this?' I said, holding the paper close to my nose.

'Yeah, how'd you know?'

'I was thinking that the more near-sighted he is the closer his thumb would be to what he was reading.'

'Which thumb? And wouldn't that depend on where he held the paper and what part of the page he was reading? If you are playing detective again, Wahlnut, you got your thumb up your . . . are you listening at all? Come on, I don't feel right about this. I'm not worried about your finding anything out, 'cause there isn't anything to find out. It's just prying, you know what I mean. It doesn't feel right. Let's go for a walk on the beach. I know a little bar up aways where we could watch the sunset.'

'Sally,' I said, 'I'd love to watch the sunset with you. But first let's go down to the Navy yard and watch the ships.'

The US Navy does not gladly welcome sightseers. A large sign at the gate marked 'passes and decals' pointed to a temporary contractor's hut alongside the pier 17 entrance to the base.

I went up to the counter and after thirty seconds of being ignored by the three sailors on duty I said loudly that I would like a pass to the base.

A tired sergeant who had probably been there since the temporary hut was built in 1957 looked up at me from a stack of badly mimeographed forms. 'You want to walk in, look around, get your foot run over by a fork-lift and sue the government for sixty-five million dollars 'cause you was lookin' the other way at the ships?' he said. 'First you got to fill out the form. Contractors only. You got no business on this base if you got no business on this base. You understand what I'm saying?' He registered a tic of disgust the Navy keeps handy for civilians and handed me a mimeographed sheet which read:

CIVILIAN PERSONNEL EMPLOYED ON BOARD THE STATION. CONTRACTORS OR REPRESENTATIVES OF CIVILIAN COMMERCIAL FIRMS WHICH PROVIDE SERVICES TO NAVAL ACTIVITIES ON BOARD THE STATION ON A REGULAR BASIS. APPLICATION MUST BE MADE ON COMPANY LETTERHEAD PAPER,

SIGNED BY AN OFFICER OF THE COMPANY, FAVOR-
ABLY ENDORSED BY A SPONSORING ACTIVITY SUP-
SHIPS, PWC, NAVRESSO, ROICC, ETC. THE LETTER
SHOULD BE MAILED TO THE SECURITY OFFICER
(ATTN: CODE 33, 92132–5000). APPLICATIONS MUST
SPECIFY THE FREQUENCY OF THE REQUIREMENT
TO COME ON BOARD; MOTOR VEHICLE IDENTIFI-
CATION BY MAKE, MODEL, STATE LICENSE; MOTOR
VEHICLE INSURANCE BY NAME OF CARRIER, TYPE
AND AMOUNT AND POLICY NUMBER; INCLUSIVE OF
EFFECTIVE DATES; AND NAMES OF PERSONNEL
REQUIRING REGISTRATION. RENEWAL PROCE-
DURES ARE THE SAME AS FOR APPLICATION.

I handed the sheet to Sally in the car. 'Do you think your
Dad has Empire letterhead paper in his office?'

'You know, Evers, you do mystify me. How come you feel
you got to go sneaking around the back door when you could
just walk in the front. Sure he has letterhead. And yes, you
could falsify a document and give it to the US Navy. I'll type
it up for you. Let you commit a Federal crime, if you are so
damn sure my Father is committing some infraction of the law.'

'I don't think this is some minor infraction, Sally. Minor
infractions don't generate five million dollars in loose change.
There is something large and nasty here and Barnes was finding
out about it.'

'Oh, Barnes,' she said looking out to the highway where the
cars were sliding by. 'Barnes is dead.'

She turned those astonishing blue eyes on me and put her
hand on my knee. 'Well, Wahlnut,' she said, sounding weary,
'if you are so hot in pursuit of a bigger truth, why don't we
just take the van out of the garage back at the house. It's got
a Navy decal on it.'

'We?'

'The deal is, Wahlnut, if you find something out about my
Daddy, I want to be the first to know. You want to drive in
that base in an Empire van, I have the keys, I have the pass
they send me every six months and I am coming with you. Or,
alternatively, you can always try to sneak under the fence.'

'Sally, it is a Naval base. You'd stick out like a peach on a banana tree.'

'Peaches don't stick out, Wahlnut. And where've you been the last twenty years? You think you have to have a dick to be in the Navy? There's lots of women on that base. I've seen 'em because I've been there lotsa times. Used to go there all the time with Daddy. You drive, tell 'em you're Bobby. I'll show you where to turn left,' she said, 'and where to turn right.'

chapter twenty-four

Good ol' bounce-around van comin' on down the road. It's a fine state of mind to be in. Call it Van Man Country, where the dogs are smart enough to answer the phone, the men are at ease in the piney woods, and the women are glad to see you. Yessirree, United States Navy decal on the windshield, Empire decal on the door, Evers' elbow hanging out the window, one hand on the wheel. And alongside, a gorgeous woman, wearing a blue work-shirt, old blue jeans and scuffed work boots, a bandage on her head and only a little pissed off.

The driver is probably the kind of man has a six-pack in the cooler alongside on the front seat. Kinda man goes fishin', huntin' and general good-time foolin' around with a buncha good-guy buddies. Except you never see his buddies these days because they're too busy making beer commercials. The passenger is the kind of woman who cleans her own gun, drinks beer straight out of the can, and will sic the dogs on any fool dumb enough to try and mess with her. Tough, but inside even tougher. A working man and a working woman, in their blue denim working shirts, in their working Van on their way to work with today's working Navy. Evidently the Cavanaugh name opens the gates around here.

Calls himself Bobby Roberts.

It is sunset, the hour when the sky changes from blue to dayglo red, orange, pink and that thigh-bruise purple just before dark. The street lights are just coming on with a buzz. I sign us in, Bobby and Mr Cavanaugh's little girl, Sally, at the gate, and we are waved in, on our way into United States Naval Base, San Diego.

We drove straight in, down the main road, slow enough to read the signs but not so slow as to attract attention. We followed the main road across the railroad tracks, past the naval barracks and rec rooms, towards the docks, sign-posted straight ahead. For one goofy moment, I wished I had that six-pack. Something about the orderly, super-clean, white-line and scraped-off landscape of a military base makes me want to fling beer cans around. Makes me lose my concentration.

Still, slowly cruising down the main drag from Gate 17, I had plenty of time. Time to concentrate on why the arrival of a cargo ship in a Navy dockyard would cause a man with five million dollars in spare change to go sweaty in the thumbs and squeeze a newspaper. 'Look up ahead,' Sally said. 'Isn't that the ship you're looking for?'

The far end of a long grey shed sprouted aerials, flags, the top of a smoke stack and the radar antennas of a large grey ship were all lit up against the dark sky. Protruding from the right side of the far end, the bow of the ship showed the letters . . . ORBES. The *Commander Melvin Forbes* was in from Panama. With a cargo of what? Cocaine, sugar cane, bananas, reject dictators?

A Naval MP was waving us down. Sergeant Ramirez, with short sleeves, razor blade creases and a chrome .357 magnum in a blonde leather holster and a mirror shine on the black boots. 'HOLD IT. HOLD IT RIGHT THERE, MISTER.'

A serious man. He came up to the van, looking it up and down as he walked towards us. Sticking his head in the window, looking me in the eyes. Taking a good look at Sally. Big on flexing his biceps with a little tricep flexing thrown in for rhythm backing.

'You blind,' he said, standing back. 'Back this unit up. You are off-limits beyond this perimeter line.' His jaw stuck out like a football coach. 'You park it over there,' he said pointing behind me, 'with the other Empire vehicles.'

Over there was inside the end of the shed where six grey Empire vans were backed against a loading dock. Ours was a little conspicuous because it hadn't been washed for a while. Didn't matter. Parked alongside the other Empire vans with its back against the concrete dock, the Cavanaugh van was still one of the family. We got out and didn't see anybody so we climbed up the steel pipe on to the dock.

The sky overhead was no longer blue, purple and red. It was

a distant pattern of blazing lights in solid black, a hundred feet overhead, stretching three hundred yards into the distance and a hundred yards either side. This was a warehouse designed for the rapid deployment of whatever the hell they wanted to rapidly deploy. There were rows of big wooden crates, jeeps, trucks, tanks, guns, and the aisles twenty yards wide in between. 'Whatever else it may lack,' I said, 'the US Navy has space.' The air was filled with the sound of distant machinery, of whirs and whines and grinding and the smell of hot electric motors.

'HEY YOU!!!' A thin, nervous man with thick glasses and a mop of curly black hair on his head, and a clipboard in his hand, short sleeve white shirt, button-down collar, and a silk tie with a pattern like spilled soup. An expensive fawn leather belt in baggy chinos and expensive soft loafers. A middle-management man looking after the store. 'Who the hell are you?' he said.

A question, I thought, I have been trying to answer. What I said was, 'Bobby Roberts.' Roberts, I thought, might sound familiar, might ring the right bells. But for all I knew he knew Bobby. So I could be a relative, cousin Buddy. Like, you misheard me, not Bobby, Bobby's little brother Bubba. Something like that.

He looked at me, blank, still my move. I said, 'This is Mr Cavanaugh's personal truck. He asked me to come down and give him my assessment of the efficiency of the operation.'

'Who the hell are you?' Sally said.

That took him back for a moment and Sally waded in. 'I'm Sally Cavanaugh,' she said, 'and Daddy sent me to keep an eye on this turkey and on you?' she said it like a question. Like he could disagree with it, but he better be able to back it up.

He looked at his clipboard, doubtful, and back at us. 'I just had a couple of phone calls about you. Jimmy said you were coming out. I don't like it.'

I looked over at Sally. She hadn't told me she'd made any phone calls. Or who Jimmy was. But she had said she had the connections. Evidently she did. The woman was full of surprises. She gave me a look and I said to the man, 'You are not supposed to like it. Check out the plates if you are worried about it.'

He looked at me through thick lenses, screwing his face up like something tasted bad. He had other worries.

'You got his home phone number here in San Diego?' I asked, sounding helpful. 'He was going out to dinner with Admiral Corl tonight but he might still be at the house. He doesn't like being interrupted, but if you need confirmation, the number is two-five-four, four-five-four-five.'

'Admiral Corl? I don't know any Admiral Corl.'

Neither did I. Never heard of the man before. I said, 'Chief of Naval Air Operations, SUNYAC,' I said. 'Just flew in from Washington.'

Clipboard was still worried. 'What's SUNYAC?' he said.

'Security,' I lied. 'There something I can do to help out?' I said.

He said, 'Fuck,' looking at Cavanaugh's van, running his hand behind his neck. 'OK, we're half an hour behind schedule and I am down four guys. We should be loading these vans now. You tell Cavanaugh that the assholes running this thing, they are fucking dinosaurs. They still think raising productivity means doing more work with less guys. It's not that simple. And this is not the time or the place to cut. You tell him I said that, OK? You want to do me a favour, you drive a fork-lift?'

Does a Formula One driver, winner of the Monaco Grand Prix whose hand has been shaken and cheek has been kissed by Princess Caroline, drive a fork-lift?

'Sure,' I said.

'Lotsa times,' Sally said.

He looked at Sally like she had two heads and she said, 'Since I was a kid.'

He thought about it for a second, looking like this was a problem he didn't need. He said, 'Go down to the end of the dock where they're off-loading. I'll radio down, let them know you're on your way. God knows we need the help tonight. If there is anything you don't understand, come back here and I'll explain it. In the mean time, I'll check you out.'

I looked at him blankly. He looked back for a moment, then he said, 'Yeah, right. The fork-lifts are over there, on the end aisle. Just around the corner. For Christ's sake don't forget to unplug them.'

There were three of them parked against the wall. Bright

orange battle-scarred CLARKs with a full roll-cage, low-profile solid Goodyear slicks, zero suspension movement, zero suspension. Fully enveloping bodywork extending to two and a half inches above the floor; not quite close enough for ground-effect aerodynamics. On the other hand, with a solid-steel monocoque giving the beast a power to weight ratio of say, one horsepower, who knows, maybe even two horsepower, for every two thousand pounds of unsprung weight, aerodynamics were probably not going to play a major part in its performance. Up front two long steel forks stuck out like giant birds' feet. Judging by the track they rolled up and down on in front of the truck, the forks could be raised almost ten feet high. Sally was already in the seat of the one on the far end, fiddling with the levers.

The one in the middle had the fewest battle scars. I unplugged a black electrical cable as thick as an anaconda, coiled it up against the wall and climbed up into the saddle.

WARNING. DO NOT OPERATE WITHOUT TRAINING AND AUTHORIZATION. READ AND UNDERSTAND THE OPERATING MANUAL, a plate said in block letters on top of the dashboard. Can't be that difficult, I thought. The ignition key looked like a good place to start. I turned it on and the machine went hmmmmmmmmmmmmmm. Like it was wondering what I was going to do to it next. Hmmmmmmmmmmmmmmm.

The stalk sticking out of the steering column said F-N-R and the three pedals on the floor looked as normal as any standard shift. Two levers by my right hand. The one closest me did nothing. Until I pressed the accelerator on the floor and CLAAAANGGG the monster surged four inches into the wall. Making its mark in the cinderblock. Judging by the gouges up and down the line, I wasn't the first to do that trick. So backward on that lever, slowly press down on the accelerator to the first click and I move backwards going SCRAAAAAYYYYYPE.

Off the accelerator and time to explore the possibilities of the other lever which, yes, raises the forks. One foot off the ground looks about right. Forward with the lever, the forks tilt forward. Back tilts them back. Right. Pedal to the metal and we are off. Going forward, I stop and look back at Sally. She smiles at me and backs across the aisle into a pile of wooden crates with a loud crash. She smiled sweetly at me, her machine lurched forward then squeaked to a sudden stop four feet away.

'I thought you knew how to drive these things.'

'Give me a couple of minutes, Wahlnut,' she said, 'and I will. I reckon I'm about as fast as you are right now.' She rolled past me, her machine going whirrrrrrrrr. And turned the corner into the stacks, out of sight.

When I floor the accelerator the beast goes from slow all the way up to not quite as slow. The first time I turn a corner I think that I have hit a patch of oil, but it is just rear-wheel steering. I am riding as high as a camel jockey with a good view and a strong curiosity about the stability of the beast. It can't roll all the way over on its head, it's too tall. On the other hand it feels like it falling over on its side wouldn't take much.

I try a sharp corner flat out at maybe nine miles an hour, lift the inside wheels and have a few moments when it feels like it could fall as I steer out and the thing comes down with the clunk of several thousand pounds of steel and lead acid batteries. Lesson: It doesn't want to skid, but it's happy to fall over. A little more respectful, I turn left, following Sally towards the noise at the end of the warehouse.

Under the high arching ceiling and a glare of lights, I can only see two naval personnel. They stand inside directing traffic, watching the fork-lift trucks move in and out of the wide-open doors, watching the fork-lifts carry wooden pallets with burlap sacks piled on top into neat five-high loads, carry them into the aisles and place them carefully on top of other piles of sacks and go back outside. Into the blazing light, the grey side of the *Commander Melvin Forbes* rising as a backdrop. I pull into line, still following Sally through an open doorway big enough to fly a helicopter through.

More naval officers were outside on the dock, directing traffic. A large crane was lifting pallets of burlap sacks out of the hold of the ship and lowering pallets down on to the dock. The fork-lift trucks were picking up the pallets, wheeling them inside, and stacking them where another naval officer told them to. The first time I approached a pallet I had my forks too high and I smashed into it, knocking two of the top burlap bags on to the dock. The naval officer was not happy about this. 'You fucking land crabs couldn't find your ass with both hands,' he said. 'Well don't just fucking sit there, asshole,' he said, 'get off your ass and get those bags back on the pallet.'

I climbed off the machine while Sally, who had been watching, carefully rolled up to a stack of burlap bags, slipped her machine's forks into the pallet, lifted it and drove off. If you didn't know better you would think that she had done it for years.

The bags were marked with naval code and said RICE MEDIUM GRAIN COMMERCIAL GRADE 100 K. Around two hundred and twenty pounds each. Too heavy for one man to lift over his head, I think, picking up the fallen bag. And too light for gold. Whatever is inside is packed solid, no rattles. I shifted it on to my shoulder and levered it on top of the four high stack.

My second pass at getting the pallets on the forks was more cautious. I crept up to it with the forks scraping along the concrete of the dock and all I did was push the pallet and its stack of burlap bags forward. The trick is to lift the forks two to three inches off the ground, then drive into it, then lift the pallet up and tilt it back. You don't need to raise the pallet a lot, not so much you can't see over it, just enough to clear the tracks of the sliding warehouse doors.

Never mind how I found out about this last little fork-truck driving tip.

Each bag was numbered, and the officer on the dock and the officer inside the warehouse paid a lot of attention to the number, marking it on his clipboard. The officer inside would check the numbers on the bags and flash his fingers three times, five, two, four; meaning aisle five, row two, stack four. After the first few laps, I fell into the rhythm of it, picking up the pallet off the dock, taking it inside, getting my instructions and putting it down in the designated stack.

Sally was four fork-lifts ahead of me and looked like she was enjoying herself. When I was headed inside the warehouse she passed me going the other way and gave me a little wave.

On the way back outside there was a small puddle on the dock where I found that if I cornered the fork-lift hard into it, flat out, I could get the front wheels to slide for at least twelve and sometimes as much as sixteen inches, but the officer in charge noticed and his attention was not really what I was looking for. Besides, the other men driving the fork-lifts did it with an easy grace and smoothness, nudging the forks into the pallets just right. I concentrated on getting it right.

I did a quick calculation and figured that at nine, say two-hundred-pound bags, forget the extra twenty, make it easy, eighteen hundred pounds, round it up to two thousand, make it a ton a pallet. With eight of us picking up a pallet every thirty seconds, that would be a two tons a minute or around a hundred and twenty tons or two hundred and forty thousand pounds an hour. The *Commander Melvin Forbes* must have been in dock for several hours. Judging by the size of the piles of crates inside the dock, and by how high she was riding out of the water, they had unloaded most of her cargo.

Curly-head with the clipboard at the front of the warehouse was bound to be checking our stories. The plates on the van would check out and I was counting on his being low enough down in the hierarchy to be afraid of calling Cavanaugh directly. But sooner or later somebody was going to say, hey wait a minute, that asshole doesn't look like Bobby Roberts.

Or, what the hell is Sally Cavanaugh doing, driving a fork-lift?

chapter twenty-five

Lieutenant Sycmanciwicz, short, stocky, crew-cut, sweat-circles under his arms from the pressure of playing air-traffic controller with fork-lift trucks, waved me left to aisle three, flashing 'three', 'nine' and 'four' with his fingers. I turned down the wide aisle, electric motor going hmmmmmmmmmmmm, headed for row nine, stack four.

Stack four was a three-pallet-high stack, just above eye level. Easy. I pulled the fork lever back as I approached, raising my pallet, turning in, the forks just clearing the stack below by two inches, off the accelerator, just a touch of brake to start sliding the pallet off as I nudged the tilt lever forward, and down an inch then two, as, at the same time I slip into reverse, the pallet slides off the forks, on to the pile of burlap bags beneath it and I am backing away, then stop.

The approach could have been a little slicker, but I thought it might be quick enough to qualify mid-grid for the San Diego Fork-lift Grand Prix. I levelled the forks, lowered them down to around three feet high, slipped the lever into forward and trod on the throttle. A wet thud: the forks punctured the top bag in the lowest pallet. Back into reverse and I backed away, withdrawing the forks like a spoon from a baby's mouth, and two streams of rice fell from the bag and then stopped. Something was keeping the rest of the rice from falling out. Forward again, into the same place. This time the forks penetrated the sack with a snapping sound. I backed away again, lowered the forks and they were covered with rice and dull little crystals, a sparkle here and there picking up the overhead lights.

I got off the fork-lift to be sure. Looking in the big hole I'd punched in the crate, there were burlap rice bags, and inside the bags, packed inside the rice, black plastic trash bags filled with crack crystals. Rice, the world's basic food. What could be more innocent in the back of a van or a pick-up truck headed for the barrio? 'It's for the bodegas.' 'For restaurants, bro.' 'It's for the field workers, señor.' 'And for the kitchens at school so the kids have a nice day.'

I had been expecting cocaine, or heroin, pure stuff to be cut locally, but think about it for a moment and shipping pre-processed crack made a lot of sense if you can ship in bulk. With the Navy on board, the port of entry was secure enough so they could bring it in a shipload at a time. No more getting frightened Indian girls to swallow fifteen plastic bags and failing businessmen to hide packets in the back of their attaché cases. They didn't have to worry about the Coast Guard, Customs or, God help us, the Navy. They were operating on the scale of an international corporation, manufacturing abroad, eliminating a whole chain of middlemen. From Central America to Main Street at a hundred and twenty tons an hour.

Well, I thought, there is so much of it on the streets and schoolyards of America that it can't all be coming in smugglers' pockets and in the back of unregistered Cessnas.

I got back on the fork-lift and started to turn the wheel, thinking I would quietly find Sally and we'd roll back to where we came in, park the fork-lift where I'd found it, and we'd hop in the van, saying thanks to Clipboard, telling him we'd mention him to Daddy. I was already thinking of how good it would be, driving through the front gate, when I was aware of a hmmmmmmmmmm sound. Followed almost immediately by the WHANNNGGGG of steel lift forks striking the side of my truck and knocking me against the side of the roll-cage, forehead first.

I must have been knocked out for a moment because it seemed that in the next instant he was climbing off his truck and yelling, coming towards me. Short red hair, a gold earring in his right ear, lots of freckles on a round chubby face, bright red, mouth open screaming. And then falling, hard, face forward.

Sally had come alongside and neatly swept him off his feet on to the forks of her truck. She was already lifting him up, high overhead, easing forward and tilting the forks, dropping him on to a stack of crates as I tried to restart my truck. 'Click.' 'Click.' Nothing.

'Come on, Wahlnut,' she shouted. 'You're supposed to be the racing driver. You drive.' Sally was standing on the back of her seat waving me over. I jumped on in front of her and she settled down behind me, holding on to my neck.

I twirled the wheel, levered into F, mashed my foot to the floor and we turned around and trundled forward, zero to eight, maybe nine miles an hour, in say six or seven seconds, each second lasting around three or four minutes. By the time I reached the end of the row, we were flat out, turning left towards our van at the front of the warehouse.

Heading towards another fork-lift coming at us. We're playing chicken, I thought. See who has the most nerve. But after a few microseconds of entertaining that thought (We'll see who's chicken, the big man said), while we were headed towards each other at the combined speed of eighteen miles an hour, I had a more realistic idea. He wasn't going to be the first to turn. He *wanted* to ram us. When we were just a little over a foot apart and I saw him bracing himself, shutting his eyes, Sally tightened her grip on my throat and I went sharp right putting the fork-lift up on two wheels, the front left wheel skidding. It fell back down on its wheels with a clunk and I headed down row ten. Trundle, trundle. Whirrrrrrrrrrr. Nice peaceful ride. Row ten we had all to ourselves picking up speed the way an elephant does, shifting from a slow walk to a walk.

All to ourselves until another fork-lift turned into row ten two aisles behind us. A long ways away. Flat out. 'Come on, Forrest, put your foot down, find another gear,' Sally said. 'I can make it go this fast.'

This time I was a little more cautious coming into aisle four, trying to head back in the direction of our van, taking the turn wide and letting up just enough to check if there was a fork-lift coming up towards us. There were. Two. Side by side. I'd slowed up enough to see what was coming but not quite enough to change direction so I was still turning down aisle four towards them. I jammed my foot down on the accelerator and spun the wheel and the little five-thousand-pound donkey spun on its heels and we headed up aisle four towards the ship. Whrrrrrrrrrrrrrrr.

It took just a little while to get back up to speed and the two fork-lifts behind me closed up to within ten yards.

Flat out down the straight at nine, maybe even ten miles an hour. But they weren't gaining. I looked back over my shoulder and the driver on the left was talking on a telephone, something, letting them know where we were. Still, the aisle stayed clear past row eight. Past row seven, six, five.

I kept expecting a fork-lift to pop out from one of the rows on either side, but we stayed clear past four, past three, past the rows of guns, rocket launchers, office copiers, and toilet paper. Straight ahead, another fork-lift turned into our aisle, outlined against the lights of the dock and the grey side of the *Commander Melvin Forbes*. It was headed straight for us, ten yards away. Closing fast, as they say in the Navy.

I turned left into row one, the machine tipping and the top of the fork track just laying a groove along some cartons labelled doc. paper. Row one had another fork-lift, coming towards us. 'Where are the two following us?' I yelled to Sally.

'They're right behind us, just turning in to row one now. But they're not getting any closer.'

With a fork-lift heading straight for us and another ten yards behind we were trapped.

'Keep your eye on them,' I said. I turned right, into the stacks of cartons on pallets. Labelled, among the jungle of Navy numbers, CUTL. It was a good impact and the boxes of CUTL exploded in a shower of plastic knives, forks and spoons. 'I don't see them,' Sally said.

We hit another row of boxes labelled COTWAD, but we weren't going fast enough to burst them, we just pushed them in front and alongside, one of them impaled on one of the truck's forks. The men on the other side of row one must have seen the row of boxes bulge and grow like a blister before we came trundling out on to the dock because about ten of them were running towards us.

They were about thirty yards away which gave me plenty of time to head out the door and on to the open dock alongside the ship. 'They're awful close, Wahlnut,' Sally said. I looked over my shoulder and there were two fork-lifts five yards behind us.

Must be the two that had followed us into row one had followed us through the stacks, gaining time while we had been shoving boxes aside. 'I don't want to be a backseat driver,' Sally said, 'but don't you think we're headed in the wrong direction?' True. The original plan had been to head for the van.

The open dock was bumpier than the polished concrete floor of the warehouse, the forks of our truck going clang, clang, clang. And in the confusion, the bright spotlights, the piles of boxes, the men yelling and running towards us and the two fork-lifts just behind us it took just a little while to appreciate that the reason that the man closest to me, no more than ten feet away, the reason that he was standing still, not moving, the reason was that he was bracing himself, pointing a gun at my head. I was aware of other fork-lifts, heading towards me, but the naval man, with the pressed trousers and the white shirt with the black epaulettes holding the large-barrelled gun pointing at me got all of my attention.

It was a reflex reaction. I didn't think about it, I just lifted the forks a foot, jerked the wheel left and the forks slammed into his shins, knocking his feet out from under him, knocking him flat out, dragging his gun, across my forks.

'Beautiful, Wahlnut,' Sally shouted in my ear.

'I've seen it done better,' I said.

This was not a stable situation. The forks were bouncing and he could easily jounce off and I would roll over him with five thousand pounds of fork-lift. I twirled the wheel, the fork-lift spun, gently flinging the man off its prongs, and, flicking the lever into 'R' and mashing the accelerator to the floor, we were rolling backwards. Picking up speed and a passenger. About six two, I guessed, I couldn't see his face. He was holding on to the roll-cage and kicking me with his crepe-soled dirty orange leather workboot. The first kick was a surprise, I was looking up, expecting him to drop down, grab me, grab Sally, do something so I didn't see the kick coming and he kicked me in the soft place just under my ribs.

I guessed his plan was to kick me out of the saddle and one more would have done it, the air exploding out of my lungs followed by another explosion of pain that makes you think ruptured kidney. But as he drew back I couldn't help but notice that his balls were about the height of my head and as he started his second kick I drove my fist straight up into his balls with a lot of ill-will. It stopped his kick, but he didn't let go. So I put a little more into the second hit. This time he made a kind of wounded bull sound and he let go, falling to the dock with his knees drawn up. Two of the fork-lifts following us had to swerve to keep from hitting him.

Judging by the speed of the fork-lifts chasing me across the dock, a fork-lift can go backwards just as fast as it can go forwards. And as long as they weren't gaining on me . . .

This little ray of hope was interrupted by Sally saying 'Forrest!' about the same time I had the thought Backwards towards what? I was just turning my head around to have a look when the whole machine tilted back and the motor whirred up to scream whatever revs electric motors rev to when they are set free. The rattling of the forks stopped, and we were seriously tilting, backwards. The whole fork-lift was falling backwards, through the night air and I was surprised how black the sky was after the brilliant white spotlights over the dock. That was my thought when we hit the San Diego Bay.

And yes indeed, a three-ton fork-lift, falling backwards from a height of fifteen feet, makes a hell of a splash, and it does not pause on the surface on its way to the bottom.

The rush and the force of the water was hard, Sally mashed against me, the two of us trapped against the top of the wire cage. I grabbed hold of Sally's body with both arms, she seemed to be turned the other way, head up towards the surface. I pushed off hard with my feet against the cage into the dark force of the water, trying to get us outside the cage dragging us down. Not hard enough. We were still trapped and we were falling fast and every moment meant we would have further to go to the air on the surface.

I felt Sally struggle, push my arms away, and I felt her do a slow turn in the water, putting her head down and her feet up against the cage. I was seriously considering taking a nice deep breath of water when her arms were around me, giving me a hard squeeze and we both pushed off, and banging my head against the roll-bar we were free, floating up through the murk, towards the shimmering surface which looked as if it was several hundred yards away.

We let go of each other and started to swim up towards the surface, both of us crawling like climbers up a rope ladder, hands and feet churning, heading for the edge of darkness that we could see where the dock cut off the light from the spotlights.

chapter twenty-six

You will not inhale. Not one sip. Don't even think about it. Not.

The surface of the water shimmers darkly overhead. Looks like fifty yards away. It can't be that far away, you'd never see it. Never make it.

Wait. Wait for it. It's not that far.

Time drags.

And drags. Because you are not moving fast enough. Swimming hard uses up too much air. You are out of air. Swim hard and you won't make it. Any slower will take too long. Much too long.

Fuck.

Another quarter of a second slides by while your muscles and your lungs scream that your brain has fucked up again. Your brain is not in charge here. Does not know what it is doing. The whole inside of you screams, bloody screams that every fibre of muscle knows what it needs and if you lose consciousness your body will get what it needs, a deep breath of oxygen. Mixed with two parts hydrogen or four parts nitrogen. Either way, doesn't matter. Your lungs don't know or care about these abstractions. They will INHALE. A good, deep breath.

Another quarter of a second.

Sally, murky, green, her hair flowing down her back, is clawing away at the water alongside, five feet away.

The surface, a little closer, blooms red.

I closed my eyes with the effort to stay conscious for another fraction of time and felt lazy, dreamy, floating in the cool dark water. Nothing to do.

And then there was a burst through the surface into the fresh night air. I couldn't wait to get my jaw clear even though I was shooting up out of the water. With the suction of a swimming-pool drain, I took in a half-quart of oily seawater with my first breath, blind with coughing and spitting like a new-born walrus while I was thinking that making any noise was a bad idea.

Coughing and spitting and blinking the salt out of my eyes. I was not the only one coughing and spitting and I turned in the water and Sally was just behind me, the underside of the dock over our heads, the edge of the side of the dock not more than ten feet away.

We couldn't stop for a while, the seawater was in our eyes and our lungs, our stomachs and our throats and it took some coughing, retching and splashing to get it back into the sea. As we started to calm down we realised we didn't have to worry about making too much noise.

All hell had broken loose over our heads. We could just hear, over the roar of the machinery, what sounded like several men shouting at once. The roar separated into the trundling of the fork-lifts, what sounded like at least one heavy truck and a generator.

Sally took a stroke in the water so she was treading in the water next to me. In my ear she said, 'You are a hell of a driver.'

'Take off your shoes and pants,' I said. 'It'll be easier swimming.'

'We're not thinking of swimming across the bay?'

I looked across the bay. There was a line of needles of light in the darkness. 'You're right. Even if we knew where the tides and the currents are, it's too far. They'd see us. The Navy has to have patrol boats, searchlights, helicopters . . . '

'Sonar detectors,' Sally added helpfully. 'What do you think about going back on the base?'

'Listen to them,' I said. We listened to the roar overhead. There was still a lot of shouting.

'They've been unloading for, what, two hours, maybe two and a half? From what I saw, I'd guess they have at least a hundred tons of crack in the warehouse by now. What's a hundred tons of crack worth on the street? A couple of hundred million? A billion? It's like the national budget of Bolivia, it could be anything. Whatever it is they don't want to lose it. And they don't want us walking around talking about it.'

'We're not walking.'

'How far do you think it is down the shore to the edge of the base?'

'About a mile.'

'Can you swim a mile?'

'Sure, in a swimming-pool. But it's dark, Wahlnut, it's freezing. And you know there's gonna be rats and garbage.'

'Keep your wallet in your shirt pocket.'

'I don't have a pocket in my shirt. You keep it.'

I undid the laces on my work boots and pried them off. Took Sally's wallet and mine, stuffed them in my shirt pocket, undid my belt, undid my jeans, peeled them off with my socks and kicked them away. All set for a day at the beach.

Above us, on the end of the dock, there was more shouting above the roar of the generator. Then there was a loud crack and after a moment, the beam of a searchlight swung down out of the sky and shone down into the water, sending a column of white light ten feet across shooting straight down ten feet away. The column of light turned green and fuzzy as it illuminated a trail of bubbles coming up from the fork-lift. We were in the green glow of sea jello, and on our right we could just see the bottom of the *Commander Mervin Forbes*, a huge dark shape that went on out of sight.

We started swimming down the length of the dock, under the warehouse, to the shore a quarter of a mile away. When we had gone around thirty yards, and it was so dark we could barely see each other, we heard three loud splashes. Frogmen, with tanks and flippers, brilliant in the searchlight, their faces behind glass masks, crashed into the water and dove down into the column of white light, their black flippers kicking more bubbles up to the surface.

'Do you think they're after us?'

'Sure they are after us. Maybe they want to save us.'

'Maybe we should let them.'

'Maybe we should,' I said. 'On the other hand, maybe they just want to make sure that we don't come back up.'

We were treading water; Sally's face, just a few inches away, was a soft white blur against the black. With the same impulse we leaned forward and kissed, and turned towards the black shore at the end of the long dark path made by the shadow of the dock.

The light and the noise from the end of the dock grew quieter and more distant. We swam quietly, making as little noise and disturbing the water as little as possible. They were making a racket at the end of the dock but there could be somebody else looking, listening.

'Ugh,' Sally said under her breath.

'What was that?'

'I don't know. Felt like a turd.'

When we reached the shore, if you can call slimy, seaweed-covered pilings the shore, we swam cautiously out to the edge of the pier, the lights from the Naval Base cutting a sharp edge in the water between the black shadow of the pier and the shimmering green of the water.

'There's a walkway built out over the water. If we stay inside of that, in the shadow,' I said, 'we'll be out of sight.'

'Shit. That's where all the garbage is. You know what I really hate, Wahlnut?'

'Peanut-butter and egg sandwiches?'

'What I really hate, Wahlnut, is going swimming with you.'

We stayed inches from the shore, trying to keep quiet and out of sight. It was cold and there was a lot of stuff floating in the water that we could feel but we couldn't see. And there was an irregular swell that rose and fell and pushed us against the slimy pilings. Getting underneath the piers, the long wide docks that stuck out into the bay, was a relief because there was so much more cover and we didn't have the strain of trying to stay out of sight in the narrow strip of shadow. And we could get away from the pilings.

There were rats in the pilings. We never saw them but we heard them squealing and squeaking like they were hungry. It was probably a rat that dropped with a splash in front of me and I thought I brushed its tail with my hand. But I don't know. Maybe it was just my imagination. I have never been relaxed about rats and what I said was, 'AGGHHHH.'

'Christ, Forrest, what was it?'

'I think it was a sea squirrel.'

We could relax a little under the piers, protected by the vast shadow of the pier overhead. And most of the piers had at least one ladder trailing down into the water that we could hang on, and rest. We tried to keep on the dark side of the ladder, but even so we knew we ran the risk of being seen.

'Forrest you remember carrying me out from that swimming hole?'

'Sure. I remember a mere feather of a girl.'

'I am not a girl, I weigh one hundred and thirty-two pounds and that was really sweet of you. I know I've been shitty, but I've been so scared. I'm not trying to make excuses but I feel bad that I never said thank you to you.' A pause. 'And want you to know I really am grateful. I mean, thank you.' She gave me a little kiss on the cheek.

'You're welcome.'

'But I'm not in love with you.'

'You sure you want to tell me this now? Maybe it could wait,' I said.

'Wait for what, Wahlnut? I really like you. And like I said, there is this lovely connection between us where we don't have to pretend anything or be anything else. We're kinda at home with each other. But you're not in love with me, are you?'

'Oh, I've felt some twinges here and there.'

'Twinges? Give me a break.' She started swimming for the other side of the pier and I swam alongside. 'How much further do we have to go?'

'Hard to tell. I think we've gone eight or nine piers. Maybe another four to the perimeter.'

There was another ladder on the other side of the dock, close to the shore. Sally stopped, hanging on to the inside of it, an outline against the light green floodlit sea behind her, her dark hair streaming down the sides of her face down to her shoulders.

'So you don't love me,' she said, putting an arm around my neck, leaning in against me, the rise and fall of the water moving us together and apart.

'I don't know, Sally. That's a heavy word. You are bright and sexy and gorgeous and attractive and tough as an old boot. And I am powerfully attracted to you. And yeah, I feel that connection between us, like we're made from the same bone. I can't remember which one of us said that. Doesn't matter, I like it, feels good. But I don't know. I don't even know if I have a heart in there. It could be just an old ball of scars.'

'Oh, horseshit,' she said, 'you got plenty of heart in there. You're just too dumb to know where it is.'

'I'm telling you. It's hard for me to know what I feel. If it feels like love, you'll be the first to know. Right now I feel like I am freezing solid and I think we'd better keep moving.'

'That's what you do, isn't it? Keep moving. Never really settle down. Never commit yourself.'

'Sally, did you ever hear that women have a little extra insulating layer of fat so you don't feel the cold so much? I don't know if it is true or not, but if I don't get moving now I am going to shrivel into a prune pit and freeze to death. Or do you want to hang around and talk some more?'

'I want to talk some more,' she said, pushing off the ladder and moving out into the darkness, 'but I don't want to hang around this dump.'

We swam like that for a while, keeping under the dark shadow by the shore, pushing the floating refuse out of our way and resting under the piers.

We were on our way to the last pier on the base. We knew it was the last pier because we could see what looked like a perimeter fence of silver barbed-wire on the other side when Sally screamed.

I turned around and I could just make out a hump of shining black, thrashing in the water, an arm jutting free and being sucked back in again. A foot showing above the surface of the water for an instant and disappearing. I reached out and it was cold and slick to the touch. Slimy and black. Sally was struggling underneath and I pulled at the thing and it came away easily in my hand. A plastic garbage bag, one of those big black ones they use to line garbage cans. Sally was coughing and spitting.

'I thought you were going to push the crap out of the way,' she said, pulling a stripe of wet hair out of her face.

'I guess some of it slides through.'

'You are a hard act to follow, Evers.'

'You want to go first?'

'I want to cry. I want to go home and lie in a hot steaming bubble bath for about three hours.' Then she looked up, into the distance, over my shoulder. 'What is that, Wahlnut, some kind of barrier?'

Two hundred yards away, on the other side of the last pier, stretching half the length of the dock, a fence of stainless-steel ribbon coiled in and out of the water. It was about ten feet high and we couldn't see how deep it went. We swam along the edge of the dock and under the final pier for a better look. The stainless-steel ribbon was studded with barbs and the edges looked like they would slice a fish in two.

It didn't stretch so far out that we couldn't swim around it. That wasn't the problem. The problem was that there was an officers' club overlooking the water at the water's edge. From the music and the noise of their conversation, they were having a good time. Some of them standing at a large plate-glass window, drinks in their hands, looking out over the water. If we tried to swim around the wire barrier, at least ten men would see us.

'We could wait,' I said. 'They have to go home sometime.'

'Wait for the Navy to stop drinking? I'm done, Prunepit. I can't. I didn't think I was going to make it an hour ago. I'm too tired, I can't.'

'The other thing we could do is swim out to the end of this pier, and swim straight out another hundred yards and then cross over. There's a little bit of a swell out there, not too bad, and with the swell to hide us, I think it's dark enough. I don't think they'd see us.'

'Didn't you hear me?' Her voice was rising, harsh. 'I'm too damn tired to take another stroke, Wahlnut. Those are officers, Oakhead. Two minutes' conversation and they'd have a blanket around me and a nice hot Irish coffee in my hand. Where's the ladder on this damn pier?'

'Down there, on the corner,' I said. 'You've come a long way to give up.'

'Give up! Give up what? You go out there and drown. I'm going in to have a drink.' She started to take tired strokes towards the ladder. I followed her and we got to the ladder at the same time. She started to climb up.

'You didn't give up when we were stuck in the fork-lift,' I said. 'You didn't give up when you almost drowned. Or when you got tired and cold and got attacked by a garbage bag. You are going to be really pissed off when they throw you in a cold cell with the drunks.'

'My Daddy is rich and powerful and they are not going to throw me in any damn cell.'

'Your Daddy is not here. You are. If they catch you now they might give you a drink. But they are going to know that the lady who walked out of the sea is the one who fell off their pier in a fork-lift. And they might want to know about how your Daddy is connected to the hundred tons of crack on the dock and what you were doing there and what you can tell them about their brother officers who are smuggling those hundred, two hundred tons of crack. They might just want to fry you and your Daddy alive.'

'Oh Jesus Wahlnut, I'm cold and tired. Bein' fried might be better than freezing to death. Can you give me a hug?'

We held each other, wet shirt to wet shirt in the freezing water, long enough so we could almost feel warm. Then Sally pushed off.

'Let's go,' she said, swimming out towards the end of the pier, her head just above the surface, her white arms making slow and graceful circles in the black water.

She was right. They'd be glad to see her, give her a blanket and a hot drink. Get the pretty lady some dry things to wear. Get a doctor to put some disinfectant on her scalp. She was OK on the base, she had a pass. If she showed up alone, she'd be fine. She'd need a story, but she'd be fine.

'Sally.'

She was on the ladder and we were talking about it.

'Can I have my wallet back? I might want to buy them a drink.'

I fished her drowned wallet out of my shirt pocket. 'You'll have to tell them something about me. Something that will give me some time.'

'Well, I could tell them that you got your foot caught on that damn fork-lift. That you must be down there somewhere.'

'I mean they will want to know what you were doing coming in there with me. In the first place.'

Sally thought for a moment. Then she started climbing up

the ladder, her long legs coming out of the water, shining in the light.

'I know what I'll tell 'em,' she said over her shoulder. 'I'll say you kidnapped and raped me. That'll get their attention.'

chapter twenty-seven

Salt water is easier to swim in than fresh. It's denser so you are more buoyant. Less effort to stay afloat. You bet your ass. This little chop here is letting up. Wave action hides you from the yellow light at the officers' club window three hundred yards away. Keeps you safe from the brave boys in Navy blue. The warm and dry sons of bitches with the drinks in their warm and dry hands, with their warm and dry arms around Sally, are telling sea stories, keeping the pretty woman amused.

This isn't hard. This is exercise. The tide is not running against me. I am making progress. No gain without pain. Damn straight. A little sea water in the mouth cleans the teeth.

A bit early to turn in but maybe I could cheat a little, come in at an angle. There would be less light at the edges, give me a little leeway. A better chance of making it.

I altered course, cutting the corner, heading for home which was the big dark pier that stuck out alongside the Navy pier. I made a sound like a big ship, coming in to dock, HOOOOOOOT, try to keep my spirits up. Try to forget how tired and cold I was, and push away the thought that it would be so nice and easy, and good to just relax, let go, close my eyes and rest. Be so nice to take a rest.

I went HOOOOOOOT again and the wind just swallowed it up.

chapter twenty-eight

It was hard to focus. I felt dizzy, seasick. Lifting my head took planning. Wait for the trough of a wave. Get ready. Wait for the wave to start building, a little flutter with the feet and the hands, as the wave crests and then just as the wave begins to fall, lift the head and ahhh. A breath.

The waves and the wind were taking me towards a dock. And each time I lifted my head I could see the sign. I couldn't read it for a while. But when I was twenty yards away, there was no doubt about it, even in the dark. UNITED STATES NAVY MUNICIPAL PORT COMMAND.

Whatever the hell that meant.

I thought about swimming over to the next dock. The thought was enough. My arms would not go any more. I could float, feet hanging down, arms and legs relaxed, face down in the water and just lift my head for a breath when the waves lifted me up. I could do that for a good while longer but I couldn't swim any more. I'd swum enough. It seemed a hell of a long way to swim and still be on the Naval base, but that seemed to be where I was. Still. I put my hand on the ladder and pulled myself up. One rung. One more rung. One more. Like that.

Towards the flashlight shining down in my face.

'I got a gun on you,' he said. 'Don't fuck around.'

I started to speak but I decided to spit up some sea water instead.

'What're you, AWOL?' His voice had gravel in it.

The flashlight was inches from my face and all I could see was the little light bulb with the point on top, the filament glowing and the silver reflector.

'You speak English? They got a couple of foreign ships from

overseas this week.' The flashlight wobbled as he moved back a step. 'Wait a minute, I know. You're Irish?' he said. 'I got a cousin in Ireland.'

One more step. And I was amazed to find myself on the solid, unmoving dock. My head felt like it was still bobbing around in the water.

'OK: That's it. Don't move. Hands over your head.'

I sat down.

'Hey wait a minute,' he said, worried. 'I said no fucking around here. I got a gun pointed right at your head. You understand? Stand up.'

'I can't,' I said, closing my eyes.

When I opened them again, the flashlight was on the floor, shining at me, illuminating the high roof of the empty pier. He was sitting down, leaning against a pillar, a black outline in the dark, saying, 'So I drop them at emergency in St Vincents. Let them sort it out, it's what they're paid to do, right? I mean I never had a problem with the hookers, they got their lives to lead, I got mine. But after a while you start to think every one of them is a junkie and I figured, even if I cheated on the mileage like some of the cabbies, I was still behind with all the aggro, know what I'm saying?'

'What are we doing?' I said.

'What are you, "What are we doing?" ' he said, mimicking my voice. 'We are sitting on our asses, waiting for Santucci to take over my shift.'

'Just sitting here.'

'Yeah, just sitting.'

'What do we do when Santucci comes?'

'He comes around four. Maybe ten till. He covers you, I go call the coppers.'

Maybe he was a James Cagney fan. 'The coppers?'

'What, you never heard the police called that? Where you come from anyway?'

'Let's call them now.'

'No way, José,' he said. 'I am not gonna fuck this up, know what I mean. We get up, go to the office, maybe you jump me or something. Trick me. I don't want to fuck this up. There aren't that many night jobs around, you know.'

'The Navy employs a civilian to do sentry?'

'This ain't the Navy. The Navy owns the dock, they lease it to a private company. They're planning something like a corporate park, restaurants, offices. I think they're waiting for all the permits to go through. Maybe get a little more backing from the banks. In the mean time, I watch nights. Make sure nobody sets fire to it.'

'How can you be a night-watchman and watch me at the same time?'

'Watch me,' he said. 'It's what I'm doing.'

'How do you know I wasn't the point? All the other guys are swimming around the other side now. Climbing up the ladder. Coming up behind you now?'

'Yeah and they got scaly green skin and their eyes are on stalks. What's your name?'

'Forrest Evers.'

'No shit. Forrest? Like the trees?'

'What's yours?'

'Torccellino. Tommy Torccellino.'

'I thought you said you had a cousin in Ireland?'

'That's my bride's got the cousin. Margaret Mary O'Boylan Torccellino. Married fifty-two years.'

'You have any kids, Tommy?'

'I got seventeen grandchildren,' he said. I couldn't see his smile, but I could feel it.

'Tommy, what I am going to do is reach into my shirt pocket, pull out my wallet, and take out a hundred-dollar bill.'

'Whatta you think, I'm gonna risk my job for a hundred dollars?'

I took my wallet out and held the bill in my hand so he could see it. 'I want you to let me make a phone call. To the police. I'm not asking you to risk your job, I'm just asking you to do it.'

'A hundred dollars? You got a lot more than a hundred dollars in there.'

'A hundred when I make the call. Another hundred when they show up.'

He picked up on the first ring, not saying hello. He said, 'I got my feet up, I'm watching TV. Why are you interrupting?'

'Clarence Harmon?'

'You want to make this quick? The commercial's gonna be over in a minute.' I could hear a jingle in the background. How life could be in a Subaru.

'Forrest Evers.'

'I remember.'

'You said you were looking at a connection between Barnes and Bobby Roberts.' There was a pause. Maybe calls to the police in their own home were recorded and he wanted to say as little as possible. Or maybe, on the screen in front of him, Madonna was reaching for a can opener. I said, 'Who should I talk to about a hundred tons of crack on a Navy dock?'

'Talk to me,' he said, the sound of the television disappearing, his voice much clearer. 'This something you heard about?'

'I saw it. I even carried some of it.'

'Where are you now?'

'A dock in San Diego. The watchman is holding a gun on me.'

'Not where the crack is.'

'The crack could be – probably is – gone now. But I saw it, on the Navy base.'

'You want somebody to get you out from under that gun.'

'Somebody who can do something about the crack.'

'Just a minute.' He was gone for a minute. Tommy Torccellino held his .22 service revolver at his waist, pointed at mine. A .22 is a small cheap gun, and it isn't very accurate. But professional killers use it because it is so easy to conceal and at close range it will kill you just as quickly as any magnum cannon. Tommy was looking worried. He didn't like this. My hundred dollar bill was in his blue night-watchman's shirt pocket, but he didn't like it.

'I thought you were gonna call the coppers,' he said unhappily.

'I did,' I said, 'Clarence Harmon is a cop.'

'You made a long-distance call.'

'He's a cop in Phoenix.'

'What's this shit about a ton of crack. There's no crack on this dock. You bullshitting or what?'

'Evers,' the phone said in my ear. 'The guy I was talking to is Maitland Page at the DEA in San Diego. I got two numbers for him. The first is his office. Try that first because they work weird hours. The other one'll get him bleeped. You sure that was a hundred tons?'

'In bags of rice.'

'Evers, you ever hear of Silica Gel? It's the little crystals they use to keep rice dry. They call it a dehydrating agent, looks like crack.'

'This was crack.'

'If you call Page, Evers, do me a favour. Don't tell him where you got his number.'

'I have to make another phone call,' I said to Tommy.

'You said one call. Another call is another hundred.'

'It's a local call,' I said.

'I got eighteen grandchildren,' he said.

'I thought you said you had seventeen.'

'We been here a long time.'

'Page,' he said after one ring.

'My name is Forrest Evers,' I said. 'I'm on a dock on the North Bay. Lieutenant Clarence Harmon of the Phoenix Police suggested I call you.'

'What would this be in regard to, Mr Evers?'

'I saw a hundred to two-hundred ton shipment of crack come into a naval dock this afternoon.'

'You the only witness?'

'No.'

'You want to come in and talk about it?'

'Can you send a car to pick me up?'

'Give me your address. I'll call Harmon. If he checks you out, I'll send a pastel.'

'I'm worried about the other witness. She was headed into the Officers' Club on the Navy Base about an hour ago.'

'And you are worried?'

'She didn't have any pants on. You want to talk to her?'

'What I like about working nights,' he said, 'is the comedy. You got a name on her?'

'Sally Cavanaugh. She was headed for the Officers' Club about an hour ago.'

'With no pants. After she saw this hundred tons of crack on the dock.'

'Her father is Merrill Cavanaugh. He has a house on the end of Sunset Cliffs, the other side from Ladera. The number is five-eight-six, five-five-seven-eight, she might be there by now, having a bubble bath.'

'We'll find her. You want to give me a description?'

'Slim, long dark hair, blue eyes, about five foot nine or ten. About twenty-eight. She looks a little like Julia Roberts but her eyes are too close together.'

'And no pants. OK, give me your address and stay put.'

I looked at Tommy, dark circles under his eyes, holding his gun on me with one hand, scratching his crotch with the other.

'I'm not going any place,' I said. 'I don't have any pants on either.'

'I can't wait,' he said.

chapter twenty-nine

The San Diego office of the United States Drug Enforcement Agency is on the top floor of the new Federal Building, a gloomy pile of bricks in downtown San Diego just off Broadway. The DEA offices don't have windows. The FBI get the windows.

Two suntanned San Diego cops in fawn short-sleeved uniforms, with guns, beepers, twenty-four-inch batons, handcuffs and notebooks dangling from their belts, were walking and talking a step behind me down the back hall on the fifth floor.

The heavy one with the crew-cut and the sweat-stains under his arms was saying, 'He's not a fucking Angel, he's just wearing the costume. Makes him feel bad. Anyway he's got a ZR, water-cooled sixteen valve does a hole shot to a hunnerd in nine, no shit, nine seconds. Thing is the sniffer wants four grand for it, saying it's only got three thou' on the clock. I check it out and it's got to have over ten on it. Scrapes on the bars, grooves on the head from pulling the plugs. Heavy blue on the pipes. Shit like that. Still, we draw a few more nights of golden OT like this, I might go back, see the little dork. See if I can't get him to come down. I mean shit, nine seconds.'

'Whatta you got on him?' This was the slim one with the long eyelashes and a dark basset hound face.

'Sixty in a forty-mile. Possession.'

'Any priors?'

'No priors. But he's got to sell the bike to pay for a lawyer and he's acting like he's relaxed. His story is I planted the shit on him.'

'Yeah, well, what they say, José. You can fuck with Saint Peter and you can fuck with Saint Paul. But fuck with a cop and you fuck with us all. You want me come with you, face the man, give you a hand bringing him down?'

Cop talk. I am their package to be delivered.

The lights were out in the FBI offices. Just one light was shining out on the grey linoleum floor from an open door halfway down the hall. 'In the conference room,' a voice boomed out. 'It's party time.'

Was party time.

About a dozen empty folding chairs were pushed back from a long formica pine table with cigarette scars and phone numbers engraved on the surface. The table was decorated with sandwich wrappings, bread crusts, paper plates with chewed pizza, strings of melted mozzarella, broken French fries and ketchup smears. Crumpled Buds and Coke and Pepsi Light cans, paper coffee cups with a skin starting to form on the surface of the leftover tan liquid, dainty little paper cups with bits of coleslaw and mayonnaise and Russian clinging to the sides and ashtrays full of cigarette and cigarillo butts. Smoke hung over the table, blanketing a smell of old pizza and sweaty socks. A man in a grey-green silk shirt and a paisley tie was at the end of the table, standing up.

'Maitland Page,' he said, a large padded hand held out to greet me. 'Nobody remembers Maitland, so do what everybody else does. Call me Page.' He was a large man with a face like a loaf of bread and small eyes half-hidden behind his cheeks. He was about forty and his fair skin had flushed pink patches as if he had just come in out of a cold wind. In one gesture he motioned me to sit down and waved the cops away, saying, 'Welcome to the President's War on Drugs.'

I sat down and his big forearm swept a space clear in front of us.

'I like a man wears red underpants,' he said. 'Shows a strong sense of personal identity. Certain flair and individual expression. You often walk around town at night in your underpants and no shoes, Evers, or is tonight a special occasion? You look like shit.'

'Nice to see you too. It's been a long day.'

'Yeah? It's only lunchtime here. I'm fresh as a fucking daisy.' He leaned back in his chair, hands behind his head, assessing me with a long look, like he was looking at an abstract sculpture in a gallery, not sure what it was.

'Fresh,' he said, 'as a daisy that's been fucked for the last twenty-five fucking years. It's only lunchtime, the day is just beginning, and I hate to tell you I do get weary. It's the futility makes a man tired. You know what I mean by futility?' He didn't wait for an answer. 'Futility is we send these guys out, they put their ass on the line. They get hurt, they get shot. And it is a goddamn PR exercise. We take down one guy, like a dealer. A miracle happens and he goes directly to jail, no release on a technicality. Before they turn the key there are twenty-five guys shooting each other with automatic weapons for the privilege of taking the place of the dealer we took out. That is futility.' There was a paper cup of cold coffee in front of him, a little ketchup blotted on one side. He took a sip and made a face.

He put down his cup, looking at the wall in frustration, then back at me. 'I was telling them and I am telling you and any other son of a bitch I can get to listen that the only way you can have any effect is to take down the whole chain. Take it down all at once from the Mr Big Sonofabitches in Peru or Columbia who control the gangs like the Sendero Luminoso. You ever hear of the Sendero Luminoso, Evers? You ever hear of the Shining Path?'

No, never had.

'If you were a mayor in Peru you'd know about them because Sendero Luminoso have murdered ninety mayors in Peru. They are a Maoist group who see to it that the farmers produce plenty of cocaine because they know it is subversive to the health of the United States. They are very big on torture and execution. But the State Department won't do anything to interfere with the affairs of another country. That's one gang. Then you got the Mr Big Sonofabitches in the South American government, and in the South American armies, who have absolute control of what they call emergency zones. Emergency zone is another word for where they grow the stuff. But the CIA won't let you touch them because they don't want to upset a "friendly" government. Then you got a whole chain of Mr Bigs shipping it out of South America and Panama and into the US. So you need to get to those guys all the way down to the poor dumb bastard selling it on the street. But the Government doesn't want to work that way. They don't want to take the time, don't want to spend the money. All they want is bags on the table. We make a bust, put some bags on the table and they run the picture in the newspapers so everybody can say, "Hey they're doing it. President's War on Drugs is working." We aren't doing a damn thing. There's a whole ocean of the shit out there on the street and we're trying to scoop it out with a teaspoon. Fucking PR exercise.'

He yawned, his hands coming out from behind his head for a stretch, taking his time, leaning forward, putting his arms on the table, eyes never leaving me. 'What've you got for me?'

'A chance to use a bucket instead of a teaspoon.'

'You said you saw what you estimated to be a hundred tons of crack on a naval dock.'

'Maybe more. It's hard to calculate the weight because it's wrapped in rice and burlap, but from what I saw there's enough to cover a football field. I was driving a fork-lift for a company called Empire, sub-contracted to the Navy. We were off-loading a naval cargo ship called the *Commander Mervin Forbes*, dock 17 on the naval base. And the cargo that had everybody's attention was rice. I stuck a fork-lift through one of those burlap bags and it came out coated with crack crystals.'

'How did you know it was crack?'

'Tasted alkaline, made my tongue go numb.'

'You ever taste silica gel?'

'Can't say that I have.'

'It's what they use . . . '

'To keep rice dry. That's what Clarence Harmon said.'

'Yeah. I talked to him, checked you out. He said you were probably a pain in the ass. How many bags you look in?'

'Just one.'

'One bag. But you *guessed* they were all loaded like that.'

'They were all getting a lot of attention.'

'So you assumed.'

'No, I didn't assume that. It was organised to distribute the bags as fast as possible to specific locations in the warehouse and they didn't care about the rest of the cargo, just the rice.'

Men were laughing out in the hall.

'Anyway,' I said, 'why bring in just one bag when you can bring in two hundred or ten thousand? Those Empire vans weren't there to distribute one bag.'

A woman joined in the laughter. Sounded like they were having a good time, coming our way.

'What Empire vans?'

'Don't pay him any mind,' she said, before we could see her. 'He's waterlogged. Even stone dry, Ol' Pine-brain's grasp on reality is pretty slippery.' Sally was coming in the doorway, wearing a light blue naval officer's shirt and dark blue trousers several sizes too big. She'd pulled her hair up and she was wearing a big grin. The faces of four Navy officers loomed behind her, looking in. Curious.

'You go ahead and carry on eating,' she said, looking up and down at the mess on the table. 'Don't wait for me.'

'This the other witness you were talking about?'

'Sally Cavanaugh,' I said, 'Maitland Page.' Sally came into the room holding her hand out to shake hands with him. She weaved into a folding chair, knocking it into the table, but she kept right on going. 'He's with the DEA,' I said.

Page said, 'Take a seat,' and looking behind her, 'can I help you gentlemen?'

The four naval officers were just out of their teens, twenty, or twenty-one, hanging in there just inside the door, trying not to look nervous. The short one in front, freckles and nice white teeth, looking like Michael Fox with a bigger nose, put his hands up in mock surrender. 'We got a call from the gate,' he said. 'A couple of cops were looking for Miss Cavanaugh. We thought we better come with her, make sure everything is tight, you know?'

Page pushed his chair back, stood up acting weary and walked over to them, pulling his wallet out of his hip pocket. Sally leaned over me, giving me a kiss on the neck saying, 'How are you doin' Wahlnut? I was so worried about you.'

Page was showing the Navy his badge, saying, 'This is my jurisdiction here, gentlemen. We have an investigation going on and I thank you for escorting the young woman on board. Have a pleasant evening.'

'Hey, if it's OK with you man,' the one with the bony face, the big Adam's apple and the black crew-cut was saying with a Brooklyn accent, lightly touching Page's shoulder, 'we'd prefer to stick around.'

Page took the hand off his shoulder. 'It is not OK with me.

I'd like you gentlemen to cast off now and go on back to your base or wherever the hell you want to go. But if you have a problem with that I'll ring Admiral Benghauser, wake him up and tell him that the four of you are obstructing my investigation. Good night, gentlemen.'

'You OK, Sally?' the tall one with blonde curly hair and crooked teeth said. 'You know these guys?'

'I'm jess fine, Tony,' she said. 'You sail on home now. I'll be fine here. You ever get to Phoenix . . . ' she said.

They left.

'What did you tell them?' I asked Sally.

Sally sat down next to me, saying, 'God, I could eat a dog. I told them I jumped off a party boat. Said there was too much party for a poor little innocent and straight young woman like me.' Sally smiled her big straight smile, her head cocked to one side. Then, serious, 'They were glad to see me, Wahlnut. Let me use the shower, got me some nice dry clothes. I called Daddy up, woke him up out of bed. I told him all about it and he said he didn't know the first thing about any of it. You see, it's all Bobby, Wahlnut. Daddy doesn't have a thing to do with it. Goddamn,' she said a yawn crumpling her face, 'I shouldn't drink on an empty stomach.'

'A thing to do with what?' Page said, sitting down heavily. 'You want something to eat, I'll order it.'

'I want a pizza with everything on it,' Sally said, sweeping a clear place in front of her. 'With *extra* everything on it. Except for pineapple and corn. I don't want any pineapple and corn.'

'Two,' I said. Sally gave my knee a squeeze under the table.

Later, Sally was chewing on the last pizza crust, checking the box to see if maybe she'd missed a slice.

Page was thinking out loud. 'I'm not saying you couldn't be right. You saw what you thought was crack in one bag. OK, I accept that you *thought* you saw something.'

'Whatever it was,' I said, 'if it was anything you'd be interested in it's not there now. It's been over three hours since we left the dock. And they are not going to leave it lying around for somebody to find.'

Page leaned back and picked up the phone, punched in some numbers and said, 'Grey what, Ford Chevy?'

'Ford,' I said.

He raised his voice up to the level of Commander and said into the phone, 'Grey Ford vans with a white star and Empire on top of that, E-M-P-I-R-E. Should be around a half-dozen of them, maybe headed for Phoenix, maybe LA. I want the registration and the licence of the operator and if there is a hundred-kilo burlap bag of rice in the back, don't fuck around just bring it in.' He hung up.

Page nodded his head. He'd taken care of that, now he was thinking of something else. 'Jesus Christ, the Navy. Course there was that thing when Air America was flying heroin out of Cambodia for the CIA. There were Air Force guys in on that. But Jesus Christ, the Navy. If it is true, and that is one hell of an "if", if the Navy is bringing in tonnage I don't want to touch it. And if it's *not* I don't want to fuck up a good working relationship with our friends on the base over some cock-and-bull story I can't prove and you can't either. If it is true, you have to appreciate this is over my head.'

'We're not talking about the whole Navy, Page. We are talking about some crooks in the Navy.'

'We don't know how far up it goes.'

'Are you saying you aren't going to do anything?'

'Now if I knew when the next ship is coming in . . . That's a hell of a bust.' He shook his head, thinking about it. 'If this has any truth in it and I'm not saying that it does, but if it does there is another thing you should think about. If they can't find you, for sure they are not going to do it the same way again. They'd use another port. Use another distributor. And they would probably spend some effort trying to find you. I mean, suppose I look into this and I find out it is true.'

'You gonna get to the part where there is something we should be thinking about?' Sally said.

'Sure. Simply this. If I find out the Navy is bringing in crack by the ton, you want protective custody? You know we could change your name, get you a new passport, papers, give you a house in Bismark, South Dakota. Some place like that where they would never find you.'

'No,' I said. 'I'm happy with who I am.'

'Glad to hear it. Happiness is not the point, Evers. A shipment that size is worth over a billion dollars wholesale. To these guys, in this size operation, a five hundred thousand, even a million-dollar bribe to one of my men is nothing. A tenth of one per cent at the most. Or even ten customs agents and a few naval captains is no big deal when one shipload can bring in a billion to a billion five.'

'Think there's a chance they'd offer you a million?' I asked.

'There's always that possibility,' Page said, with a straight face. 'These days even the little guys are measuring money by the suitcase. They are pulling in so much money off the street they can't count it all. So they figure one Samsonite equals a hundred sixty thousand dollars. Ten Samsonites is a million six. You want to know why we got a depression on our hands, there's your answer. We're haemorrhaging money to half the governments and most of the criminals in South America and you can bet your ass it is not reported in the Balance of Payments.

'You know the US leads the world in murder? You know that? We are top of the league, two to one per capita, over Northern Ireland in second. They have an excuse. They have a war going on.'

'I'm sorry, I don't mean to interrupt,' Sally said. 'But which part of this is the part we're supposed to pay attention to?'

'What I'm leading up to is this. You're so damn sure you saw a hundred tons of crack on that dock tonight. Well if you did I have to tell you you are in deep shit. Real danger. The only reason I can think of that you got in so easily is either it wasn't crack or they have been doing it so long they got careless. If that is the case, they are not going to sit there and wait for you to tell somebody about it. They are going to come after you and kill you. Are you sure you don't want us to give you protective custody? Put you in a safe place?'

'There is no such thing as a safe place,' I said.

'What makes you think anybody would be looking for you, Wahlnut? You signed in as Bobby. Most likely thing is they're out there now, looking for Bobby.'

'Are you going to call him?' I said.

'I don't want to talk to him. I don't think I even care if they go and shoot him. You set him up, Wahlnut. You call him. Explain it to him how come he better crawl into a hole in the ground and pull the dirt over his head.'

Sally stood up and started for the door. 'Of course the one person we know they are looking for,' she said, 'is me. I'm the one who told them who I was.'

PART THREE

PART THREE

chapter thirty

There was nothing about the DEA or a drug bust in the San Diego papers at the airport the next morning. And the afternoon edition of the *Phoenix Sun* was innocent of any drug stories from San Diego. I rolled over on the vast bed and reached for the phone. It was worth a try.

'Sally there?'

'She doesn't want to talk to you.'

'Isn't she a little old to be hiding behind Daddy's skirts?'

'You are Goddamn lucky I am talking to you at all, Evers. Jesus Christ. You rummage around my desk, in my private papers, you sneak on to the Navy Base using Bobby's name, dump a fifteen-thousand-dollar fork-lift in the bay and then, *and then* you come up with the dumbest Goddamn conspiracy theory I ever heard. Calling a shipment of rice "drugs". If I had dogs I'd set 'em on you.'

'It was crack, Merrill, and it had your fingerprints all over it.'

'See? You are fucking nuts. And you Goddamn near drowned my daughter. Am I mistaken, Evers, in thinking I have chosen a dumb fuck for a team manager? Or is that question outside the limits of your intellectual capacity?'

There was a sound of scuffling. Sally's voice. Cavanaugh's voice.

Then Sally was on the phone. 'How are you, Wahlnut?' ('Let me alone, I'm all right,' she said off the phone.) 'I kinda miss you.'

'I kinda miss you too. You took off so fast from the DEA I didn't know where you'd gone. I spent another hour talking to, what's his name, Page.'

'I was scared. Being with you has not done me a whole lot

of good. I think I need to be rewired. I went straight to the airport, got on a plane. I thought being in Daddy's house was the safest.'

'Your father doesn't sound like a happy man.'

'Oh, he's all right. He just thinks you are an asshole.'

'There was crack on that dock. And those were Empire employees on that dock and Empire vans.'

'Suppose there wasn't drugs, Forrest. Suppose it really was just some stuff they use to keep the rice from going bad. Then nobody is after you. Or after Bobby. Or me. You gotta admit, Wahlnut. I mean you saw it, I didn't see any. You gotta admit the just plain old Uncle Ben's theory does have its advantages. You talk to Bobby?'

'I wanted to talk to you first.'

'Where are you staying?'

'I'm back at the Biltmore.'

'You call me to tell me they got a nice swimming-pool?'

'I wanted to see how you are.'

'I'm fine.'

'I thought you might like to have some dinner.'

'You have to give me a little time, here, Pinebrain. You never said . . . '

'No I never said.'

'But you thought it sometimes.'

'I thought it sometimes, Sally. It just wasn't strong enough to mention.'

'You were afraid of committing your good self for the rest of your life.'

'Something like that.'

'You could say something nice, you know, you won't get punished for it.' There was a pause. 'Isn't it weird, the things men find hard to say.'

'I was glad you followed me.'

'I couldn't help following you, Wahlnut. If I had time to think I doubt I would have. But it is mutual, isn't it? I mean I feel like if I was to do something a little off the wall myself, I bet you ten dollars you'd follow me. Sometimes, Oakhead, I just pull your strings and you jump.'

'And sometimes I pull yours.'

'There were those. There were indeed. How are you coming with the Formula One team?'

'I've only been back a couple of hours. I thought I'd talk to your father about it.'

'Oh, Christ, don't wait to talk to him about it. It'll take him a week to cool down. Just do it.'

'Do it with what? I can't use your father's money. I know he is your Daddy and he can do no wrong. But I am not relaxed about money from dying kids and junkies. You think drug money is OK, gets purified just because you can lay your hands on it.'

'What *are* you talking about, Wahlnut? Who the hell ever knows what goes on and where money comes from? This is America. You rise or fall on who you know and what you promise. Followed up by what you can deliver. You know a lot of people. You got the backing. And you got the money. What the hell are you waiting for? If everybody in America worried about how squeaky-clean every dollar was this country would shrivel up and die. Besides, you're the only one who thinks there was drugs on that dock. And even if there was, my Daddy didn't know about it. Why don't you talk to Bobby?'

'You keep saying talk to Bobby. A couple of days ago you spit like a wet puma when I said I was even thinking about talking to him. What happened, you get lucky and kill him?'

'Well I was madder then. I guess I've relaxed a bit about Bobby. I don't want to kill him any more, I just want to do him some physical damage.'

'What about doing some physical damage to some dinner?'

'I don't know about dinner, Forrest. Why don't you call me in a month or two.'

'I thought we were close.'

'Yeah, we were. I just lost my taste for it.'

She had that rock, all the time, in her back pocket. Just waiting to throw it. I said goodbye and I put the phone down and rolled over on the bedspread, looking for maps on the ceiling.

There are two things you can do if you miss someone so bad your bones hurt. You can nurse the pain. Take good care of it. Hold it to you like a pillow and see if you can find some comfort in the way it slices around inside you. You can still feel her touch and feel her kiss, the one she gave you there, growing cold. Hold it tight. Enjoy the cold and the pain.

Or you can let it go and let it starve. No trouble at all. Just watch the road maps on the ceiling grow. Count to ten before you think of her again.

I picked up the phone and punched in the numbers for Page, the DEA man. Maitland, his first name was. I thought they might have found a van or maybe several. I thought he might tell me that I hadn't made it up.

'Yeah.' A man's voice. A tenor, touch of a midwestern twang. Not Page.

'This is Forrest Evers. I want to talk to Maitland Page.'

'He's not here.'

'When's a good time to call?'

'He's out of here. Transferred.'

'Where to? Where can I reach him?'

'What'd you say your name was?'

'Evers. Forrest Evers. I saw Page, talked to him last night in the conference room.'

'You talked to him, huh. What was that in regard to?'

'Can you tell me where I can reach him?'

'We don't give out that information. Is there something you want to tell me?'

I hung up.

No doubt they traced the call. No doubt he had the number of the Biltmore on his screen. The incoming number. There must have been a hundred people who might have called Page, contacts he'd had. But they had my name and where I was and they would follow it up. Or was I just being paranoid? A little silica gel giving me hallucinations.

The way she tossed her hair out of her eyes, looking at you as if she was pushing everything else out of her mind. Head to the side, concentrating on you. The cocky smile she gave you just before she threw a sucker punch.

I rang Bobby.

'Forrest, my man,' he said. 'How you hangin', bro? And where the hell have you been? I have been making rapido progress. Got a lot to tell. When do you want to get together? You got plans? You want to meet me at Durants for dinner tonight?'

'You haven't heard.'

'What? What haven't I heard? The Pope has tits? Tell me about it.'

'There's not all that much to tell, Bobby. I used your name to get into the Navy dock in San Diego and I saw the Empire trucks and they were off-loading enough crack to fill the Hollywood Bowl to the brim.'

'What are you telling me?'

'Maybe we ought to pick a quieter spot for dinner.'

'You used my name to trespass on a Naval Base? Jesus Christ, you are a wonder, Evers.'

'You telling me you didn't know anything about it?'

'I don't know anything about why you'd do such a dumb fucking thing or what it was that you did or what in hell you think you are up to. I do have the distinct feeling that you are fucking around with me again and I do not like it a bit. Where are you staying?'

'I'm just changing hotels.'

'Well, why don't you stop by here on the way to wherever in hell you're going. You've been here before, you know where it is. I don't know how quiet it's going to be but it's a safe place.'

'I'll be there in an hour, Bobby,' I said. Thinking of how she had that little trick of giving my back a light scratch, just brushing like a tease with her fingernails as we walked down the street together. Thinking of her kiss in the hospital bed and the old tidal pull.

'Call me in a month. Or two,' she said. Making 'two' sound like the upbeat option.

No problem not thinking about Sally. None at all. I wasn't even going to try to stop thinking about her. Her long legs around me, drawing me in.

chapter thirty-one

Bobby was doing a slow stroll across his half-acre spread of champagne carpet, dragging his hand along a green marble conference table and pausing behind a green marble desk uncluttered by paper. Along with the plateaux of green marble his office had curvy wine-red furniture stuffed with butter-yellow leather cushions.

A TV built into the bookshelf was showing a pre-season spring-training night-ball game with the sound down low. The walls were panelled with rosewood on either side of the door. Sheet glass curved around the edge of the carpet with Phoenix winking and blinking in the night below. Hidden spots in the ceiling highlighted the professional decorator touches like an ivory statue of a nude woman on his desk. It was about two feet long, lying back on an ivory couch, legs apart, knees up, arms outstretched.

'It's Victorian,' Bobby said, running his finger over the rise and fall of the milky stomach. 'The dealer said it came from a gentleman's club in London, but I think it was probably just a whorehouse.'

Bobby looked good, for Bobby. A little baggy under the eyes, a little red-rimmed, but relaxed, handsome under the tan. Good white teeth.

'It's quite an office for a simple country lawyer.' I was standing just inside the door.

'I don't think I ever said I was simple,' Bobby said, showing the half-grin of a man who has drawn two aces to the two in his hand. 'But yeah, it's quite an office. I like to think it's kinda like a duke on top of his tower in one of those medieval Italian cities.' He was pacing, taking his time, the captain of the home team on his home ground. Soft mahogany loafers and yellow socks. Crisp white linen trousers, yellow cashmere sweater. A tasteful yellow gold chain disappearing down the sweater in the blond curls. Bright blue eyes under that casually tousled blond hair that looked like it had been blown back by a mountain wind. 'On a good day,' he said, 'I feel like I can see the whole world from here.'

Bobby sat down on the yellow sofa, reached for a cigarette in a silver and glass box, thought better of it and stood up again. 'They say a man's office is an extension of his ego, Forrest. Well I'll tell you my ego would feel a lot more extended if the floors underneath our feet filled up with paying tenants. The carrying charges on this goddamn pile are enough to ruin a normal man. It's cocktail time. Want a drink?'

'No thanks, Bobby, but don't let me hold you back.'

'No danger of that, Forrest,' he said. He took a large crystal tumbler from a cabinet in the bookshelf and pushed the rim against a chrome lever in the door of a little built-in refrigerator. Looking over his shoulder he said, 'Where the hell you get a name like Forrest?'

Discs of ice fell into the glass.

'My mother came from around here,' I said. 'She thought forests were invented in England. My father was English and she thought anything English was romantic.'

'Wrong on all counts, huh?' Bobby sliced a lemon on a little cutting board, spun the top off a quart bottle of gin and poured, saying, 'I really am very disappointed, Forrest. That's my main sentiment, here. Disappointment.'

'I'm sorry to hear that Bobby. You missing part of your crack shipment?' I sat down in a butter-soft leather chair that looked like it had never been sat in before.

'Don't you worry about it. Don't give it another thought. I'm not bullshitting you, Forrest. Our little ship is fine. Just fine.' He gave me his big professional Bobby smile, on and off in a flash. 'What disappoints me is I put in a lot of time and effort into putting together this Phoenix Formula One team. Drawing up a charter. Setting up the finances. Lining up sponsors. Not out of the goodness of my heart, you understand. I think it could work, and I would like to make it work. And I am disappointed that you seem to be determined to fuck it up.'

'There isn't any team, Bobby. I don't know what you have

in mind for a Formula One team. Maybe a toy to play with. Something to do in your leisure time. As far as I am concerned the only point of having a Formula One team is to win the World Championship. But I am not going to do that with you. The only thing I want to do with you is nail your ass to the wall.'

Bobby took a sip of his drink. Considered it. Then took another. 'No cause for you to be offensive, Forrest. Hear me out. Naturally I like to win, but let me tell you winning races ain't the only thing around here. Couple of the fellows might bitch. But you are not irreplaceable. It is down to Merrill. Merrill has been encouraging me to keep you on. He seems to think we need the credibility of your name. Big word with Merrill, "credibility". Come over here for a moment.'

Bobby beckoned to me to come join him at the wall of glass overlooking the city. 'You see over there in the north-west, that little bitty glow?'

In the distance, across the blackness of the desert, the sky was dark with just the afterglow of the sunset. 'Not in the north-west, I don't.'

'Well, you got to know where to look. And it's not really dark enough. Anyway, trust me, on a really dark night that's Las Vegas, over there three hundred miles away,' Bobby said. 'Very useful town. You know about the twenty thousand dollar disclosure law? Every time a bank does a transaction over twenty thousand dollars they have to report it to the Federal government. But the casinos are not banks and the Federal government recognises that if gambling casinos had to report every Goddamn bet over twenty thousand Washington would be buried under ten feet of paper. So the casinos don't report individual transactions.' Bobby went back to his bookcase for more ice. He tasted his gin and tonic, savouring it. 'Tell you what I did. I lined up the Condor, the biggest casino in Vegas. I've got the Condor as one of our sponsors. Let me tell you the folks who run the Condor are not only expert at moving money around, they also have the money to move around. Dovetails nicely with an operation like a Formula One team that goes all around the world. Simplifies the cash flow, if you see what I mean.'

'Bobby,' I said, 'anybody who can access a satellite dish can move money around.'

'What I am saying is I have lined up a sponsor that is happy to throw another ten million into our tin cup, and play it straight: organise tours to the races for some of their high rollers, broadcast the races in their casino, you know really make it work for them. Tell the world what a wonderful place the Condor is for throwing your money away. All that legitimate shit you expect a sponsor to do. And, God bless their black hearts, they will be our banker.' He took a deep sip, finishing the glass, swirling the ice, looking at me.

'For a percentage.'

'Of course for a percentage. You ever hear of a bank that didn't take a cut?'

'I thought money wasn't a problem.'

'It's not a problem. The problem is moving it around. Getting the cash up into the satellite systems without passing it under the nose of some Federal official, that's a whole lot tougher than it used to be before BCCI. Since that goddamn BCCI bank went bust the Feds are keeping a lot closer tabs on money and who is moving it around. Kinda takes the fun out of banking.'

'You're telling me you want to use a Formula One team to launder money.'

'Oh Jesus Christ,' he said going back to his desk. 'I got fifteen ways to work this. You go move the cars around, I'll move the money around. You remember my telling you that you are way the hell over your head?'

'That was when you were suing me.'

'I'm still suing you. I haven't dropped that case, I've just put it on the back shelf for the moment. But let me give you a little glimmer here of how deep you are. You think you found out something in San Diego. You know what, Forrest? I don't give a shit. I made a couple of phone calls. Nobody else gives a shit either. You can go back to the DEA if you like. They'll listen to you as long as you want to talk to them, because that is all they can do, listen. The only way the DEA can get on a Navy base is with the Navy's permission. Does that give you some idea? There is no substitute for power.' He held up a finger, counting off his points. 'No substitute for influence. No substitute for speed, and we have all three.' He shoved his three fingers at the air. 'We can change companies and lines of distribution so fast it's like flicking a light switch.

'By all means if you want to tell the world about it go ahead. Who do you think is going to give a shit? You know anybody these days that doesn't know a dealer? A drug dealer is part of the fabric of the modern community. The only difference is, in the poor communities they are out on the street. Not only is nobody going to listen to you. You will be dead in a week. They'll just let enough time pass to let the connection soften. Fact is, you'd be dead now if Merrill hadn't stood up for you. But go ahead, Forrest. Get up on your hind legs and speak up. It is not going to make a rat's ass difference and you will die in some shitty accident where your head gets ripped off or you will have a heart attack from food poisoning, I don't know. Let it be a surprise. That's one option you have. And that option disappoints me because the other one is so much more profitable for all of us.'

'I respond badly to threats, Bobby.'

'You respond any way you like. I'm not threatening you, I am just trying to alert you to the facts here. I'm telling you, you can kiss your ass goodbye or . . . ' he held his hands open letting the sentence trail off.

'Or what?'

'Or you can play with us. You don't have to get involved, just set up your Formula One team. I'll keep an eye on the money.'

'I'm not interested,' I said.

'Maybe you don't understand what I am laying out in front of you. On the one hand you can have serious money in your hand, in your bank, in your pocket, up your ass, wherever you want to put it. You can have your serious Formula One team. And if you don't fuck it up you will be admired as well as seriously rich. It's true, we could get another team manager. But suppose he starts nosing around, wanting to know where the money comes from. You see, you already know now. And you know that you will die if you share that knowledge. It's not great, being under that kind of pressure. But you get used to it. Especially when you consider the alternative.'

Bobby went over to his bookshelves to check the scoreboard showing on the silent TV. 'See I like the fact that you know what you've hooked up with. It makes you cautious and your loyalty is guaranteed. This is Phoenix, man. We invented the savings and loan scam. Nobody's gonna mind. Folks out here expect you to engage in a little creative finance. And look at this building you are standing in. We are building the future of America. And you might as well take a piece of it as it passes by you Forrest, because it will not pass this way again. And neither will you, brother. Neither will you.'

'So you get used to it.'

'Used to it? Man, I *love* this.' He spread his arms, ice tinkling in his glass, as if he was going to embrace the whole city winking in the dark beneath us. 'Come on, Forrest, I'm asking you. You want to enjoy the sweetness of life or you want to get your ass blown off and your head stuck up a drainpipe?'

'Bobby, when did you get used to the idea that some quiet man is going to blow your brains out because you said the wrong thing or some guy's wife has a cousin who wants your job. You are not exactly in with the family, Bobby.'

'There's no family, Forrest. The only connection you have is you do favours for friends. Then they owe you. You keep the debt in your favour. Simple as that.'

'And when did you get used to the idea that when a fourteen-year-old addict gives birth to a baby with brain damage it's from your crack, so you can have another drink?'

'Oh cut that moralistic shit, Evers. Nobody's forcing them. If we didn't supply it, there are a thousand others that would be happy to. And if those kids couldn't get crack they'd get high on something else.'

'And when did you get used to the idea of dynamiting a man in his car.'

Bobby put his drink down, and looked at me, sinking back on his yellow sofa. 'Oh, Christ, Evers. You really don't know a goddamn thing, do you? I didn't do that any more than you did.' Then he got back up, went over to his desk and sat down in his leather important-executive swivel chair. He put his empty glass down on the green marble top of his desk, leaned forward on the desk, hard muscle under the golden hair on his forearms. 'Hasn't the thought occurred to you that we share one or two similarities? I mean you didn't go into Formula One racing for the job security. Yes indeedy, I could have been a nice plain vanilla corporate lawyer and you could have been a fucking tennis player. You want to talk about addiction, let's talk about the buzz you get from getting right out there on the edge, in control and just a see-through slice of time away from snuffing it. You see what I mean? I've been there. I know the feeling. Let's go get some supper.'

'Bobby,' I said, 'I'd love to break bread with you but I promised Sally I'd take her to dinner.'

'You are a dead fuck,' he said.

On the way back to the hotel, I stopped at a bar and rang Sally.

'Forrest,' she said, 'I thought you weren't going to ring me for a while.'

'I just wanted to see how you are. Hear your voice. See if there was anything I could do.'

'Well, I'm glad you called me, Forrest, because I was just thinking about you and there is something I'd like you to do for me.'

'What's that?' I said.

'Go away,' she said.

chapter thirty-two

Stand on top of a high hill on a clear night, my mother told me when I was a boy in freezing Norfolk, in freezing East Anglia in freezing England. Stand there and let your mind cool and stop. And while the rest of the world is wrapped in blankets and dreams, she said, you will see the stars move.

Her version of a bedtime story. Her poetic side, I'd always thought. There were no hills in freezing Norfolk.

My mother, my old dead friend. We never knew each other well enough, never saw each other enough to be friends until I grew up. By then I was too busy hauling my Formula Three car around Europe to have much time for her. Her wild west spirit was off the wall in England. The county gentry in Norfolk pursed their lips as if they were afraid she was about to pull out a six gun and called her crass behind her back. Her stories and free-flowing red hair alarmed them. I could hear a sigh of relief when she left the room.

Standing on top of a bare hill, on her land and mine, I could see she was right about the stars. The stars rose up in the east and one by one and by the million they cruised through the sky overhead. There was no moon and no light in the desert to give away the presence of another human being. No cars, no houses, no buildings. There was the jagged outline of the mountains on the horizon to describe the curve of the earth, there was the black of night, and there were the stars gliding by as the world rolled east beneath my feet.

The earth and the stars were moving at light-speed and I was stalled. Not a case of shifting to a lower gear. Stalled. I pictured myself here, three weeks ago, tricked out in pimple boots and Ralphie Lauren nostalgia cowboy costume. A big man in a big land, looking for something to take on at racing speed. Today's starring role will be played by Forrest Evers, former Famous Man, former Formula One star. Former Bigtime. Show the folks your dimestore neckerchief, Forrest. Give us a little imitation cowboy shuffle in those full-quill ostrich skins. Let's see you dance to the tune of a real six-gun.

The next hill had been my mother's and my mother's gift to me. It was not mine. I had lost it and I could not get it back.

Sally would not speak to me.

God damn, I thought I knew her. I thought I knew what she wanted, what she needed and what she was hoping for. And I had thought I was a part of all of those rugged-stranger-who-came-riding-in-out-of-the-Western-sky movies with happy endings. I thought we were close. I thought we shared that old same bone, same skin feeling that went all the way back to Mesopotamia, or some damn time before we were born.

I missed by a country mile.

And then as long as I was making a list, adding it up, there was the Phoenix Formula One team, another bad joke. It didn't even exist; all I had done was stir up the sharks. I had uncovered a major shipment of crack in San Diego no one cared enough to look at. Or maybe they had looked and found it *was* just a lump of badly packed silica gel.

Dance? I was still waiting to take the first step.

It had been a hard week for a man who was used to pounding around a race track at one hundred and seventy-five miles an hour, thinking he is making progress, leaving the world behind. I had waited three more days after seeing Bobby in his office. After Sally told me to piss off. After I had gone back to the hotel and swum fifty-six laps in the dark.

As I said, the first day the *Phoenix Sun* and the *San Diego Reporter* had no news of BIG DRUG BUST in San Diego. Just a taste of what was to come. More nothing. Nothing. Not a word. But of course, that was all there was, my word. And who was I? Not a lot different from a bug on a cactus, from the viewpoint of a star. If you want a true measure of your size in the universe stand on the top of a hill in the small hours of the morning and watch the stars sail above by your tiny human frame. You won't feel small, but you will understand the proportions.

After three days of walking, running, working out and seeing nothing about DRUG BUST OF THE CENTURY in the papers, I rang Clarence Harmon, the Phoenix cop.

They put me through and he said 'Now what?'

'Nobody, as far as I can tell, cares a damn that I saw a hundred tons of crack on a Navy dock in San Diego.'

'Evers,' he said, 'what in the name of sweet Jesus do you expect me to do about it? If you want advice, my advice is to forget about it. Let the professionals handle it. I am a local cop and what I do is try to keep my ass and my neighbour's ass above ground.'

'Sounds like a job for a man with a shovel,' I said.

'What I'm telling you is it doesn't matter what I think about your story, I can't help you. Your story is way the hell out of my jurisdiction.'

'Barnes didn't think so.'

'Yeah, maybe Barnes didn't think so. And maybe that's why they blew him up. We arrested the dumb fuck who stuck the dynamite under Barnes and he is in jail awaiting trial. More than that I cannot do.'

'Do you know anybody else at the DEA I can talk to?'

'C'mon. You already talked to them. Unless you have something new to tell them, they heard you. Anyway they are not going to tell you anything. They don't give information away, they control it. But listen, if you are not satisfied, Evers, the DEA comes under the Department of Justice. You can always write to the Attorney General whoever the fuck he is these days. Give him times and dates and names and who knows, you might get an agent knocking on your door in six months asking for times and dates and names. But this is way beyond my jurisdiction, Evers.'

I could hear him shifting in his chair, warming up. 'Hey, I just thought of something. You're right about the shovel. You know what my job is, Evers? My job is to shovel up the shit that happens when the crack and the heroin and the cocaine and that ecstasy shit hits Phoenix. Just an old-fashioned cop; trying to help old ladies cross the street without getting cut in half. Anyway I gave you my best advice last week. Forget about what you saw. Go home, Evers.'

I gave it another day. Another day of swimming, running, doing sit-ups, push-ups, and forty-five-minute sets of Swiss

Army variations on personal torture. Another day of three meals, newspapers and another three hundred and twenty-five dollars plus tax to the Arizona Biltmore for the pleasure of my company.

The next morning, day six of the bad week, I did what athletes do these days when they find themselves with nothing to do. I called a press conference. First I rang Merrill Cavanaugh to see if he'd put some muscle into setting it up.

'Christ, Evers,' he said, 'you haven't got drivers, a designer, a chassis, a team manager, sponsors or an engine. You haven't got a damn thing. All you got is five million dollars of my money. You haven't done anything yet. What the hell you want to give a press conference for?'

'To start the ball rolling, Merrill. Create some news. Let the world know who we are before we knock on their door. If you are serious about the Phoenix Formula One team, the sooner we announce it the better.'

'Bobby talked to you? Took you into his confidence?' Merrill's voice sounded husky, tired.

'Bobby laid it out in black and white. He was very clear. As in not to reason why.'

'He tell you how I saved your ass?'

'He didn't tell me how, Merrill, but he told me. He said if it wasn't for you I'd be dead.'

'That's right.'

'Thank you.'

'You're welcome. Don't expect me to do it again because I can't.'

'Can you line up some press?'

'Where you want to have this shindig?'

'How about Bobby's office?'

'Bobby won't like it, they'll fuck up his carpet.'

'Bobby can shampoo his carpet. Tell him we want to set it up for tomorrow. Tell him we want to make it sound like news.'

'I'll get my PR guys working on it,' Merrill said.

'Tell Sally hello,' I said but he'd already hung up.

So the next day we had the local sports writers, both of them. The younger one was in his twenties, grey faced, no neck and no shoulders, hunched forward in his folding chair, a cigarette in his mouth trailing ashes on Bobby's carpet, not impressed. The older one was an old, tall, long-haired ex-basketball player who kept his back straight and his chin up between yawns that bared a lot of yellow teeth.

And there were the two local TV stations who each brought in their bright light on a tripod which made you squint and lit you up like Dracula. There was a stringer from *Time* and the UPI reporter for the far west who happened to be in Phoenix researching an article on water conservation. About a dozen people altogether counting the camera and sound technicians. Not exactly Presidential level, but enough.

The three of us were shoulder to shoulder behind Bobby's green marble desk; Bobby on my left, Merrill on my right. Merrill introduced 'the great' Forrest Evers, 'winner of six Formula One Grand Prix'. I won four, but this didn't seem to be the time to correct him. 'A man truly dedicated to the sport.'

The reporters looked at us, blankly, their pocket tape recorders pointed at the speaker in the corner of the room. They were impatient. We had promised them a free lunch and they looked over their shoulders at the bottles of champagne on ice, and the cold lobster in silver dishes on Bobby's green marble conference table, and they looked at their watches. How long were these windbags going to keep on blowing smoke?

'I won't take long,' I said. 'I'm sorry we don't have press kits for you. We'll have press kits as soon as we have an engine.'

They looked back at me like goldfish from a bowl. Maybe I should have explained there would be a joke. 'Joke,' I said. More fish eyes. Formula One, for them, ranked somewhere between high-school bowling and archery. I picked up the typed paper that Merrill and Bobby and I had agreed on and I read:

'At the financial, cultural and geographical crossroads of the new Southwest' – 'cultural' was Merrill's idea. 'Stick it in,' he'd said. 'Give it some class.'– 'Phoenix is taking the lead in corporate and personal finance and in corporate and personal leisure activities.' Some of the fish eyes wandered off into the sky outside. Had I really agreed to say this? Bobby and Merrill had squabbled over every word. I would have agreed to reading the menu from Pizza Hut. As long as Bobby and Merrill were happy.

I droned on and on. The official voice of corporate enthusiasm. I wanted them bored. The paper ended with the statement: 'as symbolic of Phoenix's leadership in recreation and technology it gives me great pleasure to announce today's formation and foundation of the first American Formula One team in years, the PHOENIX FORMULA ONE TEAM.'

What I said was slightly different. What I said was: 'as symbolic of Phoenix's leadership in recreation and technology and position at the cross roads of the international drug market it gives me great pleasure to announce today's formation and foundation of the first American Formula One team financed entirely by our local drug industry, the PHOENIX FORMULA ONE TEAM.'

Bobby and Merrill weren't quite sure they heard what I said and there was a pause of a few seconds while the words sank in before they both reached for the microphone. But I had it with both hands and I stood up. No more fish eyes, I had their attention, mouths open. 'As this building and several of the new office buildings in Phoenix are financed by the Phoenix drug industry, we think it is time the Phoenix drug community had a Formula One team of their own.'

Merrill yanked the microphone cord out of the wall, saying, 'I'm sorry to interrupt, gentlemen, but we don't share Mr Evers' sense of humour.'

I said, without the mike, 'Mr Cavanaugh's and Mr Roberts' most recent shipment came in on the *Commander Melvin Forbes* on dock 17 at the San Diego Naval base and they expect their next shipment,' I said taking a wild shot, based on the shipping charts in the San Francisco papers, 'on the *Alexander Hamilton*.'

Bobby had his arm around my throat and I paused for a moment to give him a sharp elbow in the chest, knocking the wind out of him. 'Last port of call, Panama City, Panama, due to dock in around twenty minutes at the US Naval base, San Francisco.'

Merrill was saying, behind me, 'Now hang on, Goddamn it.' But the two reporters were already running out of the room. Normally they would have stayed for the fight and the lobster, but the news of the ship docking in twenty minutes had them scrambling. The TV guys kept their cameras rolling and got a shot of Bobby on the floor, gasping, and throwing an ashtray in my direction.

I had the rest of that day to scan the papers and the TV news reports. And the night. And I wasn't really surprised to see that there was almost no mention of the PHOENIX Formula One Team inaugural press conference. Just another goofball out there making another noise in the din, trying to get on TV and be famous for a soundbite. Maybe if they'd found something on the *Alexander Hamilton* it might have worked. If there was something to find. If they looked. Never take a wild shot, my mother used to say. If you are going to shoot, shoot to kill.

The last day of the bad week there were a few messages. Bill Platt rang from Falcon to say that he didn't know what the hell I was trying to prove, but for the record, Falcon would not touch me with a barge pole. Some anonymous voice who said he was from the DEA rang to say that I had fucked up an extremely important high-priority operation. What the hell did I think I was doing, interfering with a government investigation? This is the new morality. If you see a crime, don't say anything, report it to the authorities, let them deal with it. They know better than you. One day Noriega is a trusted friendly drug dealer, a buddy of Bush and the CIA. And the next they flatten Panama City to get him. Let them handle it. They know what they are doing.

All in all it had been a week of sound and fury, signifying nothing.

So after the sun started to go down I drove out to my property and climbed up on the highest hill that I could find.

And despite Bobby's promise that I would not live for twenty-four hours I can tell you that if you stand on top of a hill in the small hours of the morning and watch the stars, you will not only see the stars sail across the curve of the universe, you will see them disappear.

And in their place you will see the sun rise up and set fire to the sky.

chapter thirty-three

Nothing like a needle shower to clear the mind. Ah yes indeedy, those pulsing needle sprays zing through the skull and sluice out the brain grooves. If you can't fight 'em, to hell with them. Open wide the drapes. Wave goodbye to the corporate wives strolling on the lawn in their bulging bikinis. See if any of them smile back at the naked man waving his big white fluffy towel. Let the Arizona sun come blazing through the glass sliding door. Make that carpet sizzle. The air-conditioning can handle it. The National Power grid can take the extra stress. Who gives a shit about an extra puff of smoke from the Four Corners power plant, and an infinitesimally deeper haze to blur the Grand Canyon from Evers turning his air-conditioning on 'Hi'? Everybody else was letting go, not giving a damn. Why should I?

I was going to do the first smart thing I had done since I'd landed. I was going to walk. Negative intention, the behaviourists call it. If you really want something, walk away from it, and you will be amazed at how many times it will come trotting along after you. And if it doesn't, you don't give a good Goddamn.

I wanted Sally and I wanted my land and there was nothing I could do about either one. I would board the first plane to London and leave this developer's paradise behind me. I'd go back to the reptile cages of London, the streets slick with rain, the friendly mould slithering up out of the drains to give your shoes a wet green kiss, and the little street children flashing their razor grins as they scrounge the tourists for something to eat. All in all a far more welcoming town than Resurrected Bird.

Sally would loathe London's grey skies and intricate hedges

of class, manners and prejudice. I wondered how she'd react to a ticket to Heathrow.

I had a swim and lunch and a swim again, and I was in my room, packing, when the phone rang. Thinking I never owned that land, so you can't lose what you never had. Excuses like that. Let Lawyer Judith find a handle on the property. Mortgage the half I still owned to pay her legal fees. If I didn't win the other half back, I didn't want it anyway. The phone rang again.

'Hi, Forrest,' Sally said.

'I thought you didn't want to see me.'

'Changed my mind.'

'You don't sound good, Sally.' Her voice was cracked and rasping.

'I'm not. I'm not good at all. Might even die, it's hard to tell.'

'Where are you?'

'Bobby's. I think he gave me something.'

'Is he there?'

'Somewhere. I must have passed out.'

'I'll see you in ten minutes.'

'You be careful, now, Forrest. He's been talking about you, what you did to him. I don't think he is going to be real glad to see you.'

Bobby's house was just down Camelback from the hotel. If I had driven like a maniac, gone through red lights and driven the Reatta at its middle-aged limit I might have cut the time down by a whole minute. Maybe even two. The downside was the squadron of cop cars I'd drag along with me. Cops like cruising the rich neighbourhoods. Nothing much happens and the tips are good. So an overweight Buick bowling along at ninety-five next to the Biltmore Plaza Shopping Center would have done a lot to relieve their boredom. Of course it might have been a good thing to lead a police escort to Bobby's, but I doubted it. Once you start off on the wrong foot with our guardians of public safety it can take just a little while to convince them that you are the good guy. No more than seventy-five between the lights. Eighty-five top. With just a burst here and there to ninety. OK one hundred, the speedo is probably ten miles an hour fast anyway. And that light didn't turn red until I was into the intersection almost, did it? Miraculously, no policeman picked up on the respectable Buick barge acting like a low-flying Scud.

I slid into Bobby's lot sideways for twenty-five yards, stopping in front of the outdoor lift, switching off the key, moving, lifting myself up and out of the car before it was completely stopped, and running the six steps into the lift, pushing the up button about thirty to forty times before it sluggishly consented to lift. Normally a pleasant trip, with glass on all sides to admire the spread of the city below and the back of Camelback mountain behind if you are interested in rock face. I hadn't noticed before just how slow it was. I tried to urge it upward. It made a refrigerator-humming sound. Humming right along on Slo-Mo.

After a small eternity of rising, the lift stopped humming by the pool and I pushed the door open and ran around the edge, up the steps on to the wide terrace and through the open sliding glass doors into Bobby's wrecked living-room.

Books had been torn off the shelves; some of them, lying on the shag carpet, had their covers ripped off. There were at least, judging by the broken-off bottle necks, four broken bottles smashed on the floor. Lamps had been knocked over, lampshades kicked and pictures ripped off the wall. I could hear the sound of water running, sounded like a bathtub, in another room, but it would take a little while to get to that because Sally was sitting naked on the floor, propped up against the couch. Her light blue silk panties were on the couch behind her. The phone was off the hook, lying beside her on the carpet, and she looked like she was having trouble focusing.

'Welcome to the party,' she said. 'Siddown.' Her hand made a little welcome gesture towards the carpet.

'How are you?'

She gave me a little smile. 'Never felt worse in my life.' She bent forward suddenly, a dry heave.

I knelt in front of her, touching her cool forehead. 'Where's Bobby?'

'Oh, he's around somewhere, maybe just behind the couch with an axe. I think he heard me call you. Maybe he wanted me to, I don't know, I haven't seen him since, oh, maybe couple of days or something. Not since I called you.'

I stood up, looking around. No sign of him. Just the sound of water running in the bathtub. 'You want a glass of water?'

'Oh boy, is that a possibility?'

I followed the sound of running water into the bathroom and turned off the overflowing bathtub. Sally's blue silk bra and her aquamarine dress were in a heap on the wet floor along with a man's yellow sock. I had a quick look around two other bedrooms, a game room, a dining-room and a kitchen. Most of the damage was around Sally, in the living-room, but not all of it. There were broken glasses and cups littering the floors and marks on the wall where they'd hit. A couple of plants had been tipped over in the game room, and the antique dining-room table had a paring-knife stuck in it. No sign of Bobby. I went back into the kitchen and got Sally a glass of water.

She stretched out her hands to receive the glass, and holding it carefully with both hands, as if it were the only glass of water in the world, she took small sips. 'I must look like a buzzard,' she said. 'I think things are starting to slow down but one of us is on a yo-yo.'

'You and Bobby did this?'

'Bobby did. It was like this when I got here. Or mostly like this. I mean he keeps doing it. Isn't it weird, Wahlnut? I always thought I would really like to do something like this to him, like rip his place up and then, when I saw him doing it, it took all the fun out of it. I just felt sorry for the sick, silly sonofabitch.' She looked around, noticing that she was naked but not upset. 'Have you seen my dress?'

I held the dress and her bra out to her. 'It was in the bathroom on the floor.'

'Oh, shit.'

'Your panties are right behind you on the couch.'

'Will you excuse me for a minute?'

'Are you OK to stand up?'

'One way to find out.' She put her hands on the couch behind her and pushed herself up. She wasn't steady, but she was standing. 'I'll just be a couple of minutes, Wahlnut,' she said.

'Hey, shit. No hurry, Squeezy Tits. Take your time.' Bobby was standing just inside the open glass doors, the pool blue and sparkling behind him, the sky a deep rosy red from the sunset. 'Glad you could make it too, Forrest. We've got news for you.'

'I'm taking Sally home,' I said.

'You bet your sweet ass you are taking Sally home. You bet your ass. She tell you how she GOT HERE?' His voice raised to a shout and he smashed one of the glass doors with something he had in his hand. The light was behind him and I couldn't see more than his outline. *'Tell him.'*

'I called him,' Sally said, her voice still raspy, quiet. 'I called him because Merrill told me about your press conference and I wanted to tell Bobby that I knew it was true. "You're just a cheap little drug dealer, aren't you Bobby." That's what I said. And Bobby said he was hurting. He said he was in pain and he needed me. He said he had something to tell me about Merrill. That nobody else knew.'

'Anything to get you here, darling,' Bobby said, walking slowly, unsteadily into the room. His words were slurred but he was watching Sally the way a cat watches a bird on the ground. He didn't have a shirt or shoes or socks, just loose, white trousers with no belt, a couple of the buttons undone. The gun he held was a chrome-plated .45 and he kept it pointed at me.

I have had guns pointed at me before but I have not got used to the shock of the black hole of a barrel. A gun pointed in my direction makes me obedient, alert, anxious to please. This was an old-fashioned clumsy showpiece. A kind of hand cannon for Cadillac Cowboys. But it didn't matter that there are more modern and efficient weapons. Its bullet would blow a hole the size of a fist on the way through. If Bobby had loaded it with hollow-points the exit hole would be about the size of a dinner-plate.

'Come on, tell the rest of it, Sally sweetheart. There's lots to tell, isn't THERE?' When he reached her, he put his arm around her bare shoulder. Sally started to pull away, but he held her tight enough to make her wince, keeping the gun pointing at me. His eyes were baggy and red-rimmed and there were white crusts at the corners of his mouth. He gave her another hard squeeze.

Sally said, 'When I got here he was sitting on one of those

deck chairs by the pool and he just sat there not moving and I asked him if he wasn't going to get up, say hello or anything.'

'That's right, and remember what I said? I said I was finished getting up. I was finished doing any Goddamn thing because of your friend here. Fancy-ass racing driver can't keep his mouth shut. Stumbles across the best deal of all time and all he has to do is keep his mouth shut and he can't do it. And the DEA is all over me, calling me six times a day, subpoenaed all my records, calling up all my clients, asking them if they knew anything about my drug dealing. The bastards in Las Vegas won't take my phone calls, called in my loan, and I think if I pay it they are going to have some fuck come around some night and shoot me in bed. And Merrill says he's done with me. He says don't call him, he's got his own problems. And the bank called to say they are foreclosing on my building.'

He let go of Sally to rub his eyes and Sally took a tentative half-step away from him, toward the couch. 'My business partners have pulled out the shopping mall, they won't say why they won't talk to me. It didn't make the papers or the seven o'clock news but that chicken-shit trick you pulled at the press conference has covered me with so much shit I can't see straight don't TOUCH THAT,' and he fired his gun into the couch blowing a hole three feet from where Sally was reaching for her panties.

'That's evidence,' he said quietly into the silence that followed the blast of the gun. Bobby looked mildly pleased with himself. 'Come on, Sally,' he said softly, coaxing. 'Tell him about it.'

'I don't remember.'

He pulled her by the hair so she was tight up against him, keeping his gun pointed at me. 'Try,' he said. 'For me.'

'He was drunk when I got here Forrest, and he was weeping and he said, "Come on Sally have a drink with me, no hard feelings." And I thought it would be the easiest way to get out of here, just have a drink and go only he must have put something in it.'

'Come on, now we are getting to the good part.'

'I don't remember.'

'Oh yes you do. Yes you do. You said you were never going to forget. Tell him. In the bathtub when you had my cock in your mouth you went MMMMMMMMMMMMMMM-

MMMMMMM. Don't you remember saying that? I'm sure you could if you'd try.'

Sally's face started to come apart, her face blank but her mouth twitching and fat tears making paths down her cheeks. She opened her mouth to say something, but no sound came out.

'Don't even twitch, Evers,' he said catching me starting to move towards him. 'You stay right there while Sally tells you how it felt when I fucked her from behind. Come on, darlin', you remember telling me it was the best ever, that nobody had ever fucked you like that before? You remember what you said?'

Sally looked at me, pleading. 'It was the drugs, Wahlnut.'

'You can believe that one if you want to. Here,' he said, pushing Sally towards me, 'you take her home. I'm finished with her.'

chapter thirty-four

Sally staggered a half-step towards me and stopped.

She turned around to face Bobby. 'You aren't finished with me Bobby. You're just finished.' They stood looking at each other for a moment. Sally tensed and drove her fist into Bobby's windpipe, the blow making a sound like breaking eggs. Bobby's head snapped forward and his gun went off, shattering a skylight overhead, shards of glass raining down on us. Sally screamed 'PIG, YOU FUCKING PIG,' hitting, scratching and kicking him as he sagged forward. He started to swing at her head with his gun and I caught his wrist, pulled him towards me and hit him hard on the side of his head. I let go of him and he dropped face-forward on the floor. It took Sally a couple of moments to realise he was unconscious and she stopped kicking him, her breath coming in gasps, and crying.

I held her for a moment and Bobby groaned and rolled over on his side, his face scratched, bruised and bloody, beginning to swell around the eyes. 'I'm sorry, darlin',' he said. His voice sounded painful, rasping. He started to reach towards her, 'I didn't mean . . .' She wrenched free from me to grab a brass floor-lamp and swing it one-handed, hard, catching Bobby on the side of his head as he started to look up and bring the gun barrel back in my direction. The blow hit with a wet slap, knocked him sideways, and he sprawled on the carpet.

Sally knelt down beside him, saying 'Bobby, are you OK? Oh God, Bobby, I hope I didn't kill you because I really want to see you suffer.' She looked up at me, the cloud of the drug still in her eyes, 'Did I kill him, Wahlnut? There's blood all over.'

'He's bleeding from his ear. You must have cut it,' I said. 'It's nothing serious.'

I had no idea whether it was serious or not. I didn't care. I just wanted to get out. I bent down to Sally and took her hand. 'He'll be fine. Come on now.'

She stood up slowly, the tears still running down her cheeks. 'I'm kinda shaky, Forrest. I want to go lie down. Go to sleep. Wake up in my own bed.' She started to close her eyes and sag towards the couch.

'I want to get you to a hospital. You might need help.'

She opened her eyes again, focusing on me. 'I don't need help. I need to put my dress on. Can you wait a minute?'

While Sally stepped into her dress, her arm on the sofa for support, I pried the chrome gun out of Bobby's hand, walked out of the room and on to the terrace and tossed it in the deep end of the swimming-pool.

I was watching the bright chrome spot dance on the bottom when Sally came out of the house. She had combed her hair straight and her blue dress had a design of big wet patches from lying on the wet floor.

'I'm dizzy,' she said, straightening up. 'Can you hold my hand?' She wasn't sobbing now, she was calm, distant, as if she was thinking of something else. She didn't notice the tears running down her face.

I pushed the button and the door to the lift slid open, we stepped in and pressed down.

The lift did its usual trick of waiting while it considered the meaning of life. I pressed the down button a few more times and it finally began to descend. Was it possible, I wondered, that its descent was even slower than going up? I wondered if the speed of lifts is adjustable, if you could install different gear ratios, shifting into high when you were in a rush. I was in a rush. I said, 'Is there a hospital near here?' Sally was looking out over the black carpet of the valley, lights sparkling white and red and green. I added, 'With a rape crisis centre?'

She thought about it for a moment looking out towards the last glow of the sunset. 'I can't deal with anybody now, Wahlnut. I just want to go to sleep.' She turned around to face me and managed a smile. 'I'm OK, really. Just take me home, to Daddy's house. You want to call the rape folks, do it from there. I'll talk to them in the morning. I couldn't do it now,' she said, closing her eyes. We rode down in silence, the wind blowing around the edges of our glass box.

Ten yards above the parking lot, the lift stopped.

I pressed the down button. Nothing. We heard a gust of wind. Felt the cabin sway gently. We looked at each other puzzled. There was a telephone for an emergency but who would we be calling on the other end of the line, Bobby? I pressed the down button another twenty times. I tried prying the doors open with my hands.

The lift started moving. Up.

I pressed the down button. Nothing, the lift continued to rise up along the side of the cliff. I pressed the stop button. The red emergency button. The open door. The up. The down. The close door. Sally pressed her palms against all the buttons. I tried prying open the doors again.

Nothing.

'He's up there, isn't he, Forrest?'

'It could be just a fault in the system.'

'You believe that?'

I tried working out how much time we had, how long the lift had gone down before it started up again. Two minutes? Two and a half? Plenty of time. There was a rusted service ladder running alongside the lift. If we could get out to that we could climb down. The lift was going slow enough. We could do it. I pulled off my shoe and smashed the glass. There was a dull *sproinkkkkk*. Not smashing the glass. Smashing my hand. It wasn't glass, it was a super-strong plastic like Lexan. The lift kept rising, the parking lot below and the cars in it getting smaller.

Sally pushed the buttons again. She looked up and said, 'There's that escape hatch. We could climb out on the roof except there's all those pulleys and cables up there. We could get all chewed up.'

I was looking at the plastic side panels. They were screwed in an aluminium frame with sheet-metal screws. 'I have another idea,' I said. I put my shoe back on and lay down on my back drawing my knees over my chest and kicked straight out as hard as I could against the clear plastic. The cabin shuddered and jerked against the cable. 'Did that do anything?'

Sally bent over my feet, inspecting. 'Looks like you might have loosened a screw some. Do it again.'

I did it again, making the cabin buck.

'Two,' Sally shouted. 'You got two loose, Screwloose. Keep kicking.'

I picked up the rhythm, kicking just as hard but faster, again and again and the whole frame tore off the cabin and the sheet of transparent plastic fell away, turning and disappearing in the dark. We heard it hit the asphalt below.

Sally reached out to the ladder first, reaching up as high as she could and swinging out into the night, and I rose past her leaving her below, looking up. Then I leapt out, catching the ladder, feeling it shake with my weight, and watching the cabin slowly rise above me, a bright, well-lit cube going on up overhead, into the night sky, getting smaller.

Below me, Sally was already moving down, a dark shape, her dress black and snapping in the wind.

The wind came in gusts, moaning and whistling on the steel rungs. Below, Sally was hurrying down the ladder towards the black pool of the parking lot. Above us the lift had stopped. I pictured the doors opening, Bobby finding nobody inside, the side panel missing, and getting in. Coming after us. I tried to go faster. Right, left. Left, right. I had the feeling I could go faster if I relaxed. I wasn't relaxed.

Up above, the lift started down towards us. Bobby leaned out of the side, looking down. Turning his head from side to side as if he couldn't see us. Showing a lot of blood.

Going down the ladder was hard, tiring work, like vertical cross-country skiing. The rungs were narrow, rusted steel, rasping on the hands. It looked like the lift was gaining on us, but I couldn't be sure. My eyes were tearing in the wind and I was gasping for breath.

Sally said, 'Oh fuck.'

I looked down and she was five feet below me, lying on the ground.

'I didn't see it, Wahlnut. Ground just jumped up at me. Feels like I broke my ankle.'

'How's the other one?' I said, watching the lift make its slow descent towards us, growing larger.

'Why don't you just carry me instead of trying to work it out, Screwloose?'

I picked Sally up in my arms, her head falling against my neck, and ran the few steps to the car door, opening the door and putting her gently down in her seat. I ran around to the other side, jumped in, switched the ignition, nothing, put it in park, started it, slammed it in reverse, wheels spinning, twirling the wheel in a quick one-eighty into lo, pedal to the floor, accelerating out of the parking lot, and Sally screamed, 'STOP!'

We slid to a stop.

'Look under the car.'

I looked at her puzzled. Behind us the lift was almost down to the ground. 'Goddamn it, Wahlnut, he'd do it. He said he would. I know he would.' She sat there, her face blank. In the rear-view mirror I could see the elevator descending, thirty feet off the ground.

'Do what, Sally. What are you talking about?'

'He told me he was going to have Barnes killed when I was going out with Bill. Think about it, Forrest. You know he had somebody throw those cherry bombs. Bobby said he was going to kill you. Just now. Just before I called you. Where do you think he was when you came in the house.'

I realised Bobby had not been in the house, or by the pool. I was thinking he could have been anywhere and Sally screamed, 'LOOK UNDER THE CAR! UNDERNEATH WHERE YOUR SEAT IS!'

I got out. In the distance the doors of the lift were opening, sending a cone of yellow light out across the asphalt. Bobby was running out of the lift, towards his car, his long shadow taking giant strides. I slid underneath the car on my back. I couldn't see anything, I had to feel. My forehead was against something.

Something.

I felt it with both hands, my fingers running over the surface like a blind man. A fat bundle of tubes, wired together. My fingers felt six.

Six like Barnes.

I heard Bobby start the engine in his Range Rover and race it wildly as he missed getting the car in gear. I pulled hard at the bundle and it started to give. Another pull and it came loose, falling on the ground with a soft thunk. I carefully inched backward out from under the car, carrying the package alongside, trying to keep it from dragging on the ground. We don't want to jiggle or jar anything, I thought. No little harmless vibrations to set off a hair trigger. It could be a motion switch. The first time the car goes over a bump . . . Dynamite needs a primary charge, a blasting cap to explode and the blasting cap needs an electronic charge to generate enough heat to ignite. Usually. Probably.

Bobby was backing up.

I let go of my precious bundle as carefully as I could, lowering it carefully down the half-inch on to the ground. I also stood up with great care, as smoothly as I could. Dynamite has that effect on you. Don't even think sudden thoughts.

'Goddamnit come on,' Sally said. I ran around, jumped into the car, floored it and accelerated hard for twenty yards thinking that if we just got back on to the main road it was a short run down to Camelback, before standing on the brakes and turning the wheel hard left.

Heavy red steel gates blocked the road. The car was rotating a hundred and eighty degrees, the back end just missing the gate. We stopped, facing Bobby's Range Rover. I turned off the lights, shut off the ignition and we got out of the car, hearing Bobby shift from first to second, from second to third, not lifting for the shifts, the engine screaming. He turned his lights on, the whole blaze of lights on top of his roll-bar lighting us up on the pavement and throwing our shadows behind us as we stood on each side of the Buick.

The roar stopped and there was a squeal of brakes and howl of tyres being dragged across the pavement. Bobby slid to a stop about twenty yards away.

He shut off the engine and stood up, outlined against the open doors of the lift. His face was a mess, but I wasn't watching his face. He was holding something, a small box, in his hands.

Sally screamed, backing away, 'NO, NO. BOBBY, DON'T!'

He heard her. He nodded. He smiled, showing those perfect white teeth, gave us a wave.

Sally screamed again, 'NO, BOBBY, YOU DON'T KNOW . . .'

Bobby blew her a kiss and if he heard her, he didn't show it. Bobby smiled again, the charm still there in his bloody face as he pushed the lever of the little box in his hands forward.

A white balloon, red at the edges, bloomed against the black mountainside where Bobby and the Range Rover car had been. There was no time in between, no transition. No time to see the flame bulge up through the floor, disintegrating the metal, carrying with it the jagged seven-thousand-mile-an-hour splinters that had been the aluminium and steel transmission. No time to see the fire rise around him, through him. I saw Bobby standing up behind the wheel of his car, then in the same frame of time, the same thousandth of a second, there was this rising white balloon. The light and the heat hit me in a blaze and a blow and I had just a moment to wonder at the brilliance and the pure white intensity of the explosion before it knocked me unconscious, flying slowly backwards through the air.

chapter thirty-five

'How far you throw this, uh, what was it you called it, bundle? Of dynamite?'

He was an OK cop. In shirtsleeves, a bead of sweat on his forehead and trickling down his cheeks, the night still warm from the heat of the day. The asphalt of Bobby's parking lot was warm under our feet. The cop had an owl face, glasses, black curly hair piled up. He was trying to piece together my story so somebody else could compare it to the story Sally was telling ten yards away inside a black and white, to compare with the scattered wreckage they found on the ground. The ambulance had come to pick up the body and gone away with several tagged plastic bags containing what were believed to be parts of the deceased.

'I didn't throw it,' I said. 'I put it down about three feet from where I found it. Over there, where the hole is.'

'So you could say you put it right in his path. Do you think the other guy, uh, this uh' – he consulted his notes – 'this Mr Roberts saw the dynamite?'

In the car, after midnight, I was driving Sally to her father's, and Sally asked, her voice matter of fact, 'You tell them anything about Bobby raping me?'

'They didn't ask and I didn't tell them anything. What did you tell them?'

'Same as you, Wahlnut. I mean what's the point now? It isn't like I could make them put him in jail.' We rode along Indian School Road, Sally looking out at the new car dealers. 'There's another thing,' she said. 'I've tried hard but I really can't remember anything about it. And I don't *feel* like there's anything. I mean I would know, but there's nothing. I'm not even a little sore or anything and to tell you the truth, Wahlnut, I don't think he did a damn thing to me except give me a drug that knocked me out.'

'Somebody took your clothes off.'

'Yeah, he must have done that, but maybe he was setting this up.'

'And it went wrong.'

'Not,' she said, 'necessarily.'

When I pulled in the drive alongside Cavanaugh's house, Sally put her hand on my sleeve. 'Come in with me, Wahlnut. Please? Help me tell him? I don't think I can face him alone.'

When we got to the front door on the porch Sally put her key in the lock and stopped. 'I feel numb, you know? Like I just woke up? I'll probably hate him tomorrow, Lord knows I know how to hate Bobby. But I keep thinking of Bobby when I first saw him, when he was just a twelve-year-old kid. When Daddy first brought him home. He could have been, oh, I don't know. He could have been anything he wanted to, governor or something. He was so beautiful then, and smart. I wish you knew him then,' she said, unlocking the door. She led me down the hall into the kitchen on the left, flicking on light switches as she went, checking herself in a hall mirror, and wincing at what she saw.

The kitchen lights flickered on, fluorescent tubes in an old-fashioned room with wooden counters and cupboards painted green. There was a big old cast iron stove converted to gas and a worn porcelain sink with rust stains around the drain. 'You want anything?' she asked, rummaging in the cupboards under the counter. 'I'm gonna have some coffee, see if it'll clear my head. I'm still kinda shaky.'

'Maybe he'd like a bourbon,' Cavanaugh said from the doorway, his voice rough from sleep. He had a faded yellow cotton flannel robe, hairless white bandy legs sticking out the bottom, bare feet in worn leather slippers. He seemed several years older than the last time I'd seen him. His shoulders sloped forward, his back seemed more rounded giving him a slightly stooped look, as if the earth was dragging him back down. His steel wire hair looked whiter than before, his lipless snapping-turtle mouth wrinkled and dry. His eyes, though, were not old. His small faded blue eyes had intensity, glaring out of his square and wrinkled face, a brick with eyes.

Standing in the middle of the doorway he said, 'I don't know what you are doing here, Evers. But this is my house and perhaps before I have to listen to you tell me what kind of crap you've been up to this evening you'll do me the courtesy of having a drink with me.' He was out of the kitchen and moving down the hall, not waiting for a reply.

'Y'all go ahead, Wahlnut. I'll come in soon as I get this coffee fixed. You want a cup?'

I shook my head no and went into the old man's study where he was pouring us each a half-tumbler of bourbon over the rocks. 'What the fuck has been going on?' he said, not looking up. 'Sally looks like she's been hit by a bus.'

'There's always a disadvantage in talking to you, Cavanaugh. I never know how much you know.'

'Just assume I don't know a damn thing except how to pour good bourbon,' he said, handing me a glass.

Normally I do not drink. This was not a normal night. I took a deep sip, tasting the smoke before the fire. Not fire, a nice old comfortable warm glow like a fire that has burned down to the coals under a blanket of ashes. 'Then I'll assume,' I said, 'that you didn't know that Bobby put six sticks of dynamite under my car tonight.'

His face didn't budge an inch. He took another sip, savouring the whisky. 'I didn't know that,' he said, sitting down at a round poker table covered with green felt. Chips piled neatly in the middle. 'How did you come to find that out?' he said, motioning me to another chair.

I sat down. 'Well not by getting blown up,' I said. 'Sally had an idea he might have set us up. So I looked underneath the car and pulled it out.'

'And it didn't go off,' he said.

'Bobby set it off,' I said. 'He stopped his car over it and he set it off.'

Cavanaugh sat still, his eyes fixed on me. 'What in hell are you telling me, Forrest?' he said, leaning forward suddenly. 'What happened, Goddamnit? You killed him?'

'Bobby killed himself. He blew himself up.'

Sally said, 'He was trying to blow us up, Daddy, and it

backfired.' She was standing in the doorway, holding a white porcelain pot of coffee.

As she spoke, Cavanaugh closed his eyes and eased against the table, making a moaning sound. Sally came over to him, setting the coffee-pot down on the table and putting her arm around his shoulder. 'What is it, Daddy?' she said. 'Are you OK?'

He stood up slowly, his head tilted back, his eyes still shut and his mouth opening wide as if to receive rain from the sky. A small noise came from the back of his throat and his arm swept across the table, knocking the coffee-pot on the floor, shattering the pot, scattering the poker chips across the room.

'Oh, God, *noooo*,' he said, drawing the word out in a long cry. 'Jesus Christ *noooo*. You blew him up.'

Sally had stepped back away from him, frightened. 'Forrest told you, Daddy. He blew himself up. He thought he was blowing us up. *Me*.'

'You sit down,' he said to Sally over his shoulder. 'And you keep your mouth shut,' he said to me, sinking back into his chair. An old turtle tongue licked his lips, tears in his eyes.

'My God what a waste. What a Goddamn waste. For nothing. All those years of looking after him.' Cavanaugh looked up from the table, at me. 'I know I should have done better, I had a lot to make up for. But nobody could say I didn't give him the best schools, the best every Goddamn thing. Was he in pain? Did he die right away? Where is your brother, where are they keeping him? I want to see him. Can you take me there, Sally?' He was pleading, sounding frightened.

Sally put her hand on his shoulder and knelt next to him. 'Whose brother are you talking about, Daddy? We're talking about Bobby.'

He sighed. 'Yeah, we're talking about Bobby. You should have seen him when he was a baby. The nurses called him the golden boy. I know I should have told you, Sally. I was just a boy. Then it was too late, way too Goddamn late. By the time I had the money and a house of my own your mother and I had our own life. Proper man and wife. I never told her I had another child before I married her. You remember it was after she died I brought Bobby in the house. You were all over him like butter on toast. That's why I had to break you up, honey.

Of course you didn't know it, but that's why I did that. He was a good boy. In his heart my boy was a good boy. He was. Can I see him now, can you take me to see him?'

'Nothin' much to see of your little boy, Daddy.' Her voice was hard, edgy. 'Just a lot of little bits in plastic bags with little tags on them. You stole him from me. You stole him, you mean son of a bitch. Why, for God's sake, Daddy, didn't you just tell me? Why didn't you tell me I had a brother?'

'Course that was the crazy thing,' he said, not reacting to her. 'That blonde hair of his. I don't know where that came from. His mother was just the wildest redhead you ever saw. And of course my hair was black but that little baby was just as blonde as sunshine. We were just kids, she was just hardly even seventeen and I was twenty-two just starting out then, didn't know the first thing about anything. Didn't have two dimes to rub together. Except I knew enough to avoid a scandal if I could. Christ, just starting out you got to have your credibility. Can't have credibility with a little bastard on your hands, can you. Hell, I didn't know what to do with a Goddamn baby. But by God she had spirit. She walked into a bar, doesn't sound like much but in those days weren't any women went into a bar alone. She walked into a bar in Cave Creek sixteen years old and said, "Which one of you buzzards is gonna buy me a drink?" And I swear there were twenty-five drinks on the bar before she sat down. I know 'cause I bought about ten of them. The racetrack, that's a real one, don't let go of that one whatever you do. Keep the credibility of that alive and you'll see it happen. Promise you. But she was just a kid herself, Jesus just barely seventeen, and I never blamed her for taking off. Leaving the boy in the hospital. Little Bobby. Oh God, I am tired, and there is so much to remember. Restore, restore, that's what we have to do for the human spirit, Sally. I mean Re-Create. The Re-Creation centre of the world. Only reason ever to do anything is for the human spirit. Only reason I ever did anything. You see we have the solar power here. The guy to talk to, Sally, is Empirio, Joseph Empirio in Las Vegas, the number is, I can't remember the number it's upstairs but you don't want to tell him too much. Never anything you don't have to.' He made a loud humming sound, looking around the room. 'Now they got that Dickie Esmond in jail we can forget.

UMMMMMMMMMMMMMMMMMMMMMMMMMM. Only use the fax only for stuff doesn't matter who sees it. You see the structure is crucial, Sally. Once you understand the structure. What Barnes was getting at. Sonofabitch had to know, sticking his nose in. Make an example, that's what we wanted to do, teach those sonsabitches a lesson. Get little Dickie to blow his ass sky-high.'

He was rocking in his chair, his thoughts all coming to the front of his mind at once falling over each other trying to get out. 'And Admiral Boyce, Jack Boyce, you gotta keep close to him. Sally, you call him in the morning to tell him. All for Goddamn nothing. The steering committee on the Central Phoenix Rebuilding Fund is another one, that's Friday. I was building for him. You know? I was going to give it to Bobby. How many kids' daddies give 'em an empire? Mine never gave me . . . ' Cavanaugh made that loud humming sound again, holding his head in his hands. UUMMMMMMMMMMMMMMM.

Sally started to reach out to him and he smiled at her, easing back in his chair with a warming thought, the old turtle lips stretched wide in a nice big grin, and turned to me. 'Your mother's idea, did you know that? It was your mother's idea to give him his name, Evers. "Call it Bobby," she said. She said he just bobbed up out of nowhere. Made a joke of it, said she had no idea where that baby came from. She ever tell you you had a brother, Forrest?'

chapter thirty-six

A dry, clear sunny day. The trees along the creek were deep green from the spring rains, their leaves flickering their silver bottoms in the breeze. Behind us the desert hills were bright with flowers. Sally stood up, brushing her long hair out of her eyes.

'Stick it in,' she said.

Fifty yards away, on top of a little rise on the other side of the road, the tall cowboy with tight blue jeans and a T-shirt that said FUCK LUBBOCK nodded and walked back to the cab of the tow truck. He started it up, there was a crunch of gears and then a whirring of the winch. He looked over his shoulder, through the back window to make sure he made a straight drop into the big hole. Just as it was about to sink into the earth a breeze slowly twisted the coffin sideways, turning it perpendicular to the hole, and the scratched and stained bronze casket, clumps of dirt sticking to it, gently settled on the ground, a bronze bridge across the grave. The man shut off the truck and got out of the cab.

'Brother Bobby,' I said, 'doesn't want to go back in the ground.'

'I've had enough of Brother Bobby this week,' Sally said, looking off at a flock of birds skittering among the trees and dipping down to the surface of the creek. 'It was a hell of a lot tougher getting him out of the ground than it was burying him in the first place. I never knew there were so many twenty-five-page forms in the world. Or lawyers. There were the city lawyers, lawyers for the cemetery, lawyers from Bobby's estate, lawyers from the Arizona Parks Department. Goddamn EPA lawyers, would you believe, wanted an environmental-impact statement.' Sally picked up a flat stone, threw it and watched it skip off the glittering surface of the running water.

'I finally did what I should have done in the first place,' she said, watching the spot where the stone sank. 'Went out to the cemetery and paid a couple of grave-diggers two thousand dollars apiece to dig him up with a backhoe at night. Paid a couple of motorcycle cops to escort us. The grave-diggers said they do it all the time. Said there are a lot of empty holes in the cemetery. Said some people are buried in three or four places.'

The cowboy was pushing his hat back, staring at the coffin.

Sally called out to him. 'Just roll it in, why don't you, Orrin. There's not many bits of him rightside up anyway.'

'Sally, he's your brother too,' I said, putting a hand on her shoulder. I was thinking of Bobby, telling me how he liked getting out on the edge, where it was dangerous. Slices of time so thin you could see through them, he said.

My brother; like another self I might have been.

Sally moved her shoulder an inch away and I let my hand drop. She said, 'He's had all the grief he's gonna get from me, Forrest. You know it would have been us instead of him if he had his way. I felt bad when he died. And I cried. But I think of that last night, and I think of Barnes and those Goddamn cherry bombs and I am glad, Forrest. Glad to stick him six feet down every chance I get.'

'You don't think he set the whole thing up? Got us to help him kill himself?'

'I don't think about it, Forrest. Not at all. I mean what difference does it make to any of us now? How long you staying?'

The cowboy was back in the tow truck winching the coffin off the ground, backing closer to the hole and raising the crane for a better angle. The truck eased over the freshly dug mound of earth, making the coffin swing like a pendulum against the dark blue sky.

'I just came out for this,' I said. 'I'm flying back to London tomorrow morning. How's your Dad?'

'Oh, they keep saying he'll be fine to come home in a week or two, but I'll believe it when I see it. He looks OK, even put back a little of the weight he lost. But if you saw him now you'd know he's had some wires pulled. At first I thought he was faking, giving himself an excuse in case Dickie Esmond got tired of sitting in jail and started talking. But it's real and God knows he paid Dickie enough. I see Daddy most every day and what I get is a bit of sense here, lotta gibberish there. A little nugget hiding in half a ton of garbage. Drives me nuts. I'm trying to put it together, take some of the money and fund rehab clinics, give it to charity. Try to keep the damn Government from taking away the rest. But sometimes it takes a while to track it down.'

'I kind of miss your old Airstream,' I said.

'I don't. I don't miss it a bit. I don't have the time now for messing around with that stuff.' She brushed the dirt off her hands. 'Aren't you staying for the opening ceremony tomorrow? Hear the speeches? Lieutenant-Governor's coming out and there's TV. We could get you a silver trowel or somethin'. It's your mother's park, you should be here.'

'Maybe I should, but I've got to get back to London. We're about two weeks away from launching our Formula One team and three weeks behind schedule. You know, the usual story. I just wanted to see Bobby into the ground again. See how you are. See how the place has changed.'

'The only change to the place is going to be Bobby's grave and a sign with your mother's name up by the road. "Sally Concannon State Sanctuary", like we agreed. I didn't have to agree to that, you know.'

'I know, you're just a pussy cat. I would have tied you up in court for years.'

'Oh, horse puccy. Anyway that's not why I did it. I thought it was a good thing to do with what used to be your mother's land. And Daddy in one of his clear moments really liked the idea too. He liked bringing Bobby and his mother together, burying him next to that old stone foundation where his mother was born.'

His mother and mine, I thought.

The wind stopped and the cowboy got the coffin to go in straight, and we watched it sink slowly beneath the surface of the ground. The cowboy hit the release catch and Bobby's casket fell free and hit the bottom of the grave with a boom, sending up a cloud of dust.

Sally turned back to me. 'What are you going to do with the rest of it? The five thousand acres you still own.'

'I don't know. Leave it the way it is for a while. It might be worth something someday. Hard to know what something is worth until you lose it,' I said.

Sally turned her head and looked at me with tears streaming down her cheeks. 'As long as you're here, Wahlnut,' she said, 'grab a shovel.'

All Pan books are available at your local bookshop or newsagent, or can be ordered direct from the publisher. Indicate the number of copies required and fill in the form below.

Send to: Pan C. S. Dept
              Macmillan Distribution Ltd
              Houndmills Basingstoke RG21 2XS
or phone: 0256 29242, quoting title, author and Credit Card number.

Please enclose a remittance* to the value of the cover price plus: £1.00 for the first book plus 50p per copy for each additional book ordered.

*Payment may be made in sterling by UK personal cheque, postal order, sterling draft or international money order, made payable to Pan Books Ltd.

Alternatively by Barclaycard/Access/Amex/Diners

Card No.   ☐☐☐☐☐☐☐☐☐☐☐☐☐☐☐☐☐☐☐

Expiry Date   ☐☐☐☐☐☐

_____

Signature:

Applicable only in the UK and BFPO addresses

While every effort is made to keep prices low, it is sometimes necessary to increase prices at short notice. Pan Books reserve the right to show on covers and charge new retail prices which may differ from those advertised in the text or elsewhere.

NAME AND ADDRESS IN BLOCK LETTERS PLEASE:

....

Name _____

Address _____

_____

_____

_____

6/92